"DO YOU KNOW WHAT IT MEANS TO BE A HEALER?" DR. BASHIR ASKED.

"What d'you mean?" The young Bajoran boy, Cedra, asked cautiously. "I know I'd be a good one."

"Being a healer means more than how good you are," Dr. Bashir said. "The first thing they teach you is that a doctor's prime directive is to never betray his trust. There are people here on Bajor depending on healers for life, for a future. You can't walk away from a task half-done," he said, paused, then continued. "I came here with orders to cure the camp fever. It's gone now, but only from this camp. I can't leave it at that and still be true to my trust." *No matter what further orders Commander Sisko might want to give me,* Bashir thought to himself. The doctor had no illusions: Sisko would search for him the moment they discovered he was gone.

But he had made his choice. He said goodbye to Cedra, turned his eyes toward the hills, and headed out of camp.

Look for STAR TREK Fiction from Pocket Books

Star Trek: The Original Series

Star Trek: The Next Generation

Star Trek: Deep Space Nine

STAR TREK
DEEP SPACE NINE®

WARCHILD

ESTHER FRIESNER

POCKET BOOKS

New York   London   Toronto   Sydney   Tokyo   Singapore

This book is a work of fiction. Names, characters, places and incidents are products of the author's imagination or are used fictitiously. Any resemblance to actual events or locales or persons, living or dead, is entirely coincidental.

An *Original* Publication of POCKET BOOKS

POCKET BOOKS, a division of Simon & Schuster Inc.
1230 Avenue of the Americas, New York, NY 10020

This book is published by Pocket Books, a division of Simon & Schuster Inc., under exclusive license from Paramount Pictures.

ISBN: 0-671-88116-7

First Pocket Books printing September 1994

10 9 8 7 6 5 4 3 2 1

POCKET and colophon are registered trademarks of Simon & Schuster Inc.

Printed in the U.S.A.

*For all those people whose work
lets children hold on to their childhood*

Historian's Note

The events in *Warchild* take place between the first and second seasons of *STAR TREK: Deep Space Nine.*

WARCHILD

PROLOGUE

Ahead of them, the space station twirled slowly against a backdrop of stars. Aboard the runabout, two men wearing the robes of Bajoran monks sat side by side, silently contemplating the velvet dark.

At the controls, Ensign Munson fought off a fresh wave of the uneasiness that seemed to creep up his spine every time he thought about his passengers. He had been given orders by Major Kira herself to pick up a Bajoran monk at the port nearest the great Temple, yet when he had reported there, Ensign Munson found a monk and a vedek awaiting passage to the station, both with impeccable travel authorizations.

They presented their documents without a word, replied to his formal words of welcome with no more than a nod of the head, and they had maintained the same inscrutable silence ever since. The only discernible sound Ensign Munson heard either one of them make for the entire voyage was when the vedek inclined his head slightly in the other's direction and the delicate ornament hanging from his right ear made a muted tinkling sound like wind chimes.

Munson shuddered in spite of himself. The silence between the two Bajorans was more than just the absence of sound. It seemed to have a mass and presence of its own. A small voice inside Munson's head whispered soothingly: *Soon we'll dock, and they'll be gone. Good riddance! They give me the creeps.*

"Ahhhh."

It was only a soft exhalation of breath, a mere sound of acknowledgment, but it erupted in the midst of the silence with the impact of a photon torpedo. Munson almost jumped out of his skin, and jerked his head around. The Bajorans had their heads together, one holding a pale blue scroll open for the other's perusal. It was impossible to tell which of them had been the one to break the silence.

Then from the one holding the scroll, a question: "And your cause, my brother?"

Ensign Munson straightened his shoulders and faced forward once more. The Bajorans' conversation was none of his business. He felt like seven kinds of a fool for having let their former silence unnerve him so badly.

So they don't talk much; so what? he told himself. *Not everyone in the galaxy's a chatterbox, that's all. At least they're talking now.*

And then he heard words that made him wish the Bajorans had kept their shield of silence:

"I have come because of the children." The monk's voice echoed eerily in the runabout. "The children are dying."

CHAPTER
1

"SOMEONE TO SEE YOU, COMMANDER."

Benjamin Sisko looked up from his desk sharply and tried to put on the face of a man who has just been distracted from important business. His heart wasn't in it. He knew he'd been daydreaming—something he seldom had the leisure or the inclination to do since taking command of *Deep Space Nine*. Something he had only recently found pleasure in doing, too. A mind that wandered could sometimes wander back into the past.

"Yes, what is it?" he asked, a trifle sharply.

Major Kira Nerys met his eyes with her own level gaze. "Are we interrupting something important, sir?" she asked. Her dry, slightly amused tone let Sisko know straight off that she knew he was temporarily unoccupied, but she'd be willing to go along with the act if he felt like pretending he'd been busy.

"Not at all, Major," Sisko said, dropping all pretense and giving her one of his rare smiles. "Who wants to see—?"

The words froze in his throat as the Bajoran monk came gliding into the commander's office.

Sisko felt his body tense. No matter how hard he tried, no matter how earnestly he told himself to relax, the sight of a Bajoran monk always set his entire being on edge. He remembered—he could not help but remember—his first encounter with one of that brotherhood when he and his son, Jake, were newly come to *Deep Space Nine*. Then his thoughts had been set solely on how to get out of this unlooked-for command, how to get himself and Jake back to Earth, even if it meant taking a post with less responsibility, or leaving Starfleet altogether.

That first Bajoran monk had looked him in the eye in much the same way this one was doing now, but to Jake Sisko it had felt as if the man were looking into his soul. That monk spoke words Sisko had not understood—*the Prophets? What Prophets?*—not then. Sisko brushed the words aside. He had lost track of all the exotic religions he'd encountered since joining Starfleet. He did his best to offer them all a measure of respect, if not belief. He had never expected one of them to reach out and touch him to the heart the way the faith of Bajor had done.

It had touched him deeply, helped him come to terms with his past, the death of his wife, his role as commander on *Deep Space Nine*. It was a strong source of power—strange power, unknown power—the mystic faith that permeated every aspect of Bajoran life. And like many things strong and strange and not fully known, it put Sisko on guard.

"What can we do for you?" he asked the monk, trying to sound cordial if he couldn't bring himself to sound friendly. "No trouble in the temple, I hope? The one aboard, I mean." He realized that to a Bajoran, there could be only one Temple—that vast and eerily beautiful complex of domed buildings and lush gardens that the departing Cardassians had vandalized but could not

4

utterly destroy. When Sisko spoke of the temple, he first thought of the small Bajoran shrine aboard the space station.

The monk's gaze did not waver. He stood before Commander Sisko with his hands tucked into the voluminous sleeves of his rust-colored robes. A skin-tight cap covered his head, leaving only his weather-beaten face and ears exposed. His beard was short, black sprinkled with gray. Sisko realized that this monk was no ancient sage, but a fairly young man. The few wrinkles he did have were lines of toil, not of age.

"Commander Sisko," he said. The strength behind the voice convinced Sisko he was right in his assessment of the monk's years. "I am Taren Gis, a monk in service to the Prophets. I have come to you to ask for aid."

Sisko became aware that he was clutching the arms of his chair too hard. He made himself relax his grip. "Go on. What sort of aid?"

"It's the camps," Major Kira blurted. Sisko was startled. It wasn't a rare thing for Kira Nerys to forget herself, to barge in with demands and opinions, asked for or not. But usually those were angry outbursts, brief flashes of a temper sharpened and made bitter by growing up under the brutalities of the Cardassian occupation, honed by her years as a Bajoran freedom fighter.

"Camps?" Sisko echoed.

"The refugee camps, Commander." There was no anger in the Bajoran woman's voice; only pain. "We don't have an exact tally of how many of them there are, but I'm surprised Starfleet never mentioned them to you at all. I suppose they didn't think it was important enough to bring to your attention." Now a sliver of the old bitterness slipped back into her words.

"Starfleet is aware that there are refugee camps on Bajor," Sisko countered. *One line buried somewhere in my briefing material,* he thought ruefully. *If that.* "We're working with the provisional government to speed up resettlement procedures. Most of the camps have already been emptied and—"

"Labor camps," Major Kira snapped. "The Cardassians did their best to empty those before they left. They used their own methods of resettlement." Her tone left no question that the Cardassian idea of resettlement was permanent. "The refugee camps are another story."

Sisko turned to the monk. "Brother Gis, how many camps are there?"

The monk made a sign with his hands indicating that he did not know. "Commander, what are numbers? Your people and mine speak of the Cardassian occupation as lasting sixty years. You count these years in days, I count them in lives. You believe it is over, simply because the Cardassians are no longer here, but I see it otherwise. I see it as too many deaths that did not have to be, too much land laid waste, too many lives that have become horribly transformed. I have charge of a single camp; it is all I know. It is located in the Kaladrys Valley. Once this was the choicest, most fertile farmland on all Bajor. The Cardassians knew that as well as my people."

"The Cardassian installations in the valley set up a system of forced agricultural production," Kira said. "No mercy for the farmer who didn't meet his predetermined quotas. The quotas were unrealistic, but the Cardassians didn't care. They'd take what they could get, and if they happened to find an excuse to kill more of our people in the process—" She shrugged, though it was more like a shudder. "Those who could escape, did. But they're mostly families in the Kaladrys Valley. You can't run so fast with children." She spat out the words: "They were easy to catch."

"I only ask your help for one camp," the monk continued. "The one where I and two of my brethren serve. It is near the old farming village of Lacroya. We

6

are luckier than most; the destruction of Lacroya was fairly recent and incomplete. We have been able to glean much useful material from the ruins. Many of the people originally with us were farmers, and could coax crops from rock—or so they liked to say. They rallied the children to help them plow a few fields and to plant seedlings. Our relief supplies from the provisional government have been as much as charity could make them, but to give charity to others, you must first have enough to provide for your own family. There are very few Bajorans who can say that these days. So our farmers decided to take back the land and feed themselves."

"That's commendable," Sisko remarked. "And I assure you, if there is anything we can do to help them regain their independence—"

A wistful smile touched the monk's face. "They are dead now."

"Dead?" Sisko's hands clutched the armrests of his chair again. "What happened?"

The monk held out his hands, palms upward. "We called it camp fever, for want of another name. One of my brethren is a healer of great skill. In the Temple, he studied the ancient records of sickness and health. He thought it was an affliction very like *satai,* the swelling fever. He applied all the known remedies for *satai* to the victims." He lowered his hands. "They died anyway."

"Did you contact the government for aid?"

Major Kira snorted. "Why bother? The government will give nothing because the government has nothing to give. Besides, they have their own problems, trying to keep all the factions and splinter groups together long enough to make consensus decisions. Between that and a half dozen 'leaders' only on the lookout for the opportunity to promote themselves, there's no hope of real help. In their eyes, their own political survival is more important than the lives of a few refugees."

"It is sad," the monk said quietly. "The people of the

valley have suffered so much, so long, under so many different hands. The Cardassians' brutal rule was only one burden laid across their shoulders. Then the Bajoran resistance sought to strike at the Cardassians by destroying their immediate food supplies. They burned crops, destroyed farming implements, and in the end did no great good to the cause."

Kira bridled. "The resistance knew what it was doing! We struck at the Cardassians' resources—"

The monk shrugged. "Cardassian technology was easily able to replenish all foodstuffs the resistance destroyed. Where they did not have replicators, they simply got shipments from more cooperative districts. The only ones who starved were the Bajorans. And as if that were not punishment enough, the Cardassian overlords held the farmers themselves responsible for any damage done by the resistance. There were more executions, more deportations to the labor camps. Many farmers tried to run away, but again their families held them back. The few who stayed were told in no uncertain terms that they were to meet the old quotas. No matter that those quotas were set when there were more hands and more working machinery to help meet them."

"There's no need to tell the commander all that," Kira said sharply. "Just tell him what you told me."

Sisko cupped his chin in one hand. He had seen enough of battles and their aftermath to know that there were never any winners in a war—just some victims who lost less than others. He was certain Major Kira knew that too, but to say it aloud would be the same as admitting that the resistance had done almost as much harm to Bajor as the Cardassians. He chose to say nothing and hear out the monk's words.

"We do not know where else to turn," Brother Gis went on, addressing the commander. "The government indeed has nothing for us—neither technology nor supplies nor human aid."

"I'm surprised," Sisko said. "You'd think that the provisional government would see the wisdom in investing a major effort in the recovery of agricultural lands and the people to cultivate them. Even politicians need to eat."

"You are right," Brother Gis responded. "But foresight is a gift which the Prophets, in their wisdom, have not chosen to bestow on many. There is enough land back under cultivation for our leaders to feel that they have seen to Bajor's immediate needs. Besides, they do not see the point in wasting relief efforts on refugee camps that will not be able to repay them with effective manpower for at least ten years."

"What?" Sisko was taken aback.

"The fever has already destroyed most of the adults in our care, Commander." The monk bowed his head. "Before the sickness, our camp sheltered families. Now it is almost entirely a refuge for orphans."

"Children are out in the fields, working like adults," Major Kira said. "They can barely raise enough food to feed themselves, let alone the sick ones."

"Sickness feasts best at the table of famine," Brother Gis said. "Word has reached us that there are similar outbreaks of this illness in other camps, both in and beyond the valley. The sickness is spreading, feeding on the weak. That is why I am here. This station always brought death to Bajor. Now let it open its other hand and bring the gift of life."

"What, exactly, do you need?" Sisko asked.

The monk reached into his sleeve and brought out a carefully folded piece of paper. "In consultation with my brethren, we have made this list." He handed it over. "We have concluded—with regret, but quite realistically—that if we are unable to fulfill these needs, the fatalities will mount at such a rate that—"

"That we needn't bother sending any help at all," Major Kira concluded grimly.

Sisko studied the list, feeling his heart drop a little lower with every item. Some of the things the monk requested were simple enough to provide, but not in such quantities—! He would have to contact Starfleet, and while he waited for the shipments, more people would die. As for the rest of the monk's requests—medical personnel, for example—they were impossible. You couldn't give what you didn't have.

Sisko sat back and took a deep breath. He had always known that it wasn't easy to hold a position of command in Starfleet, but he used to think it got easier with time. He knew the answer he had to give this monk, as little as he liked it.

"Brother Gis," he began, "I'm sorry—" He saw Major Kira stiffen where she stood. "We'll do what we can to help you, but it will take time to obtain all the items you've asked for."

"There is little time," the monk replied.

"I'll dispatch a call to Starfleet immediately, requesting additional medical supplies from any ships in the vicinity, on either side of the wormhole. In the meantime we will give you all that this station can spare, but—"

Brother Gis made a small but commanding gesture that momentarily silenced Sisko. "The supplies are not vital. We will gratefully accept whatever you can offer us. As for the rest, we will go on as we have in the past, making do. But what we truly need, most desperately— what we can no longer do without—are healers. What good if you give us all this"—he indicated the list in Sisko's hand—"and we lack the help to use it?"

"I see your point." Sisko pressed his fingers to his lips in thought. "Dr. Julian Bashir is our station's chief medical officer. He's acquired a number of assistants since his arrival. I'll consult with him, see if he can recommend one or two of them to help you."

"With respect, Commander, we do not need these"—

the monk held out his hands—"so much as we need these." He touched his head, then his heart.

Sisko tried to give the monk a reassuring smile. "Dr. Bashir's people are well trained. They can monitor life-sign readouts and maintain any prescribed treatments very efficiently."

"But can they determine which treatments need to be prescribed?" Before Sisko could answer, Brother Gis went on: "I have already told you that we have no name for the sickness that is devastating our people. We need a healer, one who can give it a name. To name your enemy is the first step toward defeating him. Can your Dr. Bashir's assistants do that?"

"They're not diagnosticians," Sisko admitted reluctantly.

"In the desert, if water leaks from a vessel through invisible cracks, you do not need someone to mop up the water that has already spilled so much as you need one with the skill and wisdom to find the cracks themselves and make the vessel whole. We need this Dr. Bashir, not his assistants."

Sisko had learned it was best to make the hardest pronouncements quickly and clearly. "He can't go. I can't spare him, Brother Gis. That would leave DS9 without a—a healer, and that is something I can't risk."

"The Prophets will not leave you unprotected if you permit yourself to share your healer's skills with us," the monk said.

"The Prophets are . . . generous as always, but we're talking about the overall security of *Deep Space Nine*. I'd need a better reassurance than their promised protection before I could let Dr. Bashir go. He's needed here."

"The need for him is greater on Bajor," Brother Gis calmly maintained.

Sisko set his jaw. "I'm sorry. But as for the rest—" He laid his hand on the monk's list.

The Bajoran monk folded his hands and bowed slightly to the commander. "May the Prophets show you a better path," he said, and departed.

No sooner was Brother Gis gone than Kira whirled on Sisko and blurted, "Why couldn't we spare Dr. Bashir?"

Sisko's lips tightened. "I think I gave my reasons. Obviously you don't think they were good enough."

"No, I don't," Kira said, expressing herself in the same blunt, direct way that worked against her more often than not. "There's a medical *crisis* on Bajor! There's nothing remotely resembling a crisis here. Why couldn't he—?"

"There is no crisis here *at the moment.*" Commander Sisko stressed his words carefully. "You've served aboard DS9 long enough to know how quickly that can change."

"Commander, there are *children* dying!" Major Kira persisted desperately.

"Do you think I didn't hear a word Brother Gis said?" Sisko snapped. Then, in a calmer voice: "We'll do all we can for the children on Bajor, but not at the risk of the children here."

"Of course not," Kira muttered to herself. "They're not Bajorans."

Her words were not soft enough for Sisko to miss. "May I remind you, Major Kira, that the majority of the children aboard *Deep Space Nine are* Bajoran?" He turned his chair away from her. "I'll tell you one of the most important lessons of command: Sometimes the right decision isn't the easy one."

"Sometimes the hard decision isn't the right one," she countered.

He spun his chair around sharply to face her. "Maybe so, but it is *my* decision to make. Now, let's get to work doing what we can for Brother Gis and his people. Dismissed."

Kira looked ready to say something more, but apparently thought better of it. Her mouth opened, then shut and tightened. She acknowledged her commanding officer's order with a crisp nod and marched out of his office. The air felt several degrees chillier after she left.

Sisko folded his hands over the list Brother Gis had left behind. He knew he had made the only possible decision as far as the question of Dr. Bashir went. *Deep Space Nine* was calm now, but for how long? Could he predict accidents at the docking bays, incoming starships with medical emergencies aboard, unforeseen major injuries to any one of Mr. O'Brien's people brought about by working with dicey Cardassian equipment?

"I'm not one of the Prophets," he murmured. But he was the commander, and it was his responsibility to look after the people under his command as he deemed best. That did not include depriving them of their chief medical officer's knowledge and skill for an unspecified period of time.

He began to work on Brother Gis's list. If he worked hard enough, he hoped he would not think so much about the children.

CHAPTER
2

CHIEF OF SECURITY ODO was outside Commander Sisko's office when he encountered the Bajoran vedek who had been Brother Gis's companion on the runabout. The man was acting strangely, ignoring the device that would announce his presence and instead tapping the locked door with a peculiar-looking tube. Odo moved swiftly to place himself between the monk and the door.

"May I help you?" he asked, though his tone turned the polite inquiry into the demand *Who are you and what are you doing here?*

"How does it work?" the vedek asked.

"How does *what* work?" Odo replied testily.

"This." The vedek gave the closed door a substantial rap with the tube, making Odo flinch in spite of himself.

"You need to know how a *door* works?" The shapeshifter could not help sounding amused.

"Not *a* door," the vedek responded with equanimity. *"This* door."

Odo gave a little snort of half-suppressed laughter

through his not-quite-perfectly-formed nose. "I fail to see the problem. A door is a door."

"Here." The vedek dipped his free hand into his sleeve and quickly tossed an object right at Odo. The shapeshifter's reflexes did not fail him; he snatched it from midair and stared at the object.

"What's this?" he asked, slowly rotating the small, rubbery cube.

"A ball." The vedek smiled. "Go ahead and roll it across the floor if you don't believe me."

"Roll this?" Odo snorted again. "I don't think so."

Still smiling, the vedek extended his hand for the cube. The shapeshifter slapped it into his palm unceremoniously. The vedek gave it an odd flip and the cube went bouncing down the corridor on its edges in an erratic, wandering course.

But it did roll.

"A ball is a ball," the vedek said, picking it up when it finally came to rest. "And a door is a door," he concluded in triumph.

By now, Odo was out of patience. No matter how much he owed the Bajorans, he could never bring himself to like their vedeks' roundabout way of making a point. *"Is* there something I can do to help you? Besides playing ball in the corridors?"

"I am here to see Commander Sisko," the vedek announced, holding the tube to his chest with both hands.

"Is Commander Sisko expecting you?"

"Commander Sisko is a man who has walked with the Prophets. Who can say what he expects?"

"The Prophets again . . ." Odo muttered to himself in disgust. He liked straight answers to straight questions, something he never got whenever a Bajoran brought up the Prophets. "Do you have an appointment?" he asked.

"I have a mission." The vedek's wrinkled face was

creased by an expression of pure bliss. He cradled the tube tenderly.

"If that's a message for Commander Sisko, I'll give it to him." Odo stuck out his hand.

The vedek scuttled backward, clutching the tube. "It was entrusted to me," he protested. "I cannot let it be seen by any eyes but his."

"You'll still have to let me examine it. I'm in charge of security. I can't permit any suspicious objects to be taken into Commander Sisko's presence."

The vedek backed away even farther, shaking his head violently. Odo sighed. "You have my word of honor that I won't *read* it; I'll just *look* at it. I won't even need to open it if it scans as something harmless. I only want to make sure that it is what you say it is. Then I'll personally escort you in to see Commander Sisko, all right?"

The vedek gave Odo a long, suspicious look that reminded the shapeshifter a lot of himself. Finally, though, the tube changed hands. Odo ran a small sensor over the length of it and found nothing to excite speculation. He passed it back to the vedek, whose hands closed around it as if he'd never expected to get it back at all.

"There. That didn't hurt much, did it?" Odo said dryly.

"Would you also like to scan this?" the vedek asked.

Odo looked down at the rubber cube and grumbled, "That won't be necessary." He touched his communicator. "Commander Sisko, Odo here. There's someone to see you."

"I'm very busy right now, Odo," Sisko voice came through. "I don't want to be disturbed. Tell whoever it is—"

"He appears to be a Bajoran vedek."

"He's back?" The commander's voice betrayed surprise. "Hmmmm, just as well. I have some good news for him from Starfleet Command. The medical supplies are on their way, and I'm working on the other phase of the problem. Bring him in." There was the sound of a lock being disabled and a muted hiss as the door to the commander's office slid back to admit Odo and the monk.

Sisko looked up from his desk to say, "Brother Gis, we were lucky; there are three Federation vessels in the vicinity able to—" He stopped when his eyes lit on the Bajoran's face. "You're not Brother Gis."

"With respect, no." The Bajoran made a shallow bow. "I am *Vedek* Torin, of the *Na-melis* Order. I live in service to the Kai Opaka."

Sisko frowned. "The Kai Opaka is gone."

"We are all diminished by her absence," Vedek Torin responded. "And yet, she remains among us, if we find the eyes to see her."

"More nonsense," Odo muttered.

Vedek Torin gave the shapeshifter a searching look. "My friend, I sense a certain bitterness about you. Although my order is small, we have mastered a number of remarkably effective techniques to achieve personal harmony and set the *pagh* at rest. When I have discharged my mission with Commander Sisko, perhaps I might share some of these with you?"

"What sort of techniques?" Odo asked irascibly.

The rubber cube arced into the air between them. "Well, we play ball a lot."

"I'd take him up on it if I were you, Odo," Sisko said, secretly enjoying the nonplussed expression on the normally unflappable constable's face.

"I don't need personal harmony!" Odo snapped so sharply that Commander Sisko had to smother a chuckle.

"No?" Vedek Torin sounded disappointed. "Then perhaps you would prefer to apply our techniques as a means to rise above your skeptical nature? The mind that doubts everything often finds the answer to nothing. A person in your line of work needs answers."

"With respect, Vedek Torin," Odo said, biting off the words, "I don't think your mission here was to teach me spiritual exercises."

"That is true," the vedek averred. "Commander Sisko, I must ask you to come with me to the temple. I have a message for you from the one in whose service I will ever be."

"From the Kai? But—"

The vedek forestalled his objection. "Reserve your doubts until we have spoken, I beg of you. Come to the temple."

"Can't you just give it to him here?" Odo demanded.

"If I could, why would I ask him to accompany me to the temple?" Vedek Torin asked with such quiet reasonableness that Sisko could almost hear Odo's teeth grinding together.

"I can't leave the station," Sisko said.

"That is not needful. I speak of the temple here. Will you come?"

Sisko rose from his chair and was about to leave the office in company with Vedek Torin when Odo stopped him. "Commander, I don't like this. Why the need for all this—this hole-and-corner secrecy?" He glared at the Bajoran, who returned a beatific look to him.

"Do you have any hard reasons to suspect this man of deceit, Constable?" Sisko asked. Odo was forced to admit that he had none. "Then don't worry; I'll be fine."

Odo followed Sisko and Vedek Torin out of the commander's office. In the corridor, Sisko and the vedek turned in one direction and Odo went in another, continuing his rounds. He had not gone twenty steps when he heard a short, penetrating hiss. He looked to one side and saw Major Kira Nerys motioning for him to join her.

"Is something the matter, Major?" he inquired.

"Nothing, Odo. I just have a little free time and I was wondering if I could buy you a drink at Quark's Place.

The two of us haven't had a nice, friendly chat for a long time."

"A nice, friendly chat, is it?" Odo was amused, in his own reserved way. "A nice, *specific* chat, if I know you."

"Odo, I'm hurt!" she exclaimed, giving him a look to match the words. "You don't think I'm your friend?"

"I know you are. I also know *you.*" He gave her a searching look that had extracted confessions from more than one would-be malefactor aboard DS9.

Major Kira raised her hands in surrender. "You've got me, Odo. All right, then; let's have a nice, *specific* chat over something cool."

"You know I don't drink," he reminded her.

The Bajoran rolled her eyes. "Fine, then can we have our chat without the drinks? I'll owe you one."

"You may wind up owing me more. What's on your mind?"

"I want some information."

Odo smiled sardonically. "I thought as much."

"Who was that vedek I just saw leaving Commander Sisko's office? I saw him earlier, when I went to greet Gis at the runabout docking bay."

"Hmmm . . ." Odo grew thoughtful. "You know, Major, information moves smoothest when it moves both ways. We can trade."

"Trade?"

"My answer for your question, your answer for mine: Who is this Gis you went to greet?" He watched with interest as the color of Major Kira's cheeks heightened slightly.

"Gis came to see Commander Sisko at my suggestion." Her unwillingness to share this knowledge was obvious. "He works in one of the refugee camps."

"What was his business with the commander?"

"Isn't it about time for that trade you mentioned, Odo?" Kira asked innocently. "Who was that vedek?"

"He calls himself Vedek Torin of the *Na-melis* Order."

"Na-melis!" Kira echoed in amazement. "They were the personal assistants of the Kai Opaka."

"So he said."

"But the Kai is gone. What could possibly bring one of the *Na-melis* Order here?" Kira mused. "And what would he want with Commander Sisko?"

"I'm afraid that you will have to go elsewhere for that information," Odo said. "Vedek Torin was decidedly closemouthed on the subject. What about your Brother Gis?"

Major Kira only smiled.

"I see. Very well, if that is all—" He tried to proceed on his rounds. Kira stopped him with a gesture.

"Maybe you don't have that information at the moment, Odo, but it's only a matter of time until you do. I believe in you. You make it your business to know what's going on aboard this station. If you don't know what brought Vedek Torin aboard—*yet*—you won't be ignorant for long. When you do find out, share the news with me. We'll trade again."

"Is that an *order*, Major?" Odo asked.

Kira's smile was set to disarm. "Just a request. From a friend who's helped you do your job once or twice. And one who now owes you one." The smile faded abruptly. "I'm not asking you to spy for me, Odo. As first officer, it's my duty and in the best interests of this station for me to be aware of Commander Sisko's whereabouts at all times. It's a matter of security. You do understand that?"

"Perfectly." The corner of Odo's mouth twitched slightly. "When last seen, Commander Sisko and Vedek Torin were heading for the station shrine. If I learn more, I will make it a point to pass that information on to you. All in the name of security, of course."

"Thank you," Major Kira replied with dignity. "I'd appreciate that."

As she left, Odo remarked to himself, "There goes the only person I know who could out-trade a Ferengi." He uttered a short, sharp bark of laughter at the thought of how annoyed Kira would be to hear herself compared to Quark, then resumed his rounds.

The Bajoran shrine aboard *Deep Space Nine* was a place of silences and mysteries. Although Benjamin Sisko had made it his business to acquaint himself with every aspect of the station as soon as he had settled into his new posting, his familiarity with the shrine relied more on floor plans and schematics than personal experience. He was not a frequent visitor to this outpost of Bajoran mysticism, and those few times he had set foot across the threshold, he had been too preoccupied by other matters to truly notice his surroundings.

He followed Vedek Torin through the main area of the shrine, breathing deeply the soothing scent of old incense and pausing impatiently while the monk lit a fresh cone of perfumed gum in one of the many delicately carved braziers. As they went on, Sisko saw several Bajoran worshipers in the shadows. He recognized them—shopkeepers and servicepeople from the station. There was Kova Dilvan, who ran the refreshment stand where Jake spent so much of his time and nearly all of his allowance. Sisko was used to seeing the squat, dark-haired Bajoran full of bounce and energy, an aggressive salesman fit to give even the Ferengi some hard competition. Now he stood in quiet contemplation before an abstract sculpture on the shrine wall, the picture of tranquillity.

They left the public area and passed through a doorway hung with ornaments like those peculiar to adult Bajorans' earrings. The crystal strands chimed softly as the curtain closed behind Sisko and Vedek Torin, leaving them in a small, extremely private chamber. It was unfurnished except for a smooth, cylindric pedestal holding a glimmering golden dish of oil. Vedek Torin murmured a few words, then kindled the wick floating in the oil. It was the only light in the chamber, but it was sufficient.

"Now we may speak," Vedek Torin said.

"Are you sure?" Sisko cast his eyes back to the crystal curtain. It did not seem like a substantial barrier to potential eavesdroppers.

The vedek was unperturbed. "It will suffice. I bring you a message, Commander, from the Kai Opaka herself. It is a message whose secrecy must be guarded absolutely. If you do not have the skill to preserve secrecy where there are no doors, you will do no better behind a hundred locks."

Benjamin Sisko regarded the vedek closely. "How did your order receive this message? No one has heard anything from the Kai since her departure." He was sure of that. If anyone had had word from the Kai, there were half a dozen political opportunists on Bajor ready and willing to transform the message so that it would be all to their advantage.

"I did not say we *received* this message," the vedek replied. "It is as you say: No word has come from the Kai. But these words remained behind." He removed the ornate stopper from the metallic tube in his hand and slid out the pale blue scroll within. "Since the Kai's departure, the members of my order and myself have been devoting our efforts to organizing and archiving all personal writings that she left with us. Such must be preserved."

"She was a woman of wisdom," Sisko agreed. "I am sure there is a great deal of value in any works she left behind."

"More than you know, Commander." Carefully the vedek moved the dish of oil to one side and unrolled the scroll on the pedestal. "Are you able to read Bajoran? There are several versions of our written language, you know, some used only within the Temple."

"I understand. I'll try," Sisko said, looking over Vedek

22

Torin's shoulder. "If I can't make this out, would you have any objections to my having the computer translate it?"

"None. That way you will be assured that the translation is an honest one. Is that not so?"

Benjamin Sisko was momentarily embarrassed by the vedek's insight. "The computer can also confirm that this *is* a message left by the Kai, and not something deliberately planted by someone else for your order to find."

Vedek Torin nodded. "The intrigues of Bajor. You are wise to be so cautious, Commander. Your mind is open, but your eyes remain open as well. That is good. The Kai was altogether right in placing so much trust in you. With such good judgment, perhaps you may not need to submit this message to your computer after all. See."

What Sisko saw was a closely written, beautifully lettered example of the most common, accessible form of Bajoran script, easily legible. The message was framed by a thick band of dark blue and gold decorative calligraphy that reminded Sisko of ancient Islamic art from Earth. He had no trouble reading the Kai's message.

" 'By the blessings of the Prophets, I, the Kai Opaka, have been vouchsafed a vision of the child,' " Sisko read aloud softly, occasionally glancing up at Vedek Torin for any sign that he was mistranslating the Kai's words. " 'The hour has come when the Prophets choose to reveal the place where we must seek the child, and the peace of Bajor hangs in the balance. My time may not permit me to witness the search, but if this mission is entrusted to one who has walked with the Prophets, all may yet be well. Seek her in the places of desolation, for she shall heal them. In the heart of the green valley of song, in the village where many waters dance, the prophesied one shall be found. Let her then be brought to the Temple, into the sight of the Prophets and the people, that they may behold and believe.' "

Sisko lifted his eyes from the scroll. "A child?" he asked. "What child?"

"The child of an ancient prophecy," Vedek Torin explained. "It speaks of a healer to come and make all things whole. Do your people have such prophecies?"

"Many peoples of the Federation do," Sisko admitted. "But this"—he gestured at the message—"this doesn't strike me as a matter for the attention of Starfleet. It seems to be a purely internal Bajoran concern, something the Temple itself should pursue, not us."

"I would agree with you, Commander," the vedek said, "if not for the fact that the Kai's message is no longer solely in the keeping of my order."

"What? You spoke of the need for secrecy—"

"Secrecy as far as those who do not believe in the prophecy," Vedek Torin said, folding his hands on the pedestal. "To us, the child is everything. If you have a treasure you prize above all others, what would you give to recover it should it fall into a stranger's hands?"

Sisko felt a pang as Jake's face flashed before him. "Anything," he said sincerely.

"Better, then, to do all in your power to prevent the treasure's initial loss. No matter what the differences separating the different political factions of Bajor, we are united in this belief of the prophesied healer. But those who do not believe would see the child as a pawn to further their own desires for the future of Bajor."

Sisko was inclined to agree with Vedek Torin. Yet, knowing what he did of the Bajoran religious establishment, he wondered whether this *Na-melis* vedek was not being too optimistic. His order had served the Kai Opaka; in a way, their exclusive devotion sheltered them from the realities of life outside the Kai's service. On Bajor, intrigue was not limited to politicians. It was an insidious growth that sent tendrils of plot and counterplot even into the heart of the Temple itself.

"Then other Bajorans know about the Kai's vision of

the child?" Sisko asked. The vedek indicated that this was so. "I don't see your problem. The more who know, the easier your search for the child will be."

"I wish that were so, Commander." Vedek Torin sighed. "It is not. When we discovered the Kai's message, we brought it before the Temple council, as was our duty. By rights, the matter should have remained within the Temple until our own searches and inquiries might bring the child into our midst, as the Kai directed we must. But word escaped. Rumors sped through the capital. Not every ear that heard them was bound by the silence of the Temple."

"The silence of the Temple isn't all that effective if the rumors escaped in the first place," Sisko pointed out.

"Alas, that too is so." The vedek made a gesture of resignation. "Only a directive from the council, worded in the strongest possible terms, put an end to the gossip. But it was too late; the harm was done."

"What harm? Did the rumors reach the ears of any unbelievers?"

The vedek's eyes glittered brightly by the light of the oil lamp. "You are the first such to know, and that only because you have walked with the Prophets. May you be the last, until the child is found. No, Commander Sisko; word of the child's existence only touched Bajoran ears, but that was enough. Tell me, have you heard of the *Dessin-ka?*"

Sisko thought hard. The name sounded familiar, something Major Kira had mentioned to him once. "The *Dessin-ka* . . . Isn't that the name of one of the political factions making up the provisional government?"

"A very influential faction, Commander," Vedek Torin agreed. "My brethren and I did not know precisely how influential the *Dessin-ka* were until our news escaped to their ears. They are—how would you say it?—a group given to the more traditional values of our faith."

"Then they oppose the Federation presence on Bajor?"

"Adherence to tradition need not mean refusal to accept all things new. The *Dessin-ka* recognize the many advantages your Federation may bring to Bajor. They are a strong voice in your favor . . . for the moment."

"For the moment?" Sisko repeated slowly. He didn't like the sound of that.

The vedek stared into the flame that danced above the smooth surface of the oil. "You said before that you know of many peoples besides our own who cherish belief in the prophecy of a healing child. Yet I think you will agree, these beliefs are not identical?"

"There are some variations, of course, but in general—"

"The *Dessin-ka*, too, have a prophecy. We see the promise of a healer in the Kai's words; they see more. The child of the Kai's vision is for them the *Nekor*, the one who brings a sword. She will make all Bajor one by her power."

Sisko was at a loss to comprehend Vedek Torin's words. "I thought all your people shared a single faith. How can the healer of one Bajoran prophecy be the—the sword-bearer of another?"

Vedek Torin turned from the pedestal. He walked to a wall where a plaque set with dozens of crystals glimmered in the shadows. His fingers plucked three long, tapering stones from their setting and showed them to Sisko. One was blue, one red, the third a purple so deep it was almost black.

"Beautiful, are they not?" the vedek said, letting Sisko see that the ornaments were actually hollow. With extreme care he dipped each one into the oil and held them up to the light of the flame. Beams of green, orange, and pale amethyst light shone through the facets. "What has changed?" he asked, as if speaking to a child.

"Only what we see," Sisko replied. "The crystals and the oil inside each one is the same. I see what you mean, Vedek Torin."

The vedek sighed. "Would that the *Dessin-ka* shared your willingness to be instructed. They are convinced that the vision-child is their *Nekor* and none other. They clamor for her to be found at once. Their prophecy, you see, foretells that the *Nekor*'s reign must begin with the *Berajin,* the time of the harvest festival. We have tried to explain to them the difficulty—perhaps the impossibility—of complying with their demand. The *Berajin* comes too soon for us to have hope of finding her and bringing her to the Temple by then."

Commander Sisko studied the Kai's message. "True. This doesn't give you much help about where to begin your search."

"No?" Vedek Torin looked perplexed. "What further details would you desire than the name and location of the village where the child may be found?" His gnarled finger touched a line of the text.

" 'In the heart of the green valley of song, in the village where many waters dance,' " Sisko read once more.

The vedek laughed. "With respect, Commander, your command of this form of written Bajoran is excellent, but you are reading the *meaning* of our place-names, not the names as themselves."

"Ah!" Sisko exclaimed, understanding his error. He recalled a conversation with Chief O'Brien during which the Irishman had told him that the Terran place-name *Dublin* actually meant *the black pool.* On Earth, no one bound for Dublin spoke of going to *the black pool,* and here—

"Then this says . . . ?" Commander Sisko asked, placing his finger beside the vedek's on the scroll.

"The Kaladrys Valley, Bennikar village." The vedek's hands retreated to the shelter of his sleeves. "It might as well say the abyss. The Kaladrys Valley is a wasteplace now, and no longer do waters dance in Bennikar."

"The Kaladrys Valley?" Brother Gis's visitation returned to Sisko.

"In the Kai's service, we lost track of the world's small ironies," Vedek Torin said, his eyelids lowered as he contemplated the oil lamp's flame. "Had the Prophets granted the Kai this vision a few years earlier, the Cardassian destruction was still comfortably far off from Bennikar. We could have found the child and brought her to the Temple with time to spare. Now there is no Bennikar."

"And what guarantee do you have that the same is not true of"—Sisko hesitated, hating the words, but forced to say them—"the child as well?"

Vedek Torin's eyes snapped wide open. "But that cannot be true," he insisted. "It *must* not be true. This is why you must help us, Commander. You must lend us the Federation's aid in finding the child. If she is not found, if the *Dessin-ka* do not see their promised *Nekor* before them in the Temple at *Berajin,* they will accuse us of having found her and hidden her from them—even if she is not there to be hidden! The repercussions will be terrible. They will pull all their support from the provisional government, upsetting—even smashing the balance we have worked so hard to achieve."

His hands darted out to seize Sisko's. "You have the resources we do not. You can find the blessed child where we could not begin to seek her."

"One child . . ." Sisko took a deep breath. "A child from a village that's been wiped out of existence. No other clues? Any description of what she looks like?"

The Bajoran shook his head. "Neither here nor in any of the scriptures of prophecy. But she will be known to you."

"You are asking for a miracle, Vedek Torin," Sisko said. "The Federation will help as much as possible, but we can't promise miracles."

The vedek inclined his head. "When you first came to Bajor, you promised us peace. Is this not the greatest miracle of all?"

CHAPTER
3

"COMMANDER?"

Taren Gis was waiting outside the shrine when Benjamin Sisko finally emerged. For an instant, the commander imagined that the monk hailing him was Vedek Torin, who had inexplicably slipped past him to catch him off-guard for some unknown reason. It seemed impossible—he had left Vedek Torin replacing the colored crystal droplets in their settings in the wall sculpture—but Sisko had learned to redefine "impossible" since coming to *Deep Space Nine*. Quickly enough he recognized his error. In their earth-colored robes, their hair mostly concealed by the long-lappeted caps, the resemblance between the two Bajorans was uncanny.

How did the punch line of that old joke go? Sisko mused. *Oh yes: You find what you look for.*

"Brother Gis, this is a lucky chance," Sisko said. "I have some very good news for you."

"You will lend us your healer," the monk said, anticipating him.

"Hmmm, maybe not just chance after all," Sisko said, stroking his chin. He thought of the flimsy crystal curtain and how easy it made an eavesdropper's task.

"Forgive me for speaking in haste. You are thinking uncharitable thoughts of me, but I assure you, they are undeserved."

"What I was thinking, Brother Gis, was that your colleague, Vedek Torin, has much to learn about choosing the proper place for a private conversation; that is, if he wishes it to remain private."

"You were with him now?" Brother Gis asked. When the commander nodded, the monk went on: "The confidentiality of what is uttered within the precincts of the shrine is sacrosanct. I give you my solemn oath, I know nothing of what passed between you."

"Then how did you know what I was about to tell you?" Sisko asked. "You're not a mind reader, are you?" This last was uttered only half in jest. There was much about the Bajoran monks that remained unknown and more that defied explanation.

"I know none with that power, Commander, although I know many capable of giving the impression of possessing it." Brother Gis chuckled. "There is a certain advantage to be had in the appearance of omniscience. The truth is, Vedek Torin and I arrived here on the same vessel. We were the only passengers, and while in transit he shared his mission and the secret of the scroll with me. He knew I would say nothing of it elsewhere. I am trustworthy."

"Did he also tell you how news of the scroll leaked out of the Temple through some other 'trustworthy' source?" Sisko asked.

Brother Gis was unruffled. "He did. But the harm there is already done. You cannot smash the same cup twice. And even if this were not so, my place on Bajor is in the wilderness; whom would I tell? Lizards care very little for politics."

"I can think of several people who'd disagree with you

there," Sisko replied, good humor restored. "So you knew that even if I turned you down at first, Vedek Torin's mission would have to bring me around, hmm?"

The monk's face turned from cheerful to serious. "Commander, I did not come here to play games. I have no time; the *children* have no time. The child of prophecy is supposed to heal a world; I only need to heal the few lives still left in my care. Our camp lies in the heart of the Kaladrys Valley, in the general region of Bennikar. I would not be surprised to learn that we host a number of refugees from that village."

"You don't know for a fact where your people come from?"

Brother Gis shrugged. "We ask no questions besides 'Are you well?' and 'Are you hungry?' Our guests may speak of other matters only if they choose. We are not concerned with the past, merely the present and, the Prophets willing, the future."

"But surely the provisional government must ask you for background information about the citizens in your care," Sisko protested.

"The government has problems of its own," the monk replied. "If they can pretend ours do not exist, all the better. I cannot recall the last time a government representative visited us, for that matter, so I know not whether any of the other camps has received more attention than ours. It would be impossible for them to have had less. At this moment, there is no accurate account of how many displaced persons are still occupying the camps, and certainly no record of their identities. We do not urge our people to speak of the old days if that is not their choice, for kindness' sake. They have had too much taken from them already. You feel a loss less if you do not name it too often."

"I know," Sisko said. The words were heartfelt. The memory of his wife's face fluttered through his mind. It was thanks to the Bajorans—to the Kai in particular—

that it was no longer a memory forever darkened by the circumstances of her death.

"Some of our smallest guests do not even know that their villages had names. To them, it was simply *home*. Now it is nothing." The marks of sorrow on Brother Gis's face seemed to grow deeper. "Still, we are your best place to commence inquiries after the child."

"I hope so," Sisko said. "Apart from the name of the village, the Kai's vision left no other clues, not even a hint about the child's appearance, her age, nothing."

"As for that, I may be of some assistance. I have studied some of the prophecies, and perhaps you will find that my brethren in the camp have studied others. I, at least, know that the child should be between seven and twelve years of age."

"How do you know that?"

"The prophecies refer to her as one who has passed first presentation to the Prophets, but not yet reached the age of initiation. And of course you know as well as I that we must search for a girl."

"Yes, the Kai did speak of the child as 'she,'" Sisko agreed. "But that doesn't do much to narrow down the field. How many girl children must there be in the Kaladrys Valley?"

"There are fewer by the day, Commander," Brother Gis said matter-of-factly.

"We'll do everything in our power to change that, Brother Gis," Sisko promised. "The supplies you requested are on the way; they should be here within three days. In the meantime, I will be dispatching my chief medical officer, Dr. Julian Bashir, as well as Lieutenant Jadzia Dax to your encampment."

"This Lieutenant Dax is also a healer?"

"Not as such, but she is my science officer, and a person of wide experience."

That was an understatement, and Sisko knew it.

Although to the uninformed eye, Lieutenant Dax appeared to be an entrancingly lovely young woman in her twenties, she was in reality a Trill—a life-form made up of a humanoid host and a wormlike symbiont within.

The inner part of Dax's being had lived for centuries, surviving one host after another but always preserving the memories and experiences it had shared with each. Both parts benefited enormously from the relationship. Sisko himself had originally encountered Dax while the symbiont was lodged in the body of a mature male. The change in Dax's outer looks made for some occasionally awkward moments between old friends.

Perhaps, Sisko reasoned, there was some shred of information somewhere in Dax's shared memories that would provide the crucial clue to finding a cure for the Bajoran camp fever.

"Only one true healer, and so much work to be done . . ." Brother Gis murmured.

"I can also spare you one of Dr. Bashir's assistants, Ensign Kahrimanis, and when the Federation ships arrive with your supplies, they ought to be able to provide some additional personnel as well."

The monk brightened to hear this news. "Well, Dr. Bashir's one more healer than I was going to get. I will pray that the Prophets reveal the cure to your Dr. Bashir swiftly. The sooner he discovers an effective treatment, the sooner we may return him to you."

"Speed is in the best interests of us all," Sisko concurred. "While Lieutenant Dax will provide some help for Dr. Bashir, her true task will be to locate the child of the Kai's prophecy. For the sake of security, as requested by Vedek Torin, no one else will know the reason for her presence; not even Dr. Bashir."

The monk made a gesture of acceptance.

"If you or your brothers happen to think of any further clues concerning this child, bring them to Lieutenant

Dax's attention at once. This is no easy task. We can use all the help we can get."

Brother Gis's lips curved up slightly. "So can we."

Dr. Julian Bashir stood at attention before Benjamin Sisko's desk, but his eyes did not remain fixed on his commander's face. Try as he might, he could not resist stealing a sideways glance at Lieutenant Dax, who had also been called into the commander's office.

Commander Sisko was speaking about Bajor, about the necessity for the Federation to take a more active role in helping the Bajorans recover from sixty years of Cardassian occupation and surmount the local factionalism that reasserted itself almost as soon as the oppressors departed. Naturally Commander Sisko stressed that while simple humanity cried out for the Federation to act, the Prime Directive put certain unavoidable barriers in the way of total involvement.

If he had not been standing at attention, Dr. Bashir would have shaken his head and sighed in perplexity. Why was Commander Sisko bringing up all this now? It was common knowledge. More to the point, why was the commander going over such familiar territory solely for the benefit of his medical and science officers?

While still a medical student, Dr. Bashir had developed the extremely useful ability to split his attention. Thus he was able to make rounds under the tutelage of one doctor while picking up additional useful insights from the lecturer of a second group of students just across the ward. When Julian's teacher marveled aloud at the handsome young man's apparently miraculous ability to learn twice as much, twice as fast as his peers, they never suspected it was because Julian could benefit from two teachers at the same time.

It was this same gift that now allowed him to hear every word Commander Sisko said while his mind cast back over the circumstances that had brought him here.

Less than fifteen minutes ago he had been strolling on the Promenade, feeling rather pleased with himself. A brief visit to Garak's shop had turned into a lengthy conversation with the Cardassian clothier.

Garak was an anomaly, and Dr. Bashir's inquisitive mind never could resist such a tantalizing puzzle. As a member of the race that had bled Bajor for sixty years, the clothier had nonetheless chosen to remain behind on *Deep Space Nine* when his fellow Cardassians pulled out. Garak was no fool; he *had* to realize that his continued presence aboard the station would be viewed with suspicion, to say nothing of out-and-out hostility by the Bajorans. It was not the safest place for him to be, even with the Federation standing guard, maintaining the peace of the station. Yet he stayed.

Privately, Julian thought of Garak as the Brave Little Tailor from the old Earth fairy tale. Just as privately, he pondered the real reason for Garak's choice. He was not the only one. The Cardassian dealt in more than the latest fashions, and secrets were changed just as frequently as styles behind the curtains of his fitting rooms. But whose secrets, and at what price?

There had already been more than one occasion on which Garak's subtle aid had helped the Federation. Such actions seemed to indicate that Garak was an agent who would act however and for whomever it would benefit himself most, but was his cooperation a blind? When you dealt with someone like Quark, you knew the Ferengi was only out for personal gain. With Garak . . . ? Bashir wasn't ready to hand in a final diagnosis just yet. The Cardassians were not the sort of people to forget their expulsion from Bajor, especially since the discovery of the wormhole. Would Garak pull back the curtain someday to reveal a door through which his people could retake all they had lost?

Unasked, Dr. Bashir had made it his business to keep an eye on this potential threat to the security of *Deep*

Space Nine. He told himself it was his duty, but the truth was he would have done it anyway, just for the thrill of dabbling in intrigue. A medical student's life was circumscribed by long hours of classes followed by longer hours of study and practice. There was little time left over for relaxation, and definitely none for adventure.

Adventure! The word, the very thought of it thrilled Dr. Bashir. When he was younger, before he sank himself body and soul into his medical studies, he loved to spend every free moment steeped in all sorts of adventure stories, everything from tales of swashbuckling swordsmen and Wild West cowboy heroes to the latest real-life news of Starfleet actions across the galaxy.

He often told himself that he'd chosen a career in medicine first of all as a result of that incident during the ion storm on Invaria II, when simple medical knowledge might have saved that poor girl's life. Having his career as a professional tennis player pop like a soap bubble during his first match merely confirmed his choice. But he knew as well that he had chosen to become a physician because it satisfied the many different urges of his soul. As a doctor, he would be able to solve a thousand fascinating human puzzles—puzzles that *must* be solved, with stakes of life and death in the balance. His expertise would earn him as much admiration as any of his boyhood heroes, and even if dashing bladesmen no longer existed outside of holosuite programs, he could still save the lives of countless damsels in distress with a scalpel if not with a sword.

But even the many promises of a medical career were not enough for him. He refused to become just another doctor; he would become the *best*. He joined Starfleet because their standards were almost as high as his own, and because the dream of adventure on some distant frontier still beckoned.

His posting to *Deep Space Nine* seemed like the fulfillment of his every desire. And once here, finding

Garak was icing on the cake. Julian was never more pleased with himself than after having a long and—he hoped—revealing interview with the Cardassian. He couldn't for the life of him understand why no one else on the station seemed to recognize or appreciate his efforts.

That didn't stop him from trying to make them see what a good job of amateur espionage he was doing.

He viewed it as pure luck when he ran into Commander Sisko on the Promenade. "I've just had the most fascinating chat with our Cardassian friend Garak—" he began.

"You can tell me all about it in my office," Sisko replied, and hustled him away before he could get another word out.

When they entered the commander's office, instead of sitting down and asking Julian to describe the conversation with Garak, Sisko motioned for the young doctor to keep silent while Lieutenant Dax was summoned. Dr. Bashir couldn't help preening a bit when he heard that. At last his efforts were being appreciated! Better; Commander Sisko was taking his contribution seriously enough to want Lieutenant Dax to share Julian's revelations.

It was easy for Julian to remain silent while they waited for Dax to arrive. He was mentally reviewing every detail of his talk with Garak, the better to present it in a way that would force the lovely lieutenant to take him seriously.

Why won't *she?* he wondered, and the thought rankled as much as it always did. *I know she's a Trill, that she's lived hundreds of years—at least her symbiont has—but that doesn't make Jadzia a crone. So what if she shares the symbiont's memories? I've studied the writings of Hippocrates, but that doesn't make me an ancient Greek. Sometimes I get the feeling she thinks of me as just a little boy.*

Strangely enough, this thought did not irritate Julian;

it only strengthened his determination to show her how wrong she was. He had been underestimated by others before this. His youth, his good looks, his healthy self-confidence, all together or separately managed to make certain people prejudge him. He had proved himself to every one of them, and he intended to prove himself to Dax, too. It was only a matter of diligence and patience.

But as soon as Lieutenant Dax presented herself in the commander's office, Julian realized to his dismay that his latest effort would have to wait. Without saying a word about Dr. Bashir's recent talk with Garak, Commander Sisko launched into this speech about the need to give more help to the Bajorans. Julian failed to see the connection, but he was a good Starfleet officer. He bit his tongue and bided his time.

"We are now fortunate enough to have an opportunity to aid the Bajorans without treading on any Starfleet regulations," Sisko went on. "Our assistance has been requested for a purely humanitarian effort on the surface of Bajor. Dr. Bashir, you've often said that the main reason you wanted to come to *Deep Space Nine* was to have the chance to practice . . . frontier medicine?"

"Yes, sir," Julian replied, with some small hesitation. Something odd was afoot here; another puzzle. That was all right, he liked puzzles.

"Well, you're going to get that opportunity. There's a new sickness ravaging the displaced-persons camps on Bajor, a kind of fever like none their healers have ever encountered before. The situation is growing graver by the day. Repatriation efforts are going slowly, and the refugees still in the camps were not in perfect health when they arrived—"

"Small wonder," Lieutenant Dax commented.

"As you say," Sisko acknowledged. "They're easy prey for this epidemic."

"Excuse me, sir, but *is* this an epidemic?" Dr. Bashir inquired.

"I'm not familiar with the exact circumstances that must exist before someone with your training could call it an epidemic, but I intend to treat is as such. It's a sickness that is invariably fatal, there is no known cure for it, and it is spreading rapidly." Sisko was grim. "Yes, I'd call that an epidemic."

News of the medical crisis on Bajor had an astonishing, immediate effect on Dr. Bashir. He was no longer concerned with impressing Lieutenant Dax or making Commander Sisko admire him for his exploits at espionage. His whole mind, his whole being, focused on the problem at hand and the plight of the afflicted Bajorans. "How far has the contagion spread?" he asked intently.

"I'm afraid we have no reliable information on that," Sisko admitted. "Only rumors that it's been found in several camps in the Kaladrys Valley and it might be spreading beyond."

"Have any measures been taken to isolate the patients?"

"Not to my knowledge, no. No extraordinary measures have been taken, although the camps themselves are fairly well isolated."

"The Cardassians did a pretty thorough job of destroying the Kaladrys Valley," Lieutenant Dax put in. "It's currently impossible for the resources of any one area to maintain an extended group of people. Therefore, the Bajorans have planted their refugee camps as far apart as possible, so that the survivors have a fighting chance of supporting themselves on the land they've been given."

"I'm sending you and Lieutenant Dax to head a small landing party," Sisko told Dr. Bashir. "You're being sent to the camp that seems to be the originating point of the infection. Your assignment is to help care for the sick, naturally, but I want you to give top priority to diagnosing this illness and developing a cure."

"I'll do better than that," Dr. Bashir said boldly. "I'll come up with a vaccine to prevent the disease."

"I'll be satisfied if you can just find a way to hold it in check, and to do that as quickly as possible," Sisko replied. "Lieutenant Dax will be working with you closely on this; her experience might provide a crucial insight."

Dr. Bashir grinned. "An excellent idea, Commander."

Dax made a sound that might have been a laugh but ended up as a cough.

"You won't have much to work with," Sisko continued. "Not at first. I'm sending as much of the station's medical supplies with you as we can safely spare, though it's far from sufficient. We're expecting additional supplies in three days—that is, if nothing comes up in the meantime to divert the ships bringing them."

Dr. Bashir nodded crisply. "Am I correct in assuming that we'll be operating under, well, primitive conditions?"

Sisko's mouth twisted into an indulgent half-smile. "You might say that. From what Brother Gis has told me, only self-contained diagnostic tools can be operated in the camp. They have no power source."

"None?" Dr. Bashir looked doubtful.

"I thought it was your dream to practice frontier medicine?" Dax teased gently. "It sounds to me as though this assignment will be the answer to your prayers."

"I was only trying to learn as much as possible about what's waiting for us." The heat behind his own words startled Dr. Bashir. His face felt as if it were on fire. "Who is Brother Gis?" he asked, to divert attention from himself.

"He's the monk who came to us for help," Sisko answered, "and he's a healer in his own right. He'll brief you on conditions in his camp and give you as much information as he's got concerning other settlements. I'd pay close attention to what he says if I were you, Doctor. Major Kira tells me that Bajoran monks of the healing orders have access to a body of medical knowledge predating ours by centuries. Their technique relies less on technology and more on a combination of physical and spiritual healing, but it's said to work wonders."

"According to Major Kira," Dr. Bashir commented.

"You doubt her word?" Sisko sounded amused.

"No sir, it's just that . . . Major Kira isn't exactly objective when it comes to all things Bajoran."

Dax smiled at Dr. Bashir, a radiant look he wished he could freeze in time and hold on to forever. "Dr. Bashir's right there, sir," she said. "Major Kira's patriotism does tend to color her judgment at times."

"Fortunately, neither one of you will need to evaluate Major Kira's judgment," Commander Sisko said cheerfully. "You'll be getting firsthand experience of Bajoran healing; you can make your own reports on it afterward. And Dr. Bashir—"

"Yes, Commander?"

"Don't worry too much about the primitive working conditions. You'll be able to return to the station at any time, if you should need to use the diagnostic equipment here. But whether you do the bulk of your work here or on Bajor, there is one factor I can't stress strongly enough: *time*. The refugees have very little of it left."

"I'll begin preparations immediately, sir," Dr. Bashir said. "Can Brother Gis meet me in the infirmary? He can brief me while I pack."

"An excellent plan, Dr. Bashir. I'll see to it. Dismissed."

As Dr. Bashir turned on his heel and started from the commander's office, he heard Sisko add, "Lieutenant Dax, I'd like to have a further word with you."

Now what's that all about? Julian wondered. Another puzzle. And the sickness defying Bajoran healing powers was yet another puzzle awaiting him.

That was all right. Dr. Bashir liked puzzles, especially when solving them might mean another chance for

Jadzia Dax to see that he was not the little boy she thought. A puzzle, a chance to impress Jadzia, and the opportunity for Dr. Julian Bashir to practice medicine under primitive conditions and prove that he didn't need the technological bag of tricks of Starfleet to triumph over this unknown disease—perfect! Any other doctor might feel just a little nervous, going into strange territory like this, but he was not just any other doctor.

He had never felt so confident in his life.

CHAPTER
4

CHIEF OF OPERATIONS Miles O'Brien leaned on the control console of the runabout and asked the pair of legs sticking out from under it, "What do you make of it, McCormick?"

Ensign McCormick's muffled voice came from deep within the bowels of the machinery. "Never seen anything like this before."

"And not likely to again, if you're lucky." O'Brien slapped the console. "Blasted Cardie technology. When it works, it works . . . barely. They're the misers of the universe."

McCormick's legs vanished. There was a short scuffle; then he popped his head out and looked up at the chief of operations. "Don't you mean the Ferengi, sir?" he asked.

"No, I do not," O'Brien replied, giving the console a look of disgust. "There's worlds of difference between a cutthroat merchant and a miser. The Ferengi may be greedy, but they know the value of reinvesting what they've got with an eye to bigger profits in future. The

Cardies just take what they can and hold on to it with both hands and a tractor beam. Their machines are designed to meet the bare minimum when it comes to function specs. No thought to adaptability, no thought to possible future needs, just so it works enough to do the task of the moment. There's no—no *elegance* to it!" It was the worst judgment Miles O'Brien could pronounce on any technology.

McCormick scooted out from beneath the console. "I think that's done it. I've got it fixed."

"All right. You and Trulli run some diagnostics on it." O'Brien touched his comm badge. "O'Brien to Trulli. We're done here. How about you?"

"Trulli here," a voice replied. "I've taken care of this one. All runabout transporters should be working at peak level now."

"Good." O'Brien shuddered at the thought of what might have happened if a routine maintenance check hadn't brought the problem to light before the next time the runabout transporters were put to use. He'd been around long enough to know there was no such thing as a pretty accident, but those involving transporter malfunctions were the ugliest of all.

Of course, it was too much to hope that the runabout transporters would be the only thing to go wonky. Leave it to the Cardies to make sure that tech troubles never came by ones.

"Trulli, I want you to come here and work with McCormick, running the checkout diagnostics on the transporter systems. After that, take one of the runabouts—make it the *Ganges*—and get it into high orbit over Bajor. We'll see if we can't pick up our package."

"Aye, sir."

"O'Brien out." He cut off communication and turned back to McCormick. "After Trulli takes the runabout, join me in Ops to check out the repairs on the long-range sensors."

"Shouldn't we test all the runabouts, sir?" McCormick asked.

"We will, in time. I just want to make sure we've got at least one up and running. Don't worry, you'll get your turn."

"Aye, sir." McCormick sounded a little disappointed. O'Brien knew his two top ensigns were both keen to fly. For himself, he couldn't fathom the obsession. Give him a mechanical puzzle to solve and he'd be just as happy in a hole in the ground as in a runabout sailing through space.

Miles left McCormick to his work and headed for Ops. He wasn't a suspicious person by nature, but the way things kept breaking by twos and threes aboard DS9 sometimes made him think that it couldn't all be assigned to Cardie cheeseparing. Maybe—just maybe—the departing Cardassians had been "generous" enough to leave a few surprise packages behind, embedded in the computer system. It would explain a lot.

"A lot," he said to himself as he studied the sensor controls. "Or nothing." He was deep into the problem when Commander Sisko came in.

"Chief O'Brien, has that difficulty with the runabout transporters been cleared up yet?" he asked.

O'Brien sighed. "The transporters themselves are fine now, sir. We'll be giving them a test run shortly, just to make sure. Now there's a new difficulty with the runabout sensors, and it appears to carry over to the long-range sensors here. We got scrambled readings when we tried to get a fix on a specific target. I've got a man down there on Bajor, sitting on his thumbs, waiting for us to home in on him and pick him up. On the last run, we couldn't tell him from the rest of the crowd."

"What crowd?"

"The crowd in the Pride of Mintak, sir." An impish look twinkled in O'Brien's eye. "It's not up to the standards of Quark's Place, but it's hospitable enough to Federation personnel."

"That's saying something for a Bajoran bar. So your man's not just sitting on his thumbs after all," Sisko commented lightly.

"Well, we also needed him to be somewhere there's a few *in*animate objects to test the transporters on before we risk a man's life, sir," O'Brien said, trying to look dutiful.

"Such as a bottle or two of *kis?*" Sisko suggested.

"If there's nothing else handy for a target, sir." O'Brien continued to pretend that the famed Bajoran brew was the farthest thing from his mind. "And if a man volunteers to play guinea pig for me, I like to give him somewhere congenial to do it."

"That's very considerate of you. I'm sure he appreciates it. Now tell me: Does this difficulty with the sensors affect use of the transporters in any way?" Sisko stressed. "We've got people and supplies to deliver the fastest way possible, and I'd prefer not to have the runabout come in for a landing if it isn't absolutely necessary. We must save time. On the other hand, if there's any danger—"

"Nothing to fear." O'Brien sounded confident. "Trulli's already en route to test the *Ganges's* transporter system. I saw to that one myself. I'll wager that she'll pick up and deliver as pretty as you please, wide range or narrow. If you wanted me to beam you up a nice warm bottle of Bajoran *kis,* I could accommodate you, pluck it right from the brewer's hand. Now mind you, when the equipment's in top form, sensors fully operational, you could ask me to pick you out that same bottle by color and taste."

"All that with Cardassian technology?" Sisko tried to keep a straight face. He knew Miles's opinion on that subject; few crew members aboard DS9 didn't.

"I like to think that the longer this equipment's been in my care, the faster it'll get over being born Cardie,"

O'Brien said sincerely. He touched his comm badge. "O'Brien to McCormick. How are those tests coming?"

"McCormick here, sir. The transporters all checked out fine. Ensign Trulli's gone to try his luck with the long-range sensors and I'm on my way to Ops."

"Good. O'Brien out." He strode to another console and hailed the *Ganges*. "Trulli, report. How are the sensors?"

"Not too good, sir," Trulli responded. "I wasn't able to zero in on that case of—that test package until Goodman gave me the coordinates. And whenever I get a fix on Goodman, the reading fades out."

"So will Goodman if we leave him in the Pride of Mintak much longer," the chief muttered. "But the transporter itself is working?"

"Top-notch, sir."

"Then never mind the rest. She'll do; we can clean out the bugs in the sensors later. Have Goodman read you his own coordinates, beam him aboard, and report back here on the double. Commander Sisko's got a job for the *Ganges*. O'Brien out. Sir?" He returned his attention to Sisko.

"When Trulli gets back, have him fly a landing party of four to Bajor, to be beamed down at these coordinates." Sisko handed O'Brien a preprogrammed chip. The chief of operations slipped it into the console and double-checked the specifications.

"The Kaladrys Valley . . . Densely populated area, sir?"

"No." Sisko took a breath. "Not anymore."

O'Brien knew what his commanding officer meant without another word being said. Casually, as if he were changing the subject, O'Brien said, "You know, sir, Keiko had her pupils study poetry not too long ago; asked the children to bring in a favorite poem to share with the class, something special to them and their people."

"I'll bet that left Nog out," Sisko said, speaking of Quark's nephew. It was hard to imagine the supremely materialistic Ferengi having any sort of poetry.

"Funny thing is, he recited a whopping long selection from a Ferengi epic about a great price war that almost wiped out three whole families. There he stood, holding this absurd heroic pose and declaiming, 'Though cities burn, and all the land's consumed by ravening fire,/Go forth, my son, and buy them out! Acquire! Acquire! Acquire!' and so on . . ."

"Yes, Chief, I know all about the assignment. Jake practiced his recitation of 'Casey at the Bat' on me. What's your point?"

"My point, sir, is that one of the Bajoran children brought in a poem about the Kaladrys Valley. It was so fine, you felt as if you were actually standing there, in the midst of this grand, green, lovely land. But the poem itself dates from the days before the Cardies." Miles shook his head. "The poem went on to describe how a faction who followed the teachings of the Prophets one way set out to destroy this other group that presented the Prophets' message differently. No need to tell you what happened, or how that little difference of opinion left the land."

Sisko said nothing. He knew.

"But you see, sir," O'Brien continued, "in the end the people came to their senses and the land came back to its beauty. There've been destroyers before, but there've always been rebuilders too. What the Cardies did isn't the last word, no more than any of us has the last word to say on the grand scale."

This time Sisko did smile. "You're a bit of poet yourself, Chief."

"Why not?" O'Brien lifted his chin proudly. "I'm Irish."

Shortly later, O'Brien accompanied Sisko to the docking bay where the newly returned *Ganges* waited. The stationside bay door hissed as Brother Gis came in, escorted by Major Kira. "All is ready," he announced, beaming. "Commander, when you said you did not have much to spare us in the way of supplies, you did yourself an injustice. I have been overseeing the young doctor's preparations, and what he brings alone is more than we ever expected. We will have to share this bounty with the other camps."

"I'm glad we were able to help," Sisko responded.

"You will be rewarded for it, rest assured." The monk made a gesture of blessing that Sisko had seen the Bajorans use only infrequently.

"Commander Sisko will be the first to tell you that as a Starfleet officer, he seeks no reward," Major Kira put in. "The satisfaction he gets from having made the right decision is enough."

Sisko pressed his lips together in a frown. "Brother Gis, have you ever traveled via transporter beam?"

"Er, no," the monk admitted. He seemed a trifle uneasy.

"I thought so. This is my chief of operations, Miles O'Brien. I'd like him to explain the procedure to you so you won't have anything to be nervous about. Chief?"

"Aye, sir." O'Brien took the Bajoran monk aside. Comforting nervous first-time transporter passengers was not SOP. Usually no one even bothered asking; the whole process was accomplished so quickly, there was little need to prepare the uninitiated. Sisko's suggestion struck Miles as a diversionary tactic. Out of the corner of his eye he saw Commander Sisko motion tersely for Major Kira to come with him. They retired to a secluded part of the docking bay. While Miles dutifully explained to Brother Gis the theory, practice, and sensations of being beamed down, he also managed to steal a now-and-then glimpse of the interview between Sisko and the strong-minded Bajoran woman.

So I was right, he thought. He couldn't hear a word of

what passed between Sisko and Kira, but it was more than clear from the commander's whole demeanor that Major Kira had stepped over the line . . . again.

O'Brien *tsk*ed. He admired the major's bold, fiery disposition and her devotion to her people, but it did get her into more scrapes than need be. He wrapped up his lecture to Brother Gis in a hurry, hoping their return would save Major Kira from some of the trouble she'd gotten herself into this time.

"He's all set, Commander," O'Brien said, presenting himself to Sisko. "No more fear of the transporter now than if he'd used it since birth."

"Very good, Chief," Sisko said, breaking off with Major Kira. The Bajoran officer looked angry, not chastened. O'Brien was ready to wager there'd be plenty more to say between those two after they got the landing party dispatched.

At that moment, the docking bay door opened a second time, admitting Dr. Bashir and his assistant, Ensign Kahrimanis. They carried a fair-sized container between them, about the dimensions of a footlocker. The door barely shut behind them before it opened once more to admit Lieutenant Dax, followed by a Bajoran dollying in three similar containers on an antigrav flat.

O'Brien conferred with Trulli while the freight was loaded. "When you're in orbit, send the supplies down first," he said. "And see that it arrives safely before you beam down the landing party." He knew it might sound foolish to others, but after making any adjustments or repairs to this cursed Cardie equipment, he felt better testing it out on inanimate objects. Anyone but Keiko would laugh if they knew how strongly he felt that any technological device somehow mirrored the cultural tone and moral outlook of its developers. Klingon-made items were trustworthy—*honorable* tech, he'd call it, that functioned as promised. Ferengi-made things gave you just what you paid for, though you had to keep an eye on them. They'd shortchange you in a pinch if you let them.

Anything the Cardies created, you couldn't trust.

"Aye, sir," Trulli responded, looking doubtful. "But— how will we know what condition it arrived in? There's no one at the landing site who can communicate with the runabout, and with the sensors still—"

"Never mind, never mind. It's fixed; it'll work fine." He hoped his belief in his own tech skills outweighed the treacherous nature of the Cardie equipment in his care.

"Uh, sir?" Trulli inquired. "We've got a little something to *un*load too." He jerked a thumb over one shoulder. O'Brien peered into the rear of the runabout. Ensign Goodman sat slumped atop a case of Bajoran *kis*. He was right in the way of the crew's efforts to secure the supplies destined for Brother Gis's camp. Every time they tried to get him to move, he tried to get them to join him in a few choruses of "Klingon Women and Romulan Ale."

Gis watched with interest as Chief O'Brien escorted Ensign Goodman and the *kis* out of the runabout.

"Take tomorrow off, Goodman," O'Brien said with a wry smile as he gave his bleary-eyed ensign a light push in the direction of the bay door. "It looks to me like you've done enough for Federation-Bajoran relations today."

"What is wrong with him?" Brother Gis asked, his voice shaky at the edges. "Is that a side effect of this—this transporting we must undergo?"

"Nothing out of the ordinary," O'Brien said. The monk gave him a doubtful look and regarded the runabout with new apprehension.

Oh, fine, O'Brien thought. *I give him a full lecture on how the transporter works, take all that time, and it's undone by one crewman who can't hold his drink. Wonderful.*

He turned to his waiting passengers. "Ready for you." *Might as well see how much damage's been done.* He wasn't thinking about the sensors.

As O'Brien expected—no matter what he had hoped —Brother Gis balked. Kahrimanis and Dax boarded the runabout without a backward glance. Dr. Bashir opted to stand by and figuratively hold Brother Gis's hand.

"The Prophets have mercy!" Brother Gis breathed, eyeing the runabout. He looked to Dr. Bashir. "And we could not—we could not possibly *land?*"

"Transporting from orbit is faster," Dr. Bashir said, trying to soothe the monk's fears. "You did say time was of the essence."

"So I did." Brother Gis appeared to be regretting his words now. He clutched Dr. Bashir's wrist with a clammy grip. "And this is—safe?"

"Safe as houses," Chief O'Brien reassured him. "Safer than the trip from here into high orbit itself. Not that there's anything to fear from a ride in our runabout," he hastened to add. "It's just a matter of what you're used to."

"I admit, having spent so long in the Kaladrys Valley I have had little contact with such—" the monk began apologetically.

Dr. Bashir patted the monk's hand. "When we reach orbit, I'll have Ensign Trulli beam me down first. Then I'll contact the runabout with this"—he indicated his comm badge—"so you can hear for yourself that I've arrived safely. Will that be all right?"

"I—I suppose so."

"Excellent," Julian said cheerfully. "Then it's settled. Shall we?" He waved toward the runabout.

The monk's chest rose and fell dramatically. He boarded the runabout with the air of a man going to the scaffold, but he went. Julian followed him aboard the *Ganges.* The last sight that Commander Sisko had of

Bashir as the young doctor vanished into the runabout was a smug grin.

"Just like the Cheshire cat," he muttered as he and the others left the docking bay.

"What, sir?" Kira asked.

"A character from an old Earth children's story. *Alice in Wonderland,*" Chief O'Brien put in. To the commander he said, "Sir, I'm going to take McCormick with me and see if we can't run down the source of this sensor problem now."

"Don't waste too much time on it, Chief," Sisko said. "There are plenty of other repairs that are more urgent."

"Don't I know it." O'Brien sighed. "If we can't get it fixed in an hour, we'll do the best we can and get back to it later."

"Very good." Sisko dismissed him and Miles went briskly on his way. Sisko and Kira followed at a more leisurely pace, heading back to Ops.

As they walked, Sisko remarked, "You know, I think that later—after Dr. Bashir and the others have helped resolve this crisis—maybe we could see about sending the children some additional supplies. Staples, yes, but something extra, something special: Books. Stories. Fairy tales." He looked at Kira. "Do you have anything like fairy tales on Bajor?"

The liaison officer had a peculiar expression on her face. "I know what you're talking about, if that's what you mean. I dropped by the school a few times and overheard Keiko O'Brien reading to a group of the younger children. It was a story about a poor girl who was given many gifts by a woman even more powerful than the Kai, including a pair of glass shoes. When she lost one of them, she had to get married."

"That's definitely a new way of looking at 'Cinderella,' Major." Sisko was amused.

"My mother used to tell me stories like that, especially

nights when I was too hungry to sleep or the sound of fighting kept us all awake: stories about young girls who had nothing, but they were smart and brave and they didn't give up. Wonderful things happened to them and it all came out right in the end." Kira gazed into the past. "Even after I got too old for those stories, I still wanted to believe in them. Even when I joined the Resistance and it didn't look like we'd ever stop fighting the Cardassians, I held on to the idea that someday there'd be a—what do you say at the end of those stories?"

"Happily ever after," Sisko provided.

Kira nodded. "With your permission, sir, I'd like to help gather up storybooks for the camp children. Maybe I could work on them on my own time, use the computer to translate some of your fairy tales into Bajoran."

Sisko's teeth flashed. "Permission granted." His smile faded. If anyone ever needed a happily ever after, it was the children of Bajor. "I have some books in my personal library that I'd like to donate to the project." He wondered how Mark Twain would translate into Bajoran.

Major Kira gave him a long, hard stare. "This is a switch."

"What is?"

"Suddenly you're so eager to get involved."

"Why should that surprise you?" It disturbed him that she found his interest surprising at all.

"Because it took so much to get you to send help to the camp in the first place," she replied. "And because when I made an innocent little remark, you took my head off. Sir."

"And what innocent little remark was that?"

"When I told Brother Gis that it was reward enough for you, knowing you'd made—"

"—the right decision," he finished for her. "Major Kira, you've had a hand in this from the start, haven't you?"

"I'm the Bajoran liaison officer," she returned evenly. "It's my job to bring certain important matters to the attention of Starfleet, situations where Federation help might actually be wanted." She made the last word sting.

"I think this goes beyond just doing your job. Brother Gis doesn't strike me as the sort of man who would willingly leave his camp, not without some outside encouragement."

"Why? Because the thought of being beamed down for the first time made him nervous? He's no coward, Commander. He's been helping refugees since before the Cardassians were expelled from Bajor, under their very noses, in fact. If you don't think that takes courage—"

"I wasn't questioning his courage," Sisko said. "I was asking what could have possessed him to be the one to approach us. Why him and not someone from one of the other camps where the illness had spread? At his there's only a skeleton crew of healthy adults left to care for the sick and to tend the fields. He's a healer; he's *needed*. He's not the sort of person who would walk away from need unless he had some previous assurance that his mission was guaranteed success."

He regarded Major Kira steadily.

"All right." She gave in. "He has my sponsorship. I have distant relatives who escaped the Kaladrys Valley but who still try to keep track of the friends they left behind. I heard about the situation in the camps from them and confirmed it on my own." Her eyes flashed defiance. "I didn't simply cut off the rest of my life when I came aboard DS9!"

"No one asked you to, Major," Sisko said in his quiet manner.

Kira snorted. "That's not the way it seems, sometimes. The Federation, first, last, and always!"

"Isn't that the way you feel about Bajor?" Sisko's question was just above a whisper.

"Why shouldn't I?" she snapped.

"Because it blinds you," he replied. "No one is asking you to give up your allegiance to your homeworld. The Klingons never would have become allies of the Federation if we'd asked that of them. You have potential, Major, incredible potential. Starfleet could use more like you; leadership is not something that can be learned in the classroom. But being a leader means having to make choices, choices that affect hundreds, thousands of lives. All that I want is for you to understand that the 'right' choice may not always be the choice that favors Bajor."

"You'll have to prove that."

"Give me time." His gaze swept the bustling scene. All those people, Federation and Bajoran, depending on him. "Believe me, it's not an easy thing to prove, even to yourself." The doubts that had assaulted him when he first took command of *Deep Space Nine* came flooding back. Starfleet's idea of the "right" place to post Benjamin Sisko clashed violently with his own opinion of the "right" place to raise his son, Jake. "It's hardest when the right decision isn't the one that gives you what you want."

"Your decision got Dr. Bashir exactly what he wanted," Major Kira remarked. "Frontier medicine: ever since he got here, that's all he talked about, the chance to practice frontier medicine. I wonder if he knows what he's getting himself into?"

"Dr. Bashir's training gave him ample preparation for any medical contingency," Sisko said. "You've seen him at work long enough to know he's not just all talk. He's taken care of all of us more than once. You ought to have more faith in him."

"I'm not questioning his competence as a doctor, sir," Kira replied. "Although if I hear him tell that preganglionic/postganglionic nerve story one more time,

I can't be held responsible for my actions. But on Bajor, we have a saying: The loudest petitioners of the Prophets ask for what they desire most but know least."

"We have a similar saying, Major Kira," Sisko said. "Never wish for your heart's desire; you just might get it."

CHAPTER
5

DR. BASHIR SAT ON HIS COT in the tent Brother Gis had assigned him. His eyes were closed, his head tilted back, his mouth open as he took three slow, deep breaths, trying to regain the analytic calm he would need if he was ever going to take the first step toward saving the children.

Save them . . . for what? A malicious whisper of a thought crept through his mind. *For the next epidemic that blows through this wasteland? Or for years of backbreaking work trying to reclaim the land the Cardassians drained dry?*

Be still, Julian told the voice. He closed his mouth and took a penetrating breath through his nose, held it for a beat, let it out through pursed lips, and repeated the pattern. He had learned this technique for centering himself even before he began his physician's training. Everyone talked about the pressures of Starfleet Academy, everyone spoke of the additional pressures of exobiological studies, but no one thought to suggest how to handle those pressures. You either found a way that worked for you or you quit.

Quitting was never an option for Julian Bashir.

You see how they live here, the voice persisted. *It's amazing that this is only the first illness to take such a heavy toll. You like to think you can work fast, but will it be fast enough for them? If you fail, they die, and if you succeed . . . some other sickness will spring up and finish the work of this one.*

Julian's stomach churned. *Leave me alone. Let me think.*

He knew it was an impossible request the moment he made it. How could he escape from himself?

He could still hear the words of Selok of Vulcan, the instructor he had admired and respected above all others, telling him, "You are one of the most confident medical students I have ever known, Bashir. You are also one of the most self-critical. You believe in your abilities, yet at the same time you never cease questioning them."

"When you lecture us, haven't you stressed a doctor's need to evaluate his own performance frequently, sir?" the younger Julian protested.

The Vulcan healer's austere expression remained as it was. "There is a difference between self-analysis and self-attack. Learn it."

At times like this, alone but for the inner voice that questioned him constantly, Julian wondered if he would ever learn Selok's lesson.

Thinking about what's waiting for you out there won't change a thing, his inner voice went on. *And finding the cure for this "camp fever" won't change a thing either. You won't be saving anyone, Julian; you'll only be prolonging their misery. Is that kind?*

I am a doctor, Bashir told himself. His hands hooked under the edge of the cot, the knuckles going white. *I am a healer. It's my job to find the cure. It's my duty. It's why I was brought here, what they're all expecting of me. I can't let them down.*

A fine doctor! Laughter echoed inside Bashir's head. *Dax and Kahrimanis are already at work in the infirmary, while you're in here, hiding.*

Do you call that an infirmary? Bashir lashed out, his indignation letting him forget everything else, for the moment. *There aren't even enough beds for the sick.*

But you have a nice bed, Julian, the voice said sweetly. *Do Kahrimanis and Dax have such comfortable accommodations? Brother Gis said they would have places in the adult dormitories—more tents, only with bigger holes in the walls. But you—! You're the healer. Special privileges for you. Why aren't you out there, earning them?*

I'll do more than that. Dr. Bashir took one last deep breath and opened his eyes. *And if what I do here isn't enough to save their world, at least I can save their lives.* He felt better now. The churning in his stomach had subsided. In its place was the hot, steady fire of anger. He was angry because there was work he should be doing that was going undone. He was angry with himself for the momentary weakness that had overcome him when he first set eyes on the camp.

He got no consolation from the fact that he wasn't the only one so affected. Kahrimanis, too, had been strongly jarred when Brother Gis led the landing party down the hillock and into the midst of the settlement. Bashir distinctly remembered his assistant's pale face, his sharply indrawn breath. Even Dax registered shock at the filth, the stench, the hopelessness that hung over the entire encampment like a thick cloud of fetid smoke.

Dax, who has lived so long and seen so much! he thought. If she could stare stunned at the misery surrounding them, could he blame himself for his own reaction? The wave of pity that struck him felt like a hammer blow to the chest. It left him shaking so badly on the inside that he asked Brother Gis to show him to his quarters right away.

They don't need my pity, he told himself as he rose from the bed and strode out of the tent. *They need my help.*

Two steps out of the tent and the smell drilled him right between the eyes, stopping him in his tracks. Dr. Bashir's nostrils curled at the reek of human waste left where it had fallen, untreated and unburied. An odor of rotting garbage wove itself through the air as well, though this scent was far weaker—the refugees did not have enough food to produce many leavings, and what food they had was so thoroughly, completely used that few scraps were left over.

As Dr. Bashir stood there, a boy of about ten came by pushing a wheelbarrow full of organic refuse. The child walked with the stoop-shouldered, shuffling gait of an old man. His clothing was so tattered that it was impossible to tell what its original color had been, or even its original shape. As he trundled the barrow past Julian, he did not bother to give the doctor so much as a passing glance. Curiosity took more energy than he had to spare.

"Can I help you with that?" Dr. Bashir stepped up to the boy and tried to relieve him of the heavy barrow. Asking his permission was just a formality. To his surprise, the child clung to the wheelbarrow handles stubbornly, baring his teeth in a warning snarl. Julian released the handles and backed away fast, showing the boy his empty hands. "All right, all right, it's all yours. No one's going to take it from you."

The boy glowered at Bashir, then dug his bare, brown feet into the dusty path and continued on his way. Bashir watched him go, shading his eyes until the wheelbarrow turned around the corner of one of the camp buildings and was gone from sight.

The boy's departure left Dr. Bashir alone. Cupping his

hand over his nose and mouth, he set out to find the infirmary. After a while, his hand dropped back to his side. The reek of the camp became familiar, though no less pungent. *I suppose this proves you can get used to anything,* he thought. He wondered whether the smell would ever come out of his clothes.

Brother Gis's camp was a jumble of tents and open-sided pavilions thrown up around the ruins of an old farmstead. There was no organization to the layout of the buildings and no overall plan except to provide as much shelter as quickly as possible. It looked as if it had grown itself overnight, like some sort of fungus, rather than the work of human hands. Every solid-walled structure that Dr. Bashir passed was cobbled together from a half-dozen other cannibalized buildings. Courses of brick-work were topped with layers of unmortared stone. Roofs served as walls, floorboards were transformed into roofs, and anything that could stand was made into a wall. Some buildings had wooden sides, each one wear-ing a different-color paint, many showing the scorched scars of incomplete burnings. When the Cardassians left Bajor, they thought they'd taken everything useful with them. The refugees showed them how wrong they were.

Dirt tracks served as streets, dashed and dotted with ruts and holes. Bashir could see no order to their rambling paths, no reason for the crazy jogs and angles. At this hour, they were deserted. He found himself stepping very quietly, the better to hear any sound made by another living soul. He did not like walking with ghosts.

Julian did not have far to go in order to reach the infirmary. It was a large gray structure whose size suggested it had once been a granary or storehouse. One wall showed the black streaks of fire; another was com-pletely gone, replaced by a curtain of patchwork blankets hung between the supporting beams. That curtain was the only door the place had.

Five very young children sat playing in the dirt in front of the building. Three of them stood by watching while the fourth—a big girl with wild, brown hair like a bramble patch—gave a savage beating to the fifth, a boy much smaller than herself. The children witnessing the uneven match showed no reaction, neither cheering the bully on nor trying to go to the aid of her victim. The victim, in turn, accepted the drubbing with nothing more than stifled grunts when the blows fell. As for the bully herself, she did not appear to be enjoying the process any more than her prey. Her face was dead, her eyes empty. To Julian, that was the most frightening thing of all.

He waded into the middle of the fight and separated the children, yanking the boy to safety on his shoulder. The girl did not try to reclaim her victim, but only stood gazing at him with the patient, inhuman expression of a dog that has treed a cat and knows that the unlucky animal will have to come down sometime. She could wait. The boy's nose was dripping blood and mucus, which he did not bother to wipe away. It added to the layer of grime already encrusting his face. The stink coming from his frail, bony body was appalling.

"What's the meaning of this?" Dr. Bashir demanded. He got no answer. The children only looked at him, waiting. "You ought to be ashamed of yourself," he went on, confronting the girl.

She was not ashamed. She was nothing. Her eyes met his, but there was no spark behind them. It was like waiting for a response from a statue.

Julian set the little boy down and tried to get an answer out of him. "Why was she beating you?" All he got was a shrug. Then the boy scurried away like a rabbit, ducking around the corner of a nearby tent without sparing a word of thanks for the doctor. The remaining four trotted off after him. Julian's heart sank as he realized that if they caught up with that child, the beating would resume as if nothing had happened.

He debated whether or not to bother following them and trying to make contact. A glance at the infirmary made his mind up for him. If he didn't get to work on finding a cure for the camp fever, he was more than likely to see those children again all too soon, as patients. He lifted up a flap between two of the hanging blankets and went in.

Here was another smell, just as strong and stunning as the reek outside, but a smell he knew. Fever made its own perfume. Julian blinked, his eyes adjusting to the dimness inside the infirmary. There were few windows, most of them broken, all of them open, although the faint breeze did little to effectively circulate the air or dispel the odors. Metal cups nailed to the upright beams held candles that added their glow to the meager daylight.

By this dim light, Julian saw two rows of bedrolls laid out on the bare earth on either side of a central aisle. The few shabby cots stood out like islands of luxury. Hammocks hung in places where the upright beams were planted close enough to permit them. Ropes ran across the width of the building, holding up sagging sheets that gave a little privacy to whoever lay on the other side. The vast room was filled with the low, indistinct sound of moaning, coughing, bodies tossing and turning, and sometimes the erupting cry of delirium.

Dr. Bashir walked slowly down the aisle, turning his head left and right, noting that most of the shapes beneath the scanty covers were very small. He glanced into one of the curtained-off cubicles and surprised a woman—her face young, but her hair gray as ash—crouched on a crude stool with an infant at her breast. The baby lay very still, despite the mother's repeated attempts to encourage it to nurse. Dr. Bashir saw the small, pale lips move just a little, then relax. The mother stared at him, but her expression did not ask for help or demand privacy. To her, he was only something to look at, like a wall.

"May I?" He stepped into the cubicle the same way he had stepped into the children's fight, only this time he was not about to give up so easily. She resisted when he first tried to take the baby from her arms. He was gentle but firm as he took the child away, and she was too weak to do more than put up a token struggle. Cradling the infant in one arm, he unwrapped its dirty swaddlings and examined it. He did not use any of the medical instruments he carried, in case the sight of something so alien near her baby might panic the mother.

Observation is a doctor's first, best tool, Selok once taught. The little body in Julian's arms felt warm, but not hot, and there were no signs of swelling anywhere. He shifted the baby to his shoulder and patted its back. He was rewarded with a loud burp followed by dampness seeping through the shoulder of his uniform and the smell of curdled milk.

"Well, that's gratitude," he said, smiling at the baby as he rested it back in the crook of his arm. He stroked its cheek and got a strong rooting reflex. Now that its stomach pain was relieved, it was eager to nurse. But why was it so warm to the touch? A swift investigation of its mouth gave him the answer.

"He's teething," he told the mother. "It's normal for babies to feel a little warmer than usual when their teeth are coming in."

He gave the baby back. The young woman accepted her child from the doctor's arms, acting as if she expected the infant to explode. With one eye still on Dr. Bashir, she began rewrapping the baby as snugly as before.

"No, no, no!" Dr. Bashir said, reaching out. "Not so warm, not so tight. He's hot enough. You don't want to overheat him or the first cool breeze could give him a chill. Take off at least one layer of those swaddlings until the tooth comes in or the weather gets cooler."

The mother's eyes narrowed. She tapped the heavily

ridged bridge of her nose, flicked the naked wires hanging from her right ear, then pointed at Bashir's own ridgeless nose and undecorated earlobe.

He was puzzled only for an instant; then he laughed. "No, I'm not Bajoran," he said. "But I've studied how your people and mine are alike and different. Teething's a similar process for our babies and yours. Now, Ferengi babies, that's a different story." His tone changed to one of concern. "Is there something else wrong? Can you tell me? Can you talk?"

The woman appeared to think this over, then slowly said, "You . . . studied? You are the healer Brother Gis said he would bring us?"

"I am Dr. Julian Bashir." He moved to pat her hand, but thought better of it when she jerked away. "You may have seen others here like me?" He indicated the insignia that was his comm badge. "Lieutenant Dax and Ensign Kahrimanis. We've come from the station, *Deep Space Nine,* and . . ." His words trickled away. "You don't know a thing about space stations, do you?" he said. "Or Starfleet or the Federation or— Never mind, it's unimportant. We've come to help, that's all you need to know. Don't be afraid of any one of us. Understand?"

The woman bobbed her head uncertainly, then removed the outermost swaddling cloth and with a shy look attempted to blot away the spit-up milk from Dr. Bashir's shoulder. "Thank you," he said. "Now take your child out of here. He doesn't need to be in the infirmary. As a matter of fact, with this contagion, it's the worst place possible for him and you."

Dr. Bashir doubted whether getting mother and child out of this nexus of infection would save them, but he knew it would do them no good to remain. He escorted them to the exit personally. At the blanketed doorway, the young woman hesitated, then suddenly seized Dr. Bashir's hand and pressed it to her right ear. Then she darted through the flap and away.

"Ow," said Julian, regarding the thin scratch that the naked wires had left on the fleshy part of his palm just below the thumb.

"Ah, Dr. Bashir!" Brother Gis stood before him, pleasure lighting up his face. He was no longer clad in the long robes and cap he had worn aboard the station. Instead he was bareheaded, with a knee-length brown tunic and serviceable yellow apron covering him. He took Julian's hand and examined the scratch. "Nothing serious. Come with me and we'll put something on it."

Dr. Bashir trailed after the monk back down the aisle. At the very rear of the building, a sheet had been hung across the entrance to what looked like a stall. Julian had to duck through a slit in the sheet to enter. Inside he saw a rickety table, a back-broken chair, and a hodgepodge of chests, bins, trunks, and other storage furniture. Here the clean, spicy smell of medications was stronger than the sour smell of sickness.

"Welcome to my office," Brother Gis said. "Will you be seated?" He motioned Dr. Bashir to take the only chair, but Julian politely refused. "No? Then with your permission." The monk sat down with an audible sigh. "That feels good. Even when I am gone for so short a time, the work piles up. I had just left you in your tent and was about to escort your friends to their accommodations when Belem, my assistant, came rushing up with an emergency only I could handle. According to Belem, that is." He gave Julian an arch look. "I have been going from one emergency to another ever since. Ensign Kahrimanis and Lieutenant Dax still do not know where they are to sleep tonight. It reflects poorly on our hospitality. I hope that you, at least, are well settled?"

"Everything is fine," Julian replied. He pictured Dax and Kahrimanis, hard at work, while he huddled in his tent. The spark of anger against himself burned hotter. "If you can tell me where I can find the boxes we brought from DS9, I'd like to deploy the supplies and start setting up a field lab."

"Of course, of course." Brother Gis made calming motions. "I shall have Belem take you there at once. In fact, I shall tell Belem that for the duration of your stay, he is to be your personal aide."

"Ensign Kahrimanis is here. I really don't need—" Julian began.

"I implore you, Doctor, take him." the monk's hands joined in a sign of supplication. "He is a good lad, only a little too—how to say it?—eager. He helps where there is no need of help and there is no stopping him. He means well, yet he leaves me feeling that half the emergencies he reports are emergencies he has created."

"Surely you don't mean he causes them?" Dr. Bashir was on guard. This was not the sort of aide he wanted.

"Did I give that impression? Forgive me. It is an injustice to the boy. What I meant was, his imagination exaggerates ordinary situations to the rank of emergencies. He is very young, very excitable, and very far from home. He needs to calm down."

"I'll take him off your hands and do what I can with him," Dr. Bashir promised. He wondered whether he was blushing. While Brother Gis was describing the overeager Belem, Dr. Bashir had had a momentary vision of himself chattering at Commander Sisko about his latest dabblings in espionage with Garak. Did the few instances when he had turned up useful information make up for all the other times he had bent the commander's ear for no reason? "It's the least I can do."

"You will not regret it," the monk reassured him. "Now let me see that scratch."

Obediently, Dr. Bashir stuck out his hand. Brother Gis gave it a brief look and said, "Hardly a nick, but I would feel better if I cleaned and bandaged it for you. There is contagion in the air, and we still do not know if the disease limits itself to Bajorans. I will get my kit."

He was still rising from his chair when Dr. Bashir produced a thin, metallic instrument and ran the flashing tip of it down the length of the scratch. It vanished without leaving so much as a scar behind.

"By the Prophets!" the monk gasped. "What did you do?"

Dr. Bashir had a charming smile. "I didn't want you to waste your supplies treating something so minor."

"Er, yes." Brother Gis looked at him askance, then picked up a bronze handbell from the tabletop and rang it twice. Julian heard a scuffle of heavy footsteps from beyond the screens and was nearly bowled over by the lanky young Bajoran who came bursting into the make-shift office.

"You must be Belem," Dr. Bashir said when he recovered his balance. The boy shifted his weight awk-wardly and nodded without looking the doctor in the eye. He could not have been older than fourteen, and he, too, wore a strand of bare wire dangling from his right ear. "Brother Gis says that you'll be helping me here," Julian persisted. "I need to be taken to the supplies we brought from the station. Do you know where they are?" Again the jerky nod.

"Don't stand there like a *jeskla*, Belem; obey the healer!" the monk said severely. To Dr. Bashir he added, "After Belem has shown you where you are to work and helped you set up your things, I would like to take you on a tour of the entire camp. I say I would *like* to, barring any new emergencies." He gave the boy a significant look, but Belem was studying his own bare feet and missed it. "After that it will be time for our evening meal. We eat communally, in the square."

"The square?"

"We call it that. It used to be the exercise yard for the draft animals."

"Draft animals? How could a farm survive without machines?"

"There were machines here." Brother Gis folded his hands. "In fact, we have two of them in fair working order—a tiller and a fertilizer—and I have a man working on salvaging a third. But we were lucky that some Bajorans still enjoy the old-fashioned ways enough to make breeding *verdanis* profitable."

The word was alien to Dr. Bashir until he remembered Major Kira using it once when she and Quark got into an argument about gambling. The Ferengi thought the Bajorans were fools for not betting on the *verdanis* races and said so. "They're like horses!" Julian exclaimed with a snap of his fingers.

"If you say so," the monk replied. "Even the *verdanis* that has been trained for the racetrack can still pull a plow and tread out the grain or turn a millstone. They have been our salvation, especially now that so few adults remain to work the fields. I only wish we could give them back their old accommodations, but we need them more."

"Well, then, if I don't see you earlier, I'll meet you in the square," Julian said.

"Anyone can direct you there. In bad weather, we move into the stables, but when the sky is clear it is good to live as much as possible under the eye of the Prophets." He rose from his chair with a grunt of weariness. "Until then, Dr. Bashir."

Julian walked out of the infirmary with Belem by his side. The young Bajoran had a strange gait, a rolling limp that drew the doctor's eyes immediately. One of the boy's feet was malformed, and the calf badly bowed.

Poor fellow, he thought. *That looks congenital. Still, it's nothing I couldn't fix for him fast enough. I wonder when I ought to offer? He may be sensitive about it—I'd be surprised if he weren't! And if Bajoran adolescence is anything like ours, he's at that age when there's nothing about his body he feels at home with.* He decided he would wait until Belem got to know him better before bringing up the subject.

Belem guided Dr. Bashir to a shelter that had one stone wall, three wooden ones—one with a real door— and a wooden roof. There was a latch on the door, held closed by a complex device that looked like a hand-manipulated puzzle box. Belem pounced on it with nimble fingers, and after a series of quick twists and turns had it open. The Bajoran could not suppress a smile of pride when he opened the door for the doctor.

Dr. Bashir returned the smile and said, "Thank you, Belem. You'll have to show me how that works."

"'Seasy," Belem mumbled, and darted into a nearby tent to fetch an oil lamp. It was rancid oil, but it was the only light source available. By the flame of the rag wick, Dr. Bashir surveyed his new laboratory.

The containers from the station were there, set down neatly in a row beside three wooden tables. Julian knelt beside the first one and began to unpack. Belem hung back at first, though it didn't take long for his naturally helpful nature to manifest itself and send him to work at the doctor's side. The boy picked up all the things Julian laid out beside the chests and arranged them on the tabletops.

"Careful," Julian said automatically as Belem set out a variety of glassware and a portable microscanner.

"Don't worry, sir," the boy said. "Brother Gis told us to give you the best tables. These have their own legs, not broken, not even fixed once. They don't wobble at all, and their tops are smooth and level." He announced this as if it were the greatest miracle his world could boast.

Which it is, Julian thought. With Belem's help, they soon had a laboratory setup that was to Dr. Bashir's liking. His next step was to show the youth how to use a sampler. "I'd like you to take this into the infirmary and gather blood samples from the fever patients," he instructed him.

"There's nothing but fever patients in there now," Belem replied. He studied the slim, shining wand, awestruck. "Do you think I could? I am no healer. It would be arrogant."

"It would help me," Bashir said. The boy looked dubious. "I need the samples, and it won't hurt the patients," he went on, trying to gain Belem's confidence. "All you do is touch the blue-banded end to the patient's inner elbow—that cleans the area—then flip it around and touch the other end to the same place to take the blood. There won't be even a mark left behind. Oh, and I'll give you something to use to identify which patient each sample comes from. I could do it myself, but Brother Gis can use my skills better elsewhere. Do you see?"

"I—I think so." Belem's lower lip trembled. "But I'm so clumsy. What if I do it wrong?"

"I'll accompany you and watch you try it the first few times, then you can carry on on your own. Will that do?" Belem nodded without much conviction. "Anyway, who says you're clumsy?"

"Everyone." The boy sounded sure of that.

"Brother Gis said that?"

"Nnnnnno," Belem admitted. "But he's the only one. It's because of this." He extended his twisted foot, at the same time looking away from it as much as possible.

Dr. Bashir felt his heart leap at this unexpected opportunity. There would be no need for him to await a more favorable moment to heal Belem. It wouldn't take long, he knew it, and if he could perform the operation before it was time for the evening meal—

—*you'll redeem yourself*, the voice within whispered. *Fix the boy's leg and you prove you can be the great, romantic frontier healer of your dreams. But is that who you are? Or are you just the man who was cowering in his own tent not so long ago?*

Proving myself isn't important, Julian thought ferociously. *What's important is the boy.* "May I examine that?" he asked Belem.

"Yes, sir." The boy answered in a way that as good as said he did not dare refuse the great healer's request. He sat down on one of the empty containers and continued to look away while Dr. Bashir ran a diagnostic probe over his skin.

The boy's rigid, terrified attitude troubled Julian. He tried to relax his patient by chatting with him while he worked. "Have you been here long, Belem?"

"Five years. I was twelve when our village was—resettled."

Julian looked up sharply. Belem didn't look seventeen. His healthy growth had been stolen from him by the years of Cardassian occupation. More than his growth: Julian knew that *resettlement* was often just another word for *destruction.* He tried to keep his tone casual as he went on to say, "I should have known. I see you're well past the age of initiation." He touched the bare lobe of his own right ear where Bajorans wore the shimmering ornament that marked their status.

Belem touched his own right ear reflexively and blushed to feel the naked wires. "I had to sell them," he muttered.

"What?"

"The crystals. I was the oldest, my brothers were seven and five. I had to buy us food for our journey."

"Your journey?" Julian repeated.

Belem looked at him as though the doctor had just hatched. "The journey here, sir. We had to come, you know. There was trouble on our farm. The Underground sabotaged Father's harvester, and the Cardassian agents were coming to collect the crop. Father ordered all of my uncles and aunts and the bigger cousins into the fields to do the work by hand—even me! Only we couldn't do it fast enough. The Underground must have been watching. They came back the next night and burned the fields." The life went out of his eyes as the past came back, remorseless. "They did the same with all the other farms near our village, too. The Cardassians didn't care why we hadn't met our quotas. Father tried to reason with the Gul, but he said things—Father forgot himself and shouted back at him." Belem shuddered. "We ran into the hills when we saw what they did to Father. Then there was a bigger fire—"

"You don't have to tell me any more," Dr. Bashir said gently. Belem blinked at him, waking from the old nightmare.

"Oh, I don't mind talking about it, sir," he said. "I was able to save two of my brothers and bring them all the way here. That's something. Jin—that's my middle brother—Jin always stuck up for me after we got here. He told everyone who called me useless and a coward to shut up. Then he told them how I'd brought him and Narel—he's ten now—all the way here from home."

"I can't see anyone calling you a coward, Belem," Bashir said. He finished his examination and stood up. As he'd thought, the malformation was congenital but correctable, even here. "And Brother Gis would be the first to contradict anyone who called you useless."

The Bajoran boy's eyes filled with tears. "But I am useless, sir," he said.

"How can you—?"

"I lost it." His head dropped to his chest.

"The crystals? But you needed to sell them in order to live."

"Not the crystals." He looked up, and all Julian could see in that young face was pain and shame. "Our *name,* sir. Jin and Narel were young and terrified, and the way here was so hard that no one can blame them for forgetting, but I—I should have held on to it. It was who we *were*. It's why we're just Belem and Jin and Narel instead of who we should be." Tears flooded his cheeks. "Our *name,* sir; I lost our name."

CHAPTER
6

"JULIAN, YOU'VE GOT TO EAT." Dax slid onto the bench beside Dr. Bashir and looked pointedly at his untouched plate. A lump of grainy black bread and a dollop of meatless stew covered the chipped clay platter.

"I'm not hungry." He said it so softly that she had to have him repeat it.

"I know this isn't the Replimat's best," she said, "but it's all they've got to offer us." She picked up a piece of bread and with some effort tore off a hunk with her teeth. "Mnoff vad," she said, struggling to chew it.

Julian poked at his stew once with chopsticks, then pushed his plate away.

"You could always ask for shipments of food from the station," Dax suggested quietly. "Just do it so that Brother Gis and the rest don't find out. It would hurt them deeply."

"I'm not interested in eating station food here," Julian said, fists tightening on the table. "I'm just *not hungry.*"

The intensity of his words startled Dax. It was the first

time she'd heard him speak to her harshly. In ordinary circumstances, Julian was either trying to impress her or flirt with her, neither one with great success.

These aren't ordinary circumstances, she reflected. "What's troubling you, Julian?" she asked.

Instead of answering, he got up and walked away.

"He's still not used to this," Ensign Kahrimanis remarked.

"This is not the sort of thing anyone gets used to," Lieutenant Dax replied. *Not if you've got a heart.* Her glance swept the square, where a dozen plank-and-trestle tables had been set up for the evening meal. The sun was almost down, staining the sky shades of deep amber, peach, and purple between the camp buildings. Wooden torches smoldered and flared in their sockets, lighting the way for the children who went back and forth from the cook shack with the big serving platters or who hauled buckets of drinking water from the storage barrels.

Most of the tables were empty. Those that were occupied were packed with children who huddled near each other. The few tables where adults sat were the most thickly mobbed. As Dax watched, she saw a little girl try to squeeze onto a bench beside a grown man. The man gave her a tired smile, but the boy beside him snarled, then launched himself at her.

"Calin! Calin!" The man pulled the boy off the little girl and scolded him while the other child slunk away to take a place at another table. A heartbreaking look of yearning filled her eyes, which never left the man's face. "Why did you do that, Calin?"

"'Cause you're *my* father!" the boy shouted. "She wants to take you away from me, just 'cause her father an' mother's both dead. She can't! You're *mine!*" And he seized his father's arm fiercely.

"It is often so," said Brother Gis. The monk and his two brethren were the only ones sharing the table with the crew members of *Deep Space Nine.* "There are perhaps a dozen children for each adult here, counting ourselves. Some of them came to us already orphaned, although a number were in the care of older brothers and sisters. The fever has changed much of that. Those who came to us with parents that the fever took are like blossoms on the wind, and those who still have parents living are terrified of losing them."

"If things were otherwise, we might hope for aid from the district centers, offers of fosterage, adoption, even adult volunteers to come here and work with the children," said Mor. He was the youngest of the three monks manning the camp. He had the face of a man who was once fat. "But this is an isolated area. In the good times, pleasure-travelers seldom came this far into the Kaladrys Valley. The village of Lacroya never even had a guest-house, just a tavern. As it is, people have their own problems. To them, our hardships are unimportant in comparison. When I travel to the camp at Jabelon to trade for lamp oil, I hear rumors that there is much unrest in the cities, and it is spreading rapidly. The government is unstable, like a pavement made of broken stones. If we send them word asking for help, they send us silence. If we were to pack up the children and travel to the capital itself so that they could not pretend we are not there, they would give us excuses."

"Besides, the children have been uprooted enough," Brother Gis put in. "I would not ask it of them. They were never strong enough to make such a journey, and now that so many are sick, it is impossible."

"So here we stay," Brother Talissin concluded, "waiting for the Prophets to teach our leaders the lesson of mercy."

"It's extremely difficult for people who have been powerless to gain power suddenly." Jadzia spoke from the prior experiences of several lifetimes. "It takes time before they can think of using that power in anyone's interest but their own."

"Which makes us all the more grateful to you and Dr. Bashir for giving so much of yourselves to us," Brother Gis said.

"Please, we've barely begun. As soon as Dr. Bashir can run some tests on your patients, we'll be on our way to finding the cure for this camp fever of yours."

"Dr. Bashir has already done wonders," Brother Gis said. He gestured to where the doctor stood watching a group of the older children. They had formed a ring around Belem, who was showing off his mended foot and leg. The others gaped at it, and one tried to touch it. Belem made a mocking noise, in jest, and jumped lightly out of reach. Unfortunately, he did not look where he was going; his leap sent him bumping into the doctor.

"The healer does not have the cure for clumsiness, I see," Brother Talissin sniped. He was younger than Brother Gis, who himself was not so old, but he was steeped in bitterness.

"I'm sure the boy will discover that for himself when he's older," Dax said placidly. Brother Talissin snorted.

"If it is the will of the Prophets, a cure for the fever will be found," Brother Mor said with sincerity. "If not, we must still thank Dr. Bashir. By healing Belem's foot, he has given the children a sign they can understand, a sign that there is hope for change."

"He has changed Belem's life, at any rate," Brother Talissin said. "If he knew what sort of change he has wrought, he would not be pleased."

Brother Mor leaned forward to peer at Bashir. The doctor spoke a few words to Belem and headed slowly back toward the table. "He does not look pleased."

"That is all an act," Brother Talissin scoffed. "The long face is just to make us fuss over his accomplishment with Belem. Is one healing a triumph? The boy could have gone on as he was before and the healer could have used his time aiding those who need it more." Dr. Bashir returned to his place in time to hear the monk conclude, "I have raised enough children to know all the different tricks they try to get attention."

"Then why don't you give it to them?" he snapped.

"What—?" Brother Talissin sputtered.

"The children in this camp work like adults," Julian said. His voice was flinty, his face tense with the strain of holding back so much helpless outrage. "They have to—I accept that. If they don't do the farmwork, they won't eat. But they are so *alone*. I see it in their eyes, the nothingness, the cold. Too many of them are isolated, even in the middle of a mob. They're fed and sheltered and clothed as well as possible, but they need more than that. They want *care*."

Brother Gis regarded him with sorrowful eyes. "You think we do not care for the children, Dr. Bashir?"

Julian was abashed. "I didn't mean to imply— With respect, Brother Gis, you and your brethren are doing all you can for them, but there is a difference between maintenance and—and showing each one of them that he's more than just an interchangeable unit. You care for the children when they want you to care for the *child*. It's not your fault if they need more than you have the time to give."

"I think I see your point, Doctor," Brother Gis said, nodding, chin in hand. "As you see ours. There are not enough of us here to single out every child for individual attention. May the Prophets forgive us."

"We do our duty; the Prophets need not forgive us for that." Brother Talissin broke off a crumb of the coarse bread and soaked it to chewable softness in the liquid from his stew. "You have only arrived here today, Dr. Bashir, yet already you seem to have all the answers. Truly you must have walked with the Prophets. Share your great wisdom. Enlighten us. What will you do for our children that we have so shamefully neglected to do?"

"For a start, I'd give them the attention they have to fight for now."

"You would? How generous of you." Brother Talissin lifted the now-tender crumb to his lips and chewed it carefully. When he opened his mouth, Dax saw that many of his teeth had rotted away. "Working alone, you would have the patience to listen to every complaint, arbitrate every squabble, praise every achievement no matter how small for each of the dozen children in your care. Not only that, but find the time to see them fed, clothed, washed, and still be able to do your share in the fields, in the cook shack, fetch water, do laundry, *and* heal the sick?"

"I'm only thinking of what's best for the—" Julian began.

"For the children, yes," Brother Talissin cut him off. "Something *we* never think of. Not only are you more efficient and more insightful, but you are also more *benevolent* than we!" Brother Talissin rose from his seat. "You are in truth a gift from the Prophets. Thank you, Dr. Bashir. This has been *most* enlightening." He swept from the table and left the square.

"Is it just me or did anyone else see the size of that chip on his shoulder?" Ensign Kahrimanis muttered.

"Shhh," Dax hushed him. She could see Julian seething and thought it best to avert the imminent explosion. "You're right, you know," she said, touching his forearm. "I've noticed how badly alienated many of these children are. Their minds need as much healing as their bodies. After we've found the cause and the cure for the fever, I will make it my business to talk to Commander Sisko and Major Kira about this. If we approach the Bajoran authorities with the interest of the Federation behind us, I'm sure we can mobilize relief measures that will—"

"My God, don't you understand, either?" Dr. Bashir exclaimed. "The authorities don't see what's become of these children, and they don't care to see! They can ignore the Federation as easily as they ignore their own people. They've got their own agendas, and they don't include the children. For all the help they are, the provisional government might as well be on one of the moons! But we're here, and we owe it to them to do everything in our power to save them—not just from the fever, but from this life and what it's doing to them. Not someday; *now.*" He stormed off in the opposite direction from Brother Talissin.

Brother Mor sighed and ate an orange-colored chunk of stew. "I hope Brother Talissin's wrong about Belem. I don't think that our young healer could stand it otherwise."

"What do you mean by that?" Lieutenant Dax asked.

Brother Mor fished a green-and-white-striped bit out of the juice. "Sickness is not the only way we lose children here. The healer is right: The children need attention, they want it the way plants want rain. When there were more healthy adults to go around, the orphans would frequently be taken under someone's wing along with their own children. The whole camp felt like one big family in those days. Even the children without parents knew that they *belonged.* But since the deaths, we are shattered. The children are cut loose. Oh, we tell them what to do in the fields or when doing chores, but when they have free time it is another story."

"The healer is right," Brother Gis concurred. "Our children need more attention than we can now give them. The young ones strive to gain notice by getting into all sorts of mischief. Any attention is better than none. There have been times when the mischief escalates to downright vandalism and cruelty."

"Even so, when we are hard pressed, we put their problems to one side," Brother Mor said. He now had a limp brown stringy thing halfway to his lips. It dangled from his chopsticks like wet lace. "We told ourselves that they could wait, they were children, it was not as if their lives were in danger, they had time." He sighed and ate.

"And so we lost them," Brother Gis concluded.

"How?" Dax asked. The monks were used to speaking plainly of death, but she sensed some other form of loss behind Brother Gis's words. "How did you lose them?"

"When they grew old enough, they ran away," Brother Gis answered. "They vanished into the hills to become fighters."

"Resistance fighters? But that's over."

"They no longer fight the Cardassians, true. There is no more Underground as such. Instead, ever since the expulsion, many Bajorans who do not find our present political situation exactly to their liking strive to change it the only way they have come to know: through violence. The Resistance has smashed into scores of splinter groups, each with its own idea of what Bajor should be."

"It's not bad enough that our ministers battle among themselves in the council chamber." Brother Mor sounded disgusted. "When the Cardassians were here, at least we knew the enemy."

"As soon as a child is old enough to handle a weapon, they're gone, boys as well as girls." Brother Gis bowed his head. "Belem's younger brother left us last year, and his youngest will no doubt follow. Belem's malformed foot was all that kept him here this long. I do not care to recall how often he has been teased about it by the others of his age. They called him coward for remaining here, even though he had no choice in the matter. The fighters in the hills move like shadows and wind. He could not possibly live such a life with that handicap holding him back. That is why I made him my assistant, to do some small thing toward protecting him from his tormentors. Now that he has been healed . . ." He shrugged.

Dax looked in the direction of the group of children

that had surrounded Belem. They were still there, except now Belem was allowing them to touch Dr. Bashir's handiwork. They squatted at his feet, nudging one another and whispering excitedly. "I think Belem won't run off so fast," she opined. "He's too much of a celebrity right now."

"For the moment," Brother Mor agreed. "But later? The boy came to us without a family name. He was so scarred by the atrocities he witnessed that it was his brother Jin who had to remind him that his given name was Belem. Few of our children still recall their families. Those that do crow over their less fortunate fellows. By joining a guerrilla faction, these children acquire both a sense of belonging and a new family name. You have no idea how important that is to us, Lieutenant."

"But I do," Dax replied, thinking of Major Kira.

"It does not matter to the children which faction they join," Brother Gis added. "They know nothing of politics and care less. All that matters to them is belonging, finding a replacement for the parents they have lost. As for the guerrilla bands themselves, the leaders do not bother asking the children if they agree with the cause or not. If they can aim and shoot, they qualify."

"Several children have left us since the outbreak of the fever," Brother Mor said. "If they carried the contagion with them, it will definitely spread beyond this region."

"All the more reason for us to get back to work." Lieutenant Dax stood up; Ensign Kahrimanis followed suit.

Brother Mor's hand shot out to detain her. "But you have not finished your meal!"

"I guess we're not hungry either," Ensign Kahrimanis said.

"Sit, sit!" The monk urged them back into their places with words and motions. "When I first arrived here, I was like you and the healer. I wanted to fix everything right away. That first week, I almost killed myself with too much work and too little rest. You must trust my word: You will do us more harm than good if you drive yourselves too hard. Then we shall have you to look after in the infirmary as well as our other patients."

"Finish your meal and then go, if you like." Brother Gis backed him up. "You will be the better for it."

Ensign Kahrimanis picked up his chopsticks again and looked at the food suspiciously, but Dax settled herself to eating, following the absent Brother Talissin's technique for dealing with the rock-hard bread.

They're right, of course, she thought, chewing slowly. *There will be additional help here within three days; there's no need to exhaust ourselves. I need my wits sharp if I'm to find this holy child, the* Nekor. *I must keep fit; tired minds make stupid mistakes. I'd better remind Julian of that.* She sipped warm, tawny water from her cup. *If he'll listen.*

Julian was concentrating on the sample under the microscanner when Dax came into the laboratory shack two days later. Dr. Bashir's workspace had been improved considerably with the addition of self-powered lights sent down from the station, accompanied by a long tirade from Chief O'Brien against the "double-damned Cardie sensors that couldn't find a black dog on an ice floe!"

"I've had news from the station," she announced.

He behaved as if she hadn't spoken. He changed the sample and adjusted the instrument, then spoke into his recorder: "Possible retroviral affinities in evidence. Mutation of previously harmless organism similar to cases of *nanadekh* plague reported from Klingon Empire: Investigate." Only after he was done recording did he turn to acknowledge her presence.

"News?"

The bright overhead lights, so different from the flickering illumination of the infirmary or the dusk-hour dimness in which they ate their one communal meal of the day, shone full on his face.

Lieutenant Dax was appalled. Julian's eyes burned in red-rimmed sockets with dark shadows beneath. His skin was pasty, and his normally pronounced cheekbones jutted out so sharply that they looked ready to cut through the skin. Dax knew Julian had been pushing himself, but she had no idea he'd worked himself into this state in so short a time. It was impossible to keep track of his comings and goings, since he had a private tent.

She did not let her shock show. "Major Kira reports that the Klingon vessel *Shining Blade* docked early. They regret to report that they have no personnel they can spare to help us here. They are en route to a vital rendezvous in the Gamma Quadrant. On the other hand, they're readying a generous shipment of supplies for transport at thirteen hundred hours to our original beamdown coordinates. If I bring Ensign Kahrimanis and you bring Belem, we should be able to move them easi—"

"Belem's run away," Julian said. He turned his back on Dax and prepared a new sample for the microscanner.

Jadzia laid a hand on his shoulder. "Julian, I'm sorry."

"Don't be," he said tersely, his eye to the viewer.

"Are you sure he's gone? Maybe he's just been reassigned to the fields. The harvest festival is coming soon, and now that he's fit they can use his help getting in the crops."

Julian shrugged off her touch. "Brother Talissin saw him racing off down the road." He spun around to face her. "Brother Talissin took a great deal of pleasure in reporting that to me. The boy had too great a lead for pursuit, or so my monkish friend assured me. Besides, what good would it do to fetch him back? He would only run away again."

"Brother Talissin is a very sour mouthful," Dax commented.

"Brother Talissin is a realist. He sees things for what they are, without hanging a bunch of useless, romantic trappings all over. Why plant roses to hide a pigsty?"

One corner of Jadzia's mouth quirked up. "Maybe the pigs have a taste for roses."

Dr. Bashir made an exasperated sound and went back to his microscanner.

"Brother Talissin is an envious man," Jadzia continued. "He couldn't stand to see all you'd done to help Belem, so he had to poison it for you."

"And what have I done for the boy?" Julian wanted to know. "When he was a cripple, he was safe. I've only made it possible for him to be killed. *And* perhaps for him to spread the fever, if he's carrying it."

"Would you cripple all the children, if you thought that would keep them safe?" she asked softly.

Julian ignored her last remark. "I think I'm onto something," he said, changing the subject abruptly. "Take a look for yourself." He stepped aside so that she could check out the sample under the microscanner. "Do you see?" he asked, a touch of the old eagerness creeping back into his voice. "I've isolated that organism from samples of blood taken from fever victims only. It took me a while to find it; it's almost identical to a bioplast found in the blood of healthy Bajorans."

Dax glanced up. "A mimic?"

"Or a very clever infiltrator." He managed a grin. "Soil-borne is my guess."

"Then why hasn't it turned up before?"

"I'm theorizing that this *has* turned up before, in a different form, which was eventually diagnosed and cured by local physicians." He changed samples and invited her to take another look. "I don't need to tell you that microbes are tenacious creatures, fearsomely adaptable. Throw them out the door and they come creeping back in through the window, even if they have to build the window themselves. When this particular strain was supposedly eradicated, I'd say it went dormant, perhaps assaying a little experiment now and then with nonhuman hosts."

"There is a high population of rodentlike fauna in the area," Dax admitted. *"Hyurin.* They're rather like a cross between rats and hamsters."

"The farmers would have had their methods for keeping the *hyurin* population down, I'm sure," Dr. Bashir said. "When the Cardassians destroyed so many villages, the animals could breed unchecked."

"They have their predators, but that wouldn't keep the *hyurin* away from Bajoran settlements. On the contrary, the little creatures would seek out man-made structures as good hiding places from their natural enemies and spread the microbe through their droppings," Dax concluded. "From there it's a short step back to human hosts. Starving refugees don't have the luxury to check whether or not their food supplies are uncontaminated."

"It is related to the *nanadekh* plague. I'm hoping it will respond to the same sort of treatment."

"A specially engineered antibody." She nodded.

"Of course, given the remarkable genetic similarity between this organism and the perfectly harmless one, I'll be taking extreme precautions in designing and testing the antibody. We don't want to set up an autoimmune disaster scenario by moving *too* hastily."

"I'm glad to hear you say that, Julian." She took him firmly by the arm and steered him toward the door.

"What are you doing?" he demanded.

"I'm taking you back to your tent and putting you in your cot," she explained.

"Well, this is a switch," Julian muttered. *"You* trying to get *me* into bed."

Dax ignored the gibe. "You look awful. Talk about disasters, you're one just waiting to happen."

He yanked his arm out of her grasp. "There's nothing the matter with me. I have work to do."

"Do you trust yourself to do your best work on no sleep?" she countered. "That's the perfect formula for making mistakes—fatal mistakes." Putting on her most persuasive voice, she slipped her arm around him and steered him toward the door once more, saying, "You've done the most important work already. I think you've found the answer to our mysterious fever. Leave your notes with me and I'll take it from here. You know I've got several degrees in genetic engineering."

"Yes, but—" His protests were met by strong, steady encouragement out of the lab.

"You're our doctor, but I'm our science officer. I let you do your job, now you let me do mine. With luck, I should have a breeding batch of antibodies tested and ready for injection by this evening . . . *if* you get out of my way. Go on, rest; you'll need it when we start the immunization program. You know how children *adore* getting shots!" One final push and he was out the door. Jadzia shut it on him with a sigh of relief.

She rechecked his notes and found that despite his obvious near-exhaustion, Julian had hit the mark. All indications were that he had found the answer to a puzzle that was stealing lives. No matter what she thought of his countless attempts at flirtation, she had to confess that he was as brilliant a doctor as he prided himself on being.

Jadzia adjusted the microscanner and began her work. It would take time for her to design an antibody tailored to the task of destroying only the retrovirus and not the organism it mimicked, but the most difficult part was done: thanks to Julian, she knew the face of the enemy.

He tries to do too much, she thought. *He'll destroy himself if he doesn't learn some moderation. Oh, well, I did manage to send him off for some sleep. I don't need to worry about him now.*

She bent over the blood samples, her mind at ease.

Across the camp, in the infirmary, Brother Mor looked up to meet Dr. Bashir's wobbly smile. "I'm here to lend a hand tending the patients," he announced.

"I thought you were working in your laboratory," the monk replied, perplexed.

"I was, but I reached a good stopping point. I've discovered that sometimes when you work too close to a problem for too long, you lose insight. A different activity may give me a new perspective on the disease. I'm *very* close to an answer."

Brother Mor looked dubious. "You don't sound well," he said. "You look tired. Perhaps you would be better advised to lie down in your tent and—"

"What, my voice?" Dr. Bashir forced a creditable chuckle. "Cooped up in that lab, it's just a bit rusty, that's all. Oh, and don't be misled by these." He indicated the dark rings under his eyes. "A family quirk. We all look like raccoons half the time."

"Raccoons?"

"Brother Mor, can't you *use* an extra pair of hands in here?" Julian wheedled.

Grudgingly, the monk admitted that he could. Soon Julian was hard at work, doing what he could to clean the bodies of those fever victims who were too far gone to perform even the most basic hygiene care for themselves. It was not a pleasant task, but he did not focus on that.

It's work, he thought. *At least I'm doing something for these children, something to help them. Something to keep me from thinking about how many of them might die before Dax comes up with that antibody.*

Something to keep me from thinking about Belem.

He moved doggedly from pallet to pallet, cooling the small, burning bodies with sponge baths to ease the fever. It was primitive, but he knew it was the best solution he had to apply until Dax was ready. The retrovirus did not respond to any of the pharmacopeia at his disposal. For now, he could only deal with symptoms.

Frontier medicine, he thought as he dabbed at a little girl's flushed face with a damp cloth. *This is it, all right.*

The child's hair lay in damp tendrils across her forehead. They looked like the finest Arabic calligraphy. He stared at the patterns they made, suddenly certain that if he could stop them from weaving and blurring so badly, he would be able to read the answer to a great riddle in their pattern. The letters danced in and out of focus, mocking him, but he concentrated on their elusive message, determined that the answer would not escape.

The infirmary began to spin around him, but he knew it was just a trick of the mysterious letters to evade him. He held on, though the spinning went faster and faster, until he could reach out and seize the meaning. Yes, there it was, the answer! It was his! Another triumph for Dr. Julian Bashir!

He opened his mouth to speak the word he read in the twisting letters and pitched forward to the ground, unconscious.

CHAPTER
7

A DAMP, WARM CLOTH patted Dr. Bashir's cheek like the paw of a persistent cat. He opened his eyes to see two Bajoran children kneeling over him. Still dazed, Julian marveled at how clean and well groomed the little girl's long braid of brown hair was, a sight rare and remarkable in a place where most of the children went around scruffy and indifferent to appearances. There was something uncanny about her fragile prettiness and the luminous pallor of her skin. Although her dress was as ragged as that of any other child of the camp, there was nothing squalid or shabby about it. The taller of the two, a crop-haired boy with face and arms browned by the sun, continued to dab at the doctor's face with the wet cloth.

"Better?" he asked gruffly when he saw that Dr. Bashir was awake. He sat back on his haunches as if he intended to stare the answer out of his patient.

"I—I think so." Julian touched his forehead. "I must have—"

"You fell over on your face," the boy stated. *"Wham.*

Like that. Lucky you didn't break your nose." He snorted. "Might've improved its looks that way."

Julian smiled woozily. "Yes, I expect you'd think that." He supposed human noses must look peculiar, if not downright unattractive, by Bajoran standards.

"I think his nose is nice," the little girl whispered. She dove into hiding behind the boy's back.

Julian tried to sit up. His head still spun a little, but the feeling passed. He was surprised that his collapse hadn't brought Brother Mor running. He looked around, trying to catch sight of the monk, but saw only the rows of infirmary patients.

"He's in the office," the girl said, bobbing her head up from behind the boy like a bright-eyed ground squirrel popping out of its burrow. "He's getting my medicine."

Her words were enough to banish the last traces of dizziness from Julian's head. "What medicine?" he asked, speaking gently to her. "Are you ill?" He dreaded the thought of this exquisite child becoming yet another victim of the fever.

She ducked behind the boy again, who rolled his eyes at the ceiling in exasperation. "Don't pay attention to my sister, healer," he said. "Dejana's scared of her own shadow."

"Am not," came the muffled response from behind him, and a thump on the back that knocked him forward.

"Stop that!" he commanded. He turned back to Dr. Bashir. "She's all right, but she had this fever that's going around. Now she's better—"

"Better?" Julian echoed. "You mean she recovered on her own?"

The boy shrugged. "That's what Brother Gis said. Some do. Brother Talissin told us it meant that Dejana's specially—" He slipped into a mocking nasal singsong as he repeated the dour monk's words. "—*belooooooved of the Prophets*. As if the Prophets didn't care a pinch for all our friends who got the fever and died."

"Shush, Cedra!" Dejana hissed, scandalized. "Don't make fun of the Prophets like that!"

"I'm not making fun of the Prophets, ninny; I'm making fun of Brother Talissin," the boy replied calmly. He returned his attention to Dr. Bashir. "So anyway, Brother Gis said she's not supposed to work in the fields and she's supposed to take this special tea every six hours. It's to give her strength." He leaned closer to Dr. Bashir, and with an adult's serious intonation added, "You look like you could do with a little strengthening yourself. Drink a bowl of Brother Gis's tea and lie down for a couple of hours. Unless you like falling on your face."

"Cedra! Don't talk to him like that! He's the *healer!"* the girl wailed, and dealt the boy another thump.

Even Dr. Bashir could tell that the blows were never intended to hurt. He'd seen similar behavior countless times—one medical student congratulating another with a jab to the arm, the backslap his tennis coach gave him when he scored off an arduous volley—fake punches, skillfully pulled, given with only the friendliest intentions. He was surprised to see it here, where all the blows exchanged by the camp children were meant to hurt, and did.

He was even more surprised to notice something that set these two children apart from nearly all the others he'd seen: their eyes. Their eyes were alive.

"A healer can take medical advice as well as give it," he said to the girl. "Sometimes he'd *better* take it." His left cheek began to sting. His exploring fingers encountered a few minor contusions that made him wince. He fumbled for his instruments and treated the scrape as best he could without a mirror to guide his hand. The children watched, fascinated, as the silvery wand restored Dr. Bashir's skin to wholeness.

"Can I try that thing?" Cedra demanded, already reaching out for it.

"Later," Julian replied. "There's no one who needs a scrape or a cut treated now."

"I can fix that!" The boy sprang to his feet and started off. He looked determined to bring back an accident victim.

"Come back here, Cedra!" the little girl called. "No fair making yourself fall over something just so the healer lets you play with his magic."

"That's not magic," Cedra scoffed. "That's Federation technology. You don't know anything if I don't tell you." But he came back, reluctantly, and resumed his place on the ground beside Dr. Bashir.

"Look, I promise you I'll give you a chance to try this," Julian said, amused and impressed by the child's spirit. "But in exchange, I'll want something from you."

"What?" The boy's dark eyes narrowed, on guard.

"An introduction." Dr. Bashir made himself keep a straight face. "As one healer to another." He offered his hand. "I'm Dr. Julian Bashir of Starfleet."

The boy took his hand uncertainly, as if it were a bundle of sticks, unaccustomed to the gesture. "I am Talis Cedra, and this is my sister, Talis Dejana."

The fact that children who looked so young still recalled their family name took Julian by surprise. "Any relation to Brother Talissin?" he had to ask, struck by the similarity between the names.

Cedra gave him a look remarkably reminiscent of Selok's expression when the younger Bashir made one of his infrequent mistakes. "Talissin's not a *family* name," he said. "Besides, who'd want to be related to *him?*"

"Cedra, what you said!" Little Dejana was horrified. "Brother Talissin is—is—*holy.*"

"He's also a grouch," the unrepentant Cedra replied.

Brother Mor came bustling out of the office cubicle just as Julian forced a laugh of agreement into a cough. "Here we are, Dejana!" the monk called, a steaming clay bowl held gingerly in his hands. "You drink this as fast as you can and you'll— Ah, Dr. Bashir! What are you doing sitting on the floor? Is anything the matter?"

"It's all under control, Brother Mor." Slowly, with a few minor aches and pains, Julian got to his feet. "I've just been discussing the cure for stubbornness with my young colleague here." He gestured at Cedra.

The boy stood up and took the bowl from Brother Mor's hands. "He fell over," he explained. He held the hot brew for his sister to sip while Brother Mor turned a shocked look on Dr. Bashir.

"I am guilty as charged," Julian admitted, palms out. "I think I'll take some very good advice I was given earlier and have a little nap. I would appreciate it if some responsible person would volunteer to wake me when the additional supplies are beamed down at thirteen hundred hours."

"Me! Me! I'll do it!" Cedra perked up like a puppy, though for all his enthusiasm he never so much as joggled the bowl he held to his sister's lips. The tea had cooled enough for her to take the bowl from his hands, leaving him free to leap up and insist, "And I'll help carry them into camp, too! Please, Brother Mor? I'll go straight back to the fields afterward, I promise."

Brother Mor looked from Cedra to Dr. Bashir. "What do you think?" he asked.

Dr. Bashir smiled. "I think I have a new assistant."

"They're the most remarkable children, Jadzia," Julian enthused as he watched Lieutenant Dax load the hypodermics with her antibody solution. "You won't believe it, but they've been in this camp for two years, and they're still so—well, *cheerful's* the word I want, I suppose. I realize it doesn't sound like much but—"

"For children to keep their spirits up after two years in a refugee camp sounds like a miracle to me," Dax replied.

"Cedra was only ten when he brought his sister Dejana here—she's eight now. Brother Mor tells me they arrived unaccompanied by any adult. I don't like to think of all they must have endured to reach this place, yet here they are!"

"Many children reached the camp on their own," Dax commented, concentrating on the work at hand. She was eager to be done with it so that she might begin her real mission here. The few conversations she had been able to have with the refugees so far were short and unsatisfactory. The adults she'd approached wore faces haunted by suffering and suspicion. They disliked speaking of the past. The children often could recall no past to speak of. Sometimes she encountered a person who reacted to her questions as if he might have the answer she sought but refused to trust any words to a stranger's ears. Her quest for the *Nekor* was off to a poor start.

Given time, I might be able to win their trust, she thought, sealing another hypodermic and setting it aside. *But I don't have time. The crops are coming in, even here. The* Berajin *harvest festival isn't that far off. If the* Nekor *isn't found by then . . .*

There was little doubt in her mind that word had already reached the *Dessin-ka* that the Federation had consented to take part in the search. If the Federation failed to deliver the child, the *Dessin-ka* would quite likely do a violent about-face as far as their previous support went. Such a switch by a formerly pro-Federation group of the *Dessin-ka*'s size and influence would have seismic repercussions in the Bajoran political strata. The already unstable provisional government couldn't stand a shake-up of that magnitude.

If I find the Nekor *too late for the* Dessin-ka's *deadline, it will be as bad as if I never find the* Nekor *at all,* she thought. She hoped the council representatives of the *Dessin-ka* might be open to reason, but a host of memories from her symbiont's past experiences of dealing with such people swarmed up to remind her how hollow such hopes must be.

Jadzia's natural optimism reached out and grasped one encouraging thought: *At least Julian's stopped trying to wear himself into dust. He's accepted the fact that he can't cure everything that's wrong here by himself. I would like to meet the children responsible for this change in him. They must be remarkable.*

"There," she announced with satisfaction. "That ought to be enough for us to treat all the fever patients and immunize the rest of the camp."

"Are you sure?" Julian regarded the array of hypodermics on the table.

"As sure as I need to be. But if you're worried, there's a genetic template of my antibody design stored in the portable replicator the ship's doctor from the *Shining Blade* sent us."

Julian squatted to stare at the stark black metal oblong resting beneath the laboratory table. It was no larger than two old-fashioned tricorders set end-to-end, yet it had the capacity to duplicate any carbon-based biosample introduced to it. If he cocked his head, he could just pick up a faint humming sound coming from the unit. "All self-powered, too," he murmured in admiration.

"Did you say something, Doctor?" Dax asked.

Julian stood up and stretched. "I was just wondering what my old professor Selok of Vulcan would have to say about this. He didn't have a very high opinion of Klingon medical technology."

"Any reason?"

"With Vulcans there's always a reason. He was forever tied up in a faculty feud with Rhakh-tem, an eminent Klingon neurobiologist. All very polite, it was—Rhakh-tem never threw anything larger than a retort, the glass kind, and Selok always managed to catch it before it hit—though there were times I swear I caught a glint of some less than logical temper in Selok's eye."

"Well, Vulcans are kin to Romulans." She passed two of the primed hypos to Dr. Bashir. "You take care of the patients in the infirmary; Ensign Kahrimanis and I will organize the immunization program for the rest." *No better way to make certain I speak to everyone possible about any refugees from Bennikar,* she thought.

"Bennikar?" the man repeated as Dax administered the injection. "No, I can't say I know if any of the children come from that region. Of course, I'm not from around here." He rolled down his sleeve and gave Dax an impish look that urged her to ask where he did come from.

"Oh, I couldn't tell you that," he replied when she asked. He shook his head gravely. "The answer would be over your head."

"Try me."

"That's just it, dear lady." He pointed at the sky above. "That's where I hail from, over your head. The name's Mullibok. I used to have a farm on Jeraddo."

"The fifth moon?" Dax blinked, remembering a conversation she'd had not so long ago with Major Kira. Recognition showed on her face. "I have a friend who'll be very glad to hear you're alive and well."

"Let me guess; the stubborn one with the pretty eyes?" He chuckled. "The lady is very persuasive when she puts her mind to it."

"But what are you doing here?" Dax asked.

The farmer sighed. "When your friend . . . persuaded me to leave my home, I thought it would kill me. It didn't. So the next thought I had was to find myself a place where people would appreciate me for what I am: living proof that losing your home isn't the end of the world. A walking, breathing lesson in hope, as it were."

He lowered his voice conspiratorially and added, "Also I'm the best damn farmer on Bajor. These monks mean well, but they couldn't grow bread mold in a damp box without my help."

Dax suppressed a smile. "I'm sure of it."

"Ah, well!" He clapped his hands to his knees and stood up. "Back to work. The katterpods aren't ready for reaping yet, but Brother Talissin insists we harvest the fields according to his schedule, not nature's. Thanks for what you've done here, my dear; it's good to be able to do your job without feeling like that fever's peering over your shoulder. Give Nerys my love, won't you?"

"My pleasure."

"And a kick in the backside whenever she turns stubborn on you." He winked and strolled off, whistling.

"Any more?" Lieutenant Dax asked Ensign Kahrimanis. The two of them had set up their immunization post in a small lean-to pitched near the katterpod fields. The furnishings consisted entirely of three stools— one apiece for herself and Kahrimanis, one for each new shot recipient. It was more convenient and efficient if they brought the antibody injections to the harvest workers rather than the other way around.

"I think we got them all." Ensign Kahrimanis rolled his head slowly to work out a kink in his neck. "It feels like we've been at this forever." He checked the tally sheet Brother Gis had given him. The monk had made a special effort to take a reliable nose-count of the people in his care for the immunization program. As the harvest intensified, all able-bodied refugees were accounted for on the field workers' list, all ailing ones in the infirmary. If even one of them missed receiving the lifesaving injection, it would be tragic.

"I just wish we had something more to show for it," Dax muttered.

"Huh?"

"Nothing." Dax was annoyed with herself for that slip

of the tongue. Kahrimanis knew nothing of her search for the *Nekor*. She hunched her shoulders repeatedly and wished for a well-trained masseur to relieve the cramps that tied her shoulder muscles in knots. She had insisted on administering every shot herself, fobbing off Kahrimanis with the job of record keeper. While he checked off incoming patients, Dax was at liberty to question each and every soul for any clue to a camp child from Bennikar.

Shots do make most people nervous, she reflected. *Nervous people tend to talk more. Bajorans are no different. Too bad none of them had anything helpful to tell me.*

She stood and picked up the stool. "Let's go back to the infirmary and see how Dr. Bashir's doing."

They were a stone's throw from the infirmary when Brother Gis burst through the curtained doorway, his face a study in bliss. "May the Prophets reward you beyond all measure!" he exclaimed, clasping Dax's hand. "You have given us the miracle of our prayers!"

"Brother Gis, please—" Dax began, feeling herself squirm. As a Trill chosen to carry a symbiont, she had been schooled never to act as if she were better than her less privileged kin. Only one Trill in ten was selected for the honor, and hard feelings were common enough without the lucky ones lording it over the rest. Healthy modesty was a quality the selectors looked for in the candidates for Union. As a result, Jadzia was poorly equipped to handle such effusive praise. She slipped her hand from Gis's grasp, sidestepped the monk, and dove through the infirmary door.

"Dr. Bashir?" she called.

"Over here!" An arm sheathed in the black sleeve of a Starfleet uniform stuck out of one of the sheet-walled cubicles at the back of the building. She hurried toward it. As she strode down the aisle she noticed a great change, the miracle that had so overjoyed Brother Gis: The stink of fever was diminished. A fresher, less oppressive atmosphere seemed to have crept into the building in spite of the inadequate windows. The patients, large and small, no longer tossed in their bedclothes or stared at the ceiling with glazed eyes or moaned with pain. Here Jadzia passed a child sleeping peacefully, her breath unlabored, her face no longer flushed. There she saw a woman get up from her cot and take a few wobbling steps toward a pallet across the aisle where a little boy stretched out his arms and smiled as he said, "Mama? Mama, you better?"

The woman stumbled, but Lieutenant Dax was there to catch her and urge her back to her own bed. She paused to transfer the woman's child to a place nearer his mother's side, then told her, "You mustn't overtax yourself. I know you feel much better now, but you're still weak. You'll recover more quickly if you rest."

The woman clutched Jadzia's hand, her eyes eloquent with gratitude though she said nothing.

"Are they all reacting to the injection so well?" Dax asked as she joined Dr. Bashir inside the cubicle. The patient on the cot was deep in normal sleep. They spoke quietly, to avoid disturbing him.

"Amazing, isn't it?" he said. "Astonishing signs of initial recovery. Brother Gis hasn't stopped singing your praises."

She thought she detected something else beneath his words. "But . . . ?" she prompted.

"Well, I needn't tell you that I'd like to see whether the effects are permanent. With such a readily adaptable organism, we must be sure we've won the war, not just the first skirmish."

"Thank you, Doctor." She smiled at him. "It's a relief to hear some good, hard, scientific skepticism instead of all this talk of miracles." *I wouldn't say no to a miracle, though,* she admitted to herself. *Not if it would help me find the* Nekor. "Any theories as to how long we might have to wait to be positive we're out of the woods?"

Dr. Bashir pondered the question. "If the affinities to *nanadekh* plague are any indication, I'd say the next forty-eight hours should tell the story. That epidemic was also caused by a highly mutable retrovirus, and when it was in a humanoid host, it didn't waste much time changing itself to combat half-measures used against it. I made a special senior honors study of the phenomenon, under Selok's tutelage." For once Julian did not sound as if he were bragging about his past achievements, merely presenting them as facts. "I think we'd know still more if we spoke with Gis. He says this illness resembles another sort of Bajoran fever. If we hear how that one be-haved—"

"—we might be able to make some workable hypothe-ses about this," Dax finished for him. "An excellent idea, Doctor. Why don't I take care of that?"

"Please do. I'm making second rounds to check on the progress of the patients. Cedra is helping me, but he might miss reporting some vital detail."

Dax clicked her tongue. "Still trying to do everything, Julian?"

"That's not it." He spoke with conviction, but looked as if he'd been caught doing something he shouldn't. "Cedra's a bit preoccupied at the moment. His little sister made a natural recovery from the fever—we might want to sample her blood when she's better to see how her antibodies compare with the one you designed—but the child is still very weak. Talissin views her recovery as a sign of special favor from the Prophets. Cedra tells me that our dour friend has plans for bringing the girl to the attention of his order when the situation here betters itself."

"What does Cedra think of the religious life for his sister?" Dax inquired.

"He's all for it. Anything's better than the camps, he says. What we've done here is nothing. News comes all the time about other refugee settlements where the situation is far worse. Cedra keeps his ears open and pays attention to the monks when they talk amongst themselves. In some places they don't need this fever to kill the children; they have other illnesses that take them before the fever can arrive: dysentery, parasites, deficiencies we could set right quickly, easily, if only we could—"

"You ought to speak with Major Kira when we return to the station," Dax said, her matter-of-fact calm in strong contrast to the rising note of passion in Julian's voice.

It had the effect of a basin full of cold water dashed in the doctor's face. "Yes," he said dully. "Of course that's what I ought to do. Perhaps it will help if I show her a copy of Cedra's map. He made a rough sketch of where the other camps are located, based on what he heard from the monks. Every complaint they make about the terrain between here and the other sites went down on paper. I can't vouch for its accuracy, but still, what a project for a child to undertake! He's a bright boy."

"And his sister? Is she bright, too?"

"Dejana?" Dr. Bashir frowned. "Bright enough, but there's something else about her . . . I can't explain it. You'd have to see for yourself. At any rate, Talissin insisted she return to the infirmary. He doesn't believe Gis's course of strengthening teas is enough to encourage her complete recovery." He made a face. "I hate to say so, but I agree with him. However, Cedra's worried."

"Someone mention me?" Cedra's brown head poked around a corner of the sheet.

"Eavesdropping again?" Dr. Bashir teased him.

The boy drew himself up proudly. "You'd think it was something heroic if you called it playing spy. I learn a lot of useful things you'd be glad to know."

"Then make yourself useful, you young scamp, and find Brother Gis for us. Lieutenant Dax needs to speak with him."

"About what the old fever was like?" Cedra grinned to see Dr. Bashir's reaction. "He's in the office."

"Thank you, Cedra," Dax said. "I can find my own way." She walked to the very back of the infirmary. Behind her she heard Cedra asking Dr. Bashir if he would please take a look at Dejana.

Dax was relieved to find a much less effusive Gis awaiting her in the infirmary office. The monk looked up when she entered and said, "I apologize if I caused you any unease before, Lieutenant Dax." He rose from his rickety chair and attempted to offer it to her.

She refused it with a gesture and a courteous smile. "I understand your feelings. Let's not mention it again. It looks as if we've been able to solve one of your problems. As for the other—"

"The *Nekor*." He spoke the name scarcely above a whisper.

"None of the field-workers could give me any information. I'm hoping to do better when I can interview the recovering patients here in the infirmary. I hope you will be able to help me. I realize that the children might not know Bennikar village by name, but perhaps you might know something about it that they *would* recognize—a nearby landmark, a local festival, any detail a child might know, or recall his parents mentioning when they spoke about the place."

Brother Gis thought about it. "They did have somewhat of a reputation for brewing *kis*. But would children hear of that?"

"Hear or overhear. It's startling how many adult conversations children manage to gather."

"Especially those we do not wish them to." Gis finished Dax's thought for her with an amiable smile. "I believe Bennikar was also reputed to breed a sturdier variety of *verdanis*. Will that help you in your search, Lieutenant?"

"It's more than what I've had to go on so far. Thank

you, Gis. I think I'll begin making my own rounds of the infirmary and see if anyone is fit enough to answer a few questions."

She left the office and scanned the infirmary. She saw Dr. Bashir kneeling beside a pallet toward the front of the building. He had a length of string looped over the fingers of both hands and was weaving an elaborate cat's cradle for the entertainment of a bright-eyed little girl. The child lay with her head pillowed on a pile of folded cloth, yet even at such a distance Dax could see that Bashir's young patient was on the way to recovery. Her face was animated, and her feet fidgeted under the covers.

Maybe that's a good place to begin, Dax thought, starting toward them.

The little girl turned out to be too young to be of any help. "Lika was born in this camp three years ago," Dr. Bashir told Dax. "This is the only home she knows, can you imagine that?" He laid his hand on the child's head. "Her mother died only two weeks ago, and for a while it looked like she was going to follow her. Your injection saved her life. If you've done nothing else in your life you can be proud of, Jadzia, you can be proud of this."

"You mean *we* can be proud of this, Doctor," she corrected him.

He shook his head. "I've done nothing." He moved on to the next patient.

Dax became Dr. Bashir's shadow, following him as he made the rounds of the infirmary to check up on the vaccine's effects. While he took readings on the patients' vital signs, she engaged them in casual conversation. With adults, she sometimes asked directly whether they knew of anyone in the camp who hailed from Bennikar. With the children and the more reticent grown-ups, she jollied as much information out of them as she could.

"What d'you mean, I won't be able to manage a team

of *verdanis* for a month yet?" one fellow demanded, incensed. His hands bore the telltale calluses of reins, evidence that as good as chose Dax's point of attack for her. "I been driving *verdanis* since I was knee-high to—"

"But the camp's gotten hold of some of the really *big* ones," she said smoothly. "I heard only folk from Bennikar were used to handling that breed."

He snorted. "Then you heard wrong! Remis Jobar's from near Bennikar, and he never could drive even the small *verdanis* we've got." The man's brow furrowed. "Remis Jobar still alive?" he asked Dr. Bashir. Julian checked his list and nodded toward another male Bajoran lying three pallets farther down the line. The man relaxed. "Good. He can't drive *verdanis* worth a damn, but he's a good friend."

Dax moved on to Remis Jobar's side, leaving Dr. Bashir behind. When questioned, the man was groggy and uncertain. "Children from Bennikar . . . I'm a bachelor, myself. Been here three years. Didn't ask folks many questions about where they come from, did they have any children or not. Some of them did . . . once. I didn't want to pry. You understand?"

Dax nodded calmly, though inside she was clutching her fists in frustration. *I don't need discretion; I need information!* "You didn't ask, but did you ever just happen to hear—?"

He shrugged. "My sister came here with me. Back home, she used to do for me, keep house, like that. When we came here, she was thrilled to see some of the finer folk from Bennikar proper—we lived a good ways off from the village, you see. She knew each and every one of 'em, all their business, how it was with their families, everything. Now there was a woman who could gossip!" He chuckled softly, then grew wistful. "She's gone now."

Dax stroked his hand by way of comfort. "She must have shared some of that gossip with you, didn't she?"

He bobbed his head. "That was her second greatest pleasure, sharing what she knew. Only thing she liked better was getting the word in the first place. She said there was maybe eight, ten children from our village here. She was as proud of that as if she'd brought 'em in safe herself." He sighed. "She died nursing one of 'em. Nice little girl."

Dax perked at the mention of the child's sex. "And the little girl? Who was she? What became of her?"

Another shrug. "I don't know. I was still able to work the fields back then. When Brother Mor came to tell me Cathlys was dead, he said she'd given her life for a child's, but I don't know if that meant the girl lived. Could be he was just trying to ease my pain." He sighed again and rolled away from Dax.

Dax respected his desire to be left alone. *Eight or ten children from Bennikar,* she thought, rising from his pallet. *That's not a lot, but he wasn't sure of the count. There might be more of them . . . or fewer. Some must have survived the fever. Some probably didn't even catch it. I've got to keep asking.*

She looked around for Dr. Bashir and saw him examining a boy across the aisle. She started toward him, hoping to find fresh clues, when she felt thin, determined fingers close around her elbow and tug.

" 'Scuse me," said Cedra, steering her away from Dr. Bashir. "Would you help me some?"

"Help?" Dax echoed.

"My sister, Dejana," he replied. "Come take a look at her, please."

"Is she sick? I'll get Dr. Bashir—"

"No, don't do that!" The boy's alarm was almost comical. "He's seen her already. He'll just make it worse."

Dax frowned. "Dr. Bashir is more than qualified to—"

Cedra laid a finger to his lips, at the same time making

rapid hushing motions with his other hand. "Can you keep a secret?" he whispered hoarsely.

"That depends."

"It's nothing bad, I swear! But if Dejana found out I told you, she'd kill me."

Dax's curiosity was piqued. "I can keep secrets very well, when I have to."

The boy lowered his voice still further and hissed, "Dejana's in love with him."

"Him? You mean Dr. Bash—?"

"Shhhhh!" The child was positively mortified. "I think she's faking feeling so weak, just so she can be in the infirmary and have him see her. Dejana can get Brother Talissin to do almost anything she wants 'cause he's so soppy over how she's been touched by the Prophets. She just needs to sniffle once and he falls apart."

"What do you think I can do about this?"

"Well, I heard you're a science officer. Could you maybe do something . . . *scientific* to make her stop?"

Dax's mouth curved up. "The only scientific cure for your sister's problem is time-travel." Cedra gave her a puzzled frown. "We wait for her to outgrow it," she explained.

Cedra shook his head vigorously. "You come take a look at her and see how weak she *really* is. If you report to Brother Gis that she's faking, he'll move her out of here, no matter what Brother Talissin says. Please? She's—she's *embarrassing* me."

Lieutenant Dax patted the boy's shoulder. "I'll do what I can. Where is she?"

"Over there." He grabbed her wrist and dragged her into a sheeted alcove on the east side of the infirmary. It had only two walls, supposedly to shield patients with some hope of recovery from turning their heads to the side and seeing others, less fortunate, whose last moments might not be a pretty sight. Three pallets were laid out on the floor inside, and a box holding a clay pitcher and cups. Only the two side pallets were occupied, one by a tall girl who lay sleeping with her face to the wall, the other by Dejana.

Cedra's sister was sitting on her pallet when they entered. She looked up pertly when she saw Dax. The science officer was struck by the sharpness of the child's gaze. When she had been plain Jadzia, before the Union with her symbiont, the examiners had often fixed her with the same kind of penetrating, unnerving stare.

"Hello, Lieutenant Dax," she said. "Have you come to visit me? Please sit down." She motioned at the empty pallet with queenly grace.

Dax accepted the invitation, doing her best to keep her reactions from showing. *What did Julian call these children?* she thought. *Remarkable? The girl is, at any rate.* She settled herself tailor-fashion. From the corner of her eye she glimpsed Cedra also crouching at the foot of the pallet.

"What's it like?" Dejana asked abruptly.

"What's what like?" Dax returned, taken by surprise.

"Being a Trill. Having so many lives inside you."

"Who told you I was——?" Then Dax laughed, relieved as the answer came to her. "You've been talking to Dr. Bashir."

The girl blushed and looked away. Cedra coughed. His sister's head jerked up. "He's very nice," she said, sounding more like a child. "I like him. It's very kind of him to spend so much time showing Lika how to play that string game."

Dax glanced from side to side. With the sheets up, it was impossible for Dejana to have seen Dr. Bashir's game of cat's cradle. Still, the child was not terribly ill. She looked in perfect health, if a little delicate. She might have grown bored and crept to the end of this cubicle to peek out and spy on her beloved doctor.

"I wish he'd teach me how to play it the way you people do," Cedra said with a heartfelt sigh. "We do different shapes with the string. I'm the best at it!" He dug a length of dirty cord out of his pocket and tangled it over his fingers.

"Cedra, you awful liar!" Dejana lunged past Dax to snatch the string from her brother. Dax's eyes never left the little girl as she swiftly wove the string into a perfect replica of the figure Dr. Bashir had created for his young patient. "I'm much better at this than Cedra is," the child announced proudly.

"You are very good," Dax replied. "You're also very healthy. I'm going to have a word with Brother Gis about—"

Dejana uttered a theatrical moan and sank back onto her pallet. "I don't feel well," she announced plaintively.

Dax exchanged a knowing look with Cedra. "I see. In that case, maybe I'd better fetch Dr. Bashir?" She heard a loud groan from Cedra when she made that suggestion.

"Don't you think he's too young?" Dejana asked innocently.

"What did you say?"

"You like him, but he's too young for you. Compared to what you *know,* what you *are,* I mean. But if that's all you—all you look at, you'll never find anyone old enough for you, will you? And he *is* nice."

Lieutenant Dax stared at the girl. She recalled Commander Sisko describing the uncanny feeling he had the first time he met the Kai Opaka. *Could it have felt any stranger than this?* Dax wondered. Talis Dejana sat with hands folded in her lap, regarding the Trill as if she had said nothing out of the ordinary, and yet she had voiced Dax's thoughts about Dr. Bashir exactly.

"Dejana," she said slowly. "Dejana, where do you—?"

"My father bred the best *verdanis* in Bennikar."

CHAPTER
8

"You're sure?" Commander Sisko's voice came in loud and clear over Lieutenant Dax's comm badge.

"Positive, sir." The Trill sat at the table that served Brother Gis for a desk. The monk had given her exclusive use of his office while she relayed the good news to *Deep Space Nine.* "I have at least one adult Bajoran from Bennikar village who confirms it. When I mentioned the girl's name, it jogged his memory, and when I brought her to see him there was no further doubt in his mind. He says Talis Dejana and Talis Cedra are definitely two of the surviving Bennikar children his sister Cathlys mentioned. The little girl's older brother says that Remis Jobar's sister nursed Dejana back to health before she died."

"I hope his testimony will be good enough to convince the *Dessin-ka* representatives." Sisko did not sound at all sanguine about the possibility.

"There's more to it than that, sir. This may not sound precisely scientific but . . . there's something about her."

"What, precisely?"

"Call it a feeling she gives me."

"A hunch? That doesn't sound scientific at all, old man."

"Yet I think you can recall a time or two when my hunches turned out to be right." Dax grinned. "And didn't you tell me that your first meeting with the Kai Opaka gave you the same sort of—?"

"No argument," Sisko said quickly. "So you've informed Brother Gis?"

"He's ecstatic. Things couldn't possibly have turned out more to his liking. Even Brother Talissin stopped scowling when he heard the news."

"Why was Brother Talissin informed? I thought I made it clear to you that secrecy was vital. If the wrong people learn we've found the *Nekor*—"

"Who are the 'wrong people,' sir?" Dax asked.

"Anyone who might profit from thwarting the *Dessin-ka*. Anyone who might have a reason to see the provisional government undermined and shattered."

"Brother Talissin doesn't fall into either category. Even before he learned she was the *Nekor*, he regarded the child as something special, to be protected at all costs. He's been insisting that the best place for her is the religious life, and he's more than pleased that we've proved him right." She smiled faintly at the memory of the grim-faced monk's smug told-you-so expression.

"Proud enough to talk about it to everyone he meets?" Sisko asked.

"Sir, whom could he possibly talk to out here?"

"Even though the camp is isolated, you know the monks still travel to trade goods and news with other camps. The epidemic kept them confined to their settlement for a while, but now that you and Dr. Bashir have developed the fever cure, they'll be eager to make up for lost time. Increased commerce between the camps is a good sign that they're evolving into interdependent communities. I'd like to encourage that, but not at the cost of this project's security. In addition, there's the danger that word of this might reach the local underground factions. I don't want to put a child's life in peril because some splinter group sees her as a bargaining chip."

"You needn't worry, sir," Dax replied. "There's too small a window of opportunity for anything to go wrong. We can bring Talis Dejana to the Temple as soon as you can dispatch us a runabout. But you'd better have it land near the camp. I wouldn't advise using the transporter."

"Why not?" Sisko was puzzled.

"The girl is still in recuperation from the fever. The experience might be too intense. She's a very frail child, Commander."

"I thought you reported that your vaccine was successful?"

"She made her own recovery before we arrived, without benefit of the vaccine. Dr. Bashir thought it would be unwise to give the antibody injection to someone whose natural defenses had already dealt with the illness."

"Not a complete recovery, if what you say about her present state of health is true," Sisko opined.

"You're not taking into consideration her age and constitution. The most robust immune system in the world can't function efficiently in an undernourished, overworked young body. Benjamin, if you could see these children—" Dax's voice broke for an instant. "Dr. Bashir never stops working with them. The fever is as good as wiped out, but he continues to work nonstop. We never would have made so much progress in so short a time without his efforts."

"That's commendable."

"Can you praise a man for saving others at the risk of his own life? The *needless* risk?"

"*Is* Dr. Bashir's life in danger?"

"His health certainly is. I've cautioned him about the stress he's putting himself under; he agrees with everything I say and goes on as before. I'm—" She hesitated, glancing at the dance of passing shadows against the cubicle's cloth walls. "I'm afraid for him, Benjamin."

"Then it's a good thing I'll be recalling you both to *Deep Space Nine* once the *Nekor* is delivered to the Temple. I want this whole matter wrapped up within twenty-four hours."

"Very good, sir."

"You can begin departure preparations at once. Sisko out."

Ensign Kahrimanis knocked on the laboratory door. It opened a crack and Talis Cedra's brown, dirty face peered out. "Healer's busy," he announced in his queerly rough voice.

"I didn't expect to see you here, Cedra," Kahrimanis said pleasantly. "I thought you'd be helping your sister pack."

"Pack what?" the child asked quite reasonably. "All we've got between us is the clothes we're wearing and one of Mother's old necklaces. Just clay beads; no one would swap us any food for it on the road."

"Well, all that's about to change." The ensign leaned against the doorpost. "I overheard Brother Mor talking with Lieutenant Dax. Your sister's a very special girl."

Cedra eyed him suspiciously. If the child were full-grown, it would have been a look that promised nothing good. "What did you hear?"

"Just that she's important to a lot of people and she's going to the Temple. Hey, what's wrong?"

Cedra flung the lab door wide open and stepped out to poke a skinny finger into Ensign Kahrimanis's chest. "You keep your mouth shut about it, you hear me?" he snarled. "Being special means she'll be safe at last, once she gets to the Temple, but until then being special means *danger*. No one's going to hurt my sister just because some fool couldn't keep his mouth shut."

Kahrimanis swatted the boy's hand aside. "I can keep a secret. But you'd better watch who you're calling a fool. Now, step aside. I have to see Dr. Bashir." He did not wait for the boy to consent, but strode past him unceremoniously.

Dr. Bashir looked up from his microscanner. "Oh, hullo, Kahrimanis," he said. "I didn't hear you at the door. I've been studying samples of the drinking water. There appears to be a bacterium in some samples and not in others. I think it might have a connection with the intestinal problems some of the children have been experiencing. Odd thing: I've sampled the well water and found nothing, but it's not universally present in all the rainwater samples. I think it may have something to do with how the rainwater barrels are—" He caught himself running on and laughed sheepishly. "Listen to me babble! You didn't come here to listen to a disquisition on water supply. What can I do for you?"

"I've just come to secure a few things, sir. Don't worry; I won't be in your way." Ensign Kahrimanis walked past Dr. Bashir to where the supply chests were stacked. He took down the top one and began packing.

Dr. Bashir's face turned pale. "What are you doing? Don't tell me we've been ordered to leave already?"

Kahrimanis paused and turned around to face him. "No, sir, we haven't been ordered back; not yet. But it's only a matter of time. Lieutenant Dax told me to begin preparations. Our mission here's done."

"But it can't be!" Dr. Bashir protested. "Granted, we've stopped the fever cold, but that's not the sum total of the health problems these people—these *children* still have to face!"

Kahrimanis rested one hand on the lab table. "That's the truth, sir. Physical and mental health, both. I've been meaning to tell you, I think it's wonderful, the way you've been helping the kids. Having someone give a damn about them—" He glanced guiltily at Cedra. Sullen-faced, the boy was polishing some glassware for the doctor. "Uh, Cedra?" the ensign called. "Sorry about how I spoke to you before."

Cedra looked up and gave him a half-smile.

"This is impossible," Dr. Bashir went on, shaking his head. "If we leave now, how can we assess the long-term effectiveness of Lieutenant Dax's antibody injection? And if it *is* effective, we have to implement an inoculation program in every refugee camp in the Kaladrys Valley. Word must be gotten to the hill fighters, too. They're a dangerous vector; they could take the infection out of the valley altogether, and then where would it—?"

"Sir, calm down," Ensign Kahrimanis urged. "There's three medical aides from the Federation ship *Keppler* and one nurse from the *Shining Blade* waiting to replace us here. They'll look after things."

"The *Shining Blade* . . . a Klingon nurse . . . wonderful," Dr. Bashir muttered. "If she doesn't scare the children to death first."

"He," Kahrimanis corrected him.

"Even better." Dr. Bashir sounded ironic enough to pass for Odo.

"I wouldn't worry about how the kids react to a Klingon nurse if I were you, sir." Kahrimanis grinned. "They've seen worse."

Dr. Bashir bent over his microscanner. "When do we leave?" he asked dully, not looking at the ensign.

"Whenever the orders come, I suppose." Kahrimanis waited for the doctor to comment; there was only silence. He might as well have been invisible. He shrugged and went back to packing.

He had only secured a few items when Dr. Bashir's voice rang out, sharp and commanding: "Leave that for now, Ensign. I may need some of that equipment."

"But sir, I—"

Julian's eyes blazed. "That's an order, Ensign."

Kahrimanis gave him an odd look, but replied, "Yes, sir," and left the laboratory.

As soon as the ensign left, Dr. Bashir declared, "Thank you for your help, Cedra. You can go now. You must have lots of preparations to make for your departure."

The boy gave Bashir a sideways look that seemed to measure the doctor, inside and out. However, all he said was "All right." He set down the polishing cloth and the glassware and went without an argument.

Alone in the laboratory, Bashir leaned back against the table wearily. *Leaving . . . we can't be leaving! Not with so much left here—*

He thought of the children, sick and well. He would never forget the change he saw in their faces when those still fit enough to work the fields came back to camp to find their fever-stricken playmates on the road to full recovery.

They thought their friends would die. They had no reason to hope for anything better. Their lives were stripped of hope, and then I—we gave it back to them! We let them see that there's still a chance for something good to happen. They can go on, now. He pressed his fist to his mouth. *They can, but what of the others? The children in the camps on Cedra's map, what about them? Are their eyes dead? Do they still have the strength to dream? I can't go back yet. I was sent here to do a job. I'm not done. My work isn't done. I—I was ordered to Bajor to help the children, but—but—* Realization hit him so hard he had to voice it aloud:

"But I haven't received orders to return. Not direct orders. Not yet."

There was little time. If Dax had sent Ensign Kahrimanis to start packing, the orders must be coming soon. How soon? He couldn't lose a moment. He dashed to the laboratory door and glanced outside. There was no sign of Kahrimanis or Dax. If he avoided his crewmates, he avoided the chance of receiving the departure orders through them.

I can't hear the orders. I must not hear the orders. Once I do, I'll have no choice but to obey.

He slammed the door behind him and rested against it, eyes closed, making a swift mental listing of the bare minimum of supplies he would need to carry on his work where he was going. It was the task of moments for him to secure an array of hypodermics, all loaded with Dax's miracle-working antibody vaccine. A physician's basic field kit followed, assembled with a degree of efficiency that would have made his old teacher Selok nod approval. There were no theatrical flourishes, there was no fuss at all in Julian's preparations. He no longer acted for an unseen audience of potential admirers; he acted for a purpose, a cause that claimed his heart.

It took him a while to find a comfortable way of carrying the Klingon biosample replicator. He had no idea of how many patients in the valley camps were awaiting inoculation; with this device, he was relatively certain he could manufacture enough vaccine for all. He slipped the thick carrying strap over one shoulder and his head. It felt somewhat awkward, but he had no choice; it was necessary.

Outside the lab, the paths of the camp were largely deserted. At this hour, the refugees were finishing their day's labor in the fields, the monks were supervising rounds in the infirmary, and anyone left over was lending a hand with dinner preparations in the square. Quickly and quietly Dr. Bashir ran through the camp and sought the privacy of his own tent. He saw no one, and reasoned no one could see him. Once safely inside, he selected only the most essential personal items and stowed them in a crude bedroll.

"Where are you going, healer?"

Bashir whirled around. Talis Cedra stood just inside the tent flap. "What are you doing here?" he snapped.

"What are *you* doing?" the boy replied. He strolled over to examine Julian's preparations. "Won't you get in trouble for defying orders?"

"Defying—?" Dr. Bashir tried to turn the whole thing into a joke. "I knew this day would come, Cedra; you've been eavesdropping and for once you've gotten the story dead wrong."

The boy's mouth twisted into a skeptical knot. "Am I hearing wrong or are you pretending not to hear?" The words made Julian startle. Cedra's eyes were not dead, but they were older than his years, their stare piercing to the bone. "You like to teach us your people's games. Teach me how to play hide-and-find with the truth, healer."

"I'm doing nothing of the sort," Dr. Bashir said, strongly on the defensive. Then, more gently: "Cedra, do you know what it means to be a healer?"

"What d'you mean?" the boy asked cautiously. "I know *I'd* be a good one. There wouldn't be any more fevers on Bajor, or any more gut-cramp, or— When Dejana goes to live in the Temple, I'm going to join Brother Gis's order and become the best healer on Bajor!"

"Being a healer means more than how good you are," Julian said, wistfully hearing much of himself in Cedra. "When I was at Starfleet Medical, the first thing they taught us was that a doctor's prime directive is never to betray his trust. There are people depending on healers for health, for life, for a *future,* Cedra. Every healing is a part of that trust. You can't walk away from a task half-done. I came here with orders to cure the camp fever. It's gone now, but only gone from *this* camp. I can't leave it at that and still be true to my trust. Do you understand?"

The boy nodded. "You don't disobey orders that you don't want to hear; you just make sure you're too far away to hear 'em when they come." He ducked out of the tent without another word, leaving Julian puzzled and perturbed.

What if he's run off to tell Lieutenant Dax? Dr. Bashir threw himself back into the work of tying up the bedroll with even more haste. He had to be gone before they returned.

He stepped out of the tent just in time for Cedra to come barreling into him. The doctor staggered back. "What—?" he gasped, catching his breath.

"Here." The boy shoved a package, a flask, and a paper into his hands. "You're right: Just 'cause Dejana and I can get away safe doesn't mean the job's done. Good luck." He gave Dr. Bashir a fierce, gawky hug and darted away.

Julian stared at Cedra's offerings: food and drink for the journey, right enough, but what was that paper? He unfolded it and saw the map of the other refugee camps that was Cedra's pride. Smiling broadly, he stowed it all.

The day was fading, but there were still a few good hours of light left. Dr. Bashir consulted the map and noted where the closest camp was, then selected another, farther away. He had no illusions: they would search for him as soon as they discovered he was gone. They might not miss him at dinner, but his absence would not go unnoticed for long after that. Better a few nights' roughing it in the hills than taking the short march toward comfort and inevitable capture. He made his choice and headed out of the camp.

"Healer?"

As Dr. Bashir stood on a rocky rise to the west of the camp, a whisper from the shadows behind him brought him up short. He turned and saw Cedra leading a small, stocky creature that looked like a cross between a horse and an ostrich. "You'll go faster if you ride." The boy extended the loops of the reins. The *verdanis* snorted and tossed its head.

Dr. Bashir took the reins and regarded the beast thoughtfully. "I can't take this, Cedra," he said. "It would be stealing a valuable animal that they need here."

"Tossi's not valuable." Cedra spoke as one who knew. "Not here. He's too small to pull any carts and he's too wild to turn the millstone or the thresher. They're keeping him here only until he grows big enough to earn his keep, but he never will. You'll be doing them a favor by taking him off their hands and saving his fodder for a *verdanis* that'll give something back. Tossi's got too much racing blood in him; all he's good for is riding. My father taught me how to tell a good *verdanis* from a bad 'un, so you can take my word."

"I can, can I?" Bashir asked. He stroked the beast's pointed muzzle, and it tried to take a bite out of his hand.

"You will," Cedra replied confidently. "It's what you want to hear." He scampered back into the camp.

Julian studied his new mount. Tossi glowered at him but made no further moves to bite. The *verdanis* wore no saddle, just a folded blanket slung across its back. Grudgingly it deigned to allow Julian to pat its neck.

"I used to be a pretty fair rider," Julian remarked to the beast. "Of course, that was horses. Well, let's see." Clutching the reins, the doctor rested his hands on the animal's back and vaulted up and over to land heavily astride. Tossi did a little sideways dance but did not bolt. There was a giddy moment when it looked as if the unwieldy burden of Dr. Bashir's many packs was about to overbalance him. But he held the reins tight with one hand while steadying himself on Tossi's rump with the other.

"Ugh," he said, adjusting across his chest the set of the heavy leather strap from which the biosample replicator hung. "Nearly choked myself." The thick edge hooked itself under the tip of his comm badge, nearly tearing the insignia from his chest. "I'd better—" he began, preparing to hang the replicator at a different angle. Then he touched the badge and froze.

Orders to leave . . .

"I have my orders," he told the horizon. He left the replicator strap as it was and clapped his heels to the barrel of the *verdanis*. It launched itself into a land-devouring gait cousin to a fast canter. Dr. Bashir held on with his knees and concentrated on interpreting the landmarks they passed. The replicator strap worked its way further and further under his comm badge with every lurching step of the *verdanis*.

I really ought to do something about that, he told himself, knowing he would do nothing. *Accidents happen; they're no one's fault. I can't worry about that now. I have a job to do.*

He left the fields behind and took to the rocky upslopes of the hills.

Lieutenant Dax let the light from her searchbeam play over the faint footprints of the *verdanis*. At her shoulder, Ensign Kahrimanis asked, "Do you still see anything, sir?"

"Don't you?"

He shook his head. "He lost me when he veered off the dirt path."

"If it's any consolation, he's about to lose me, too. There's solid rock underfoot up ahead. We'll never find him this way."

"What are you going to do?"

"What I should have done in the first place: Order him back. Commander Sisko told me we're to expect the runabout at dawn." She touched her comm badge. "Dax to Bashir."

There was no answer.

"Dax to Bashir," she repeated. "Dr. Bashir, *respond.*" Still nothing. She tried a third time. "Damn it, he knows

Starfleet regulations as well as I do," she muttered. "He knows what will happen to him if he deserts—*Dax to Bashir!*"

Ensign Kahrimanis tugged at her arm. "I think I heard something. It's coming from those rocks up ahead. Do you think maybe he had an accident and can't respond? The kids say those racing *verdanis* are hell to ride. If he got thrown—"

"Come in, Dr. Bashir." Dax's sending was urgent. She dreaded discovering that Kahrimanis was right. She pricked up her ears and listened. There did seem to be a faint, echoing sound coming from that tumble of rocks. In the dark the stones held a dozen places where a running animal could catch its foot and fall, flinging its rider to the ground. She scrambled over the stones, flashing her searchbeam out in long, sweeping arcs.

Something twinkled among the rocks. She was on it in an instant. Ensign Kahrimanis came panting up behind her in time to see Dr. Bashir's torn-away comm badge nestling still and useless in the palm of Lieutenant Dax's hand.

CHAPTER
9

MAJOR KIRA was the first off the runabout when it landed
on the outskirts of the camp. She saw Lieutenant Dax
waiting for her amid a crowd of gawking, gesturing
children and adults. Most of them wore blankets
wrapped around their bodies. She wondered if they were
the patients from the infirmary. If so, word of the
curative powers of Dax's antibody hadn't done the
results justice. She leaped lightly to the ground and
hurried forward to greet her friend.

Behind her, she heard Vedek Torin come trotting after
at a more sedate pace. The *Na-melis* vedek had greeted
news of the *Nekor*'s discovery with rapture and insisted
that he be present when the child was fetched from the
refugee camp. Commander Sisko saw no harm in it—
had favored the idea, in fact. ("After all, Vedek Torin will
be in charge of the girl from now on. She should meet
him as soon as possible.")

The crowd surrounding Lieutenant Dax rushed toward Major Kira, faces alight. *What are they—?* she

thought, only to have the human wave part to either side of her and bustle past to their true goal, the runabout. The Bajoran officer understood. She recalled her own days in a Cardassian internment camp, when any distraction—however plebeian—was a major event. Some of the refugees stopped short of the runabout, preferring to make Vedek Torin their goal. He was ringed by a jabbering circle of questioning children, some of whom had never seen a Bajoran vedek in spotless, unmended robes before this. Major Kira heard one of them accuse him of being a fake. She smiled and hoped Vedek Torin would be able to talk himself out of that.

"Any sign of him?" Kira asked Dax at once. News of Dr. Bashir's vanishment had hit Ops only hours ago.

The Trill shook her head. "He's not to blame. He lost his comm badge."

"Doing what?"

"Following orders, according to Talis Cedra."

"Talis Cedra? The *Nekor*'s big brother?" Kira smirked. "Commander Sisko's going to love hearing that." She turned her gaze to the hills, where the first rays of dawn were transforming the rocky slopes to gold. "Still, you have to admire him. He always wanted to be so—*heroic*. Now, for the first time since I've known him, he's succeeded."

"Is that the defense you'll make for him when he's court-martialed?" Dax asked. As far as she knew, Dr. Bashir had no experience whatsoever in living off the land, and the terrain of the devastated Kaladrys Valley was not one of the most hospitable on Bajor. She was concerned for him, and it came out as waspishness.

"Don't exaggerate," Kira returned pleasantly. "It won't come to that. As our young friend Talis Cedra said, Dr. Bashir is obeying orders, like a good little Starfleet officer. When he's found and ordered back aboard DS9, he'll obey that directive too. *If* he's found," she added.

"What do you mean, 'if'?"

Major Kira made a gesture of helplessness. "When you

sent word of his disappearance, Commander Sisko dispatched a runabout with orders to lock on to Dr. Bashir via his comm badge and use the transporters to bring him home."

"But he hasn't got his comm badge anymore," Dax pointed out.

"So we learned. Then Commander Sisko ordered a sensor reading on Dr. Bashir's life-sign patterns to be used as a target instead. That didn't work either, from high orbit or low."

Dax was alarmed. "He can't be—?"

"—dead?" Kira finished the sentence for her. "I doubt that. If a Starfleet medical officer can't survive one night on his own out there, the Federation might as well pack up and go home tomorrow. It didn't work because the sensors are still playing games. Nasty games; you should hear what Chief O'Brien's been calling them."

Dax's brows rose. "I can imagine."

"No, you can't. Not in all your lives. This is prime stuff. If I were back aboard, I'd be taking notes." The two women laughed, but the tension remained. "So," Kira said at last. "Where's the *Nekor?*"

"In the infirmary with her brother. They spent the night there, and it would've been a bad idea for her to wait out here in the morning chill."

By this time, Vedek Torin had managed to shunt the crowd of curiosity seekers aside and join Dax and Major Kira. Together the three of them headed the procession back to the infirmary.

The body of Brother Talissin lay across the curtained doorway, half in and half out of the infirmary, blood flowing from a deep gash in his skull. Every light inside the building was extinguished; only the feeble rays of the rising sun cast dusty beams through the high windows. The children saw the body and bolted, shrieking. The few adults in the crowd caught the smaller ones in their arms and held them so that they didn't have to see the blood. Vedek Torin uttered a fearful cry.

"What's happened?" he exclaimed, pressing his hands together in panic. He grabbed Lieutenant Dax's arm. "You said she was here! I see no one, nothing but this—this—" He moaned and covered his eyes.

Lieutenant Dax dropped to one knee beside Brother Talissin's body and felt for a pulse. Major Kira drew her phaser and swept the dim interior of the infirmary with her eyes. "Kahrimanis?" she whispered for Dax's ears alone.

"He should be here, too. I left him with the children," Dax replied.

"The children . . ." Major Kira looked at the refugee children still clustering near. "Get them out of here," she ordered. No one stirred. She glared over one shoulder and barked, "I said *move.*" The few remaining adult Bajorans herded the whimpering little ones away, murmuring words of comfort.

Dax looked up. "Talissin's still alive."

Major Kira did not hear this last bit of news. She was moving fleetly down the eastern wall of the building, taking a path that would allow her to see if anyone was lurking inside the sheeted cubicles that blocked a complete, clear view of the great room. Something rustled overhead. Her eyes flew up just as a small, wiry form dropped in front of her from a rafter. Her phaser was aimed and steady on it in an eyeblink.

"Don't shoot!" Cedra shouted, flinging his hands up across his face.

Kira's phaser fell to her side as her hand darted out to seize him by the ear. "You *idiot!* Do you want to get yourself killed?"

"Ow! Lemme go!" A stream of profanity that would have left even Chief O'Brien awestruck poured from the boy's mouth. "Idiot yourself, damn it! *He's got Dejana!*"

"Who's got her? Where are they? Where's Ensign Kahrimanis?"

The boy ignored the questions. With a fantastic wriggle he broke free from Kira's grip and sprang away. "Come with me. *Now*. Just you." He pointed at Major Kira. "You're the fighter. If he sees too many coming after him, he'll kill her." Without waiting for Major Kira's consent to follow him, he spun on his heel and ran for the infirmary door.

Major Kira followed; there was no choice. Vedek Torin tried to detain her, but she sidestepped him as agilely as the boy did. "Help Lieutenant Dax with your brother," she panted, giving him a push that almost sent him tumbling on top of Talissin's body. Already the boy was well ahead of her. She could not afford to lose sight of him. Something told her that he had only been lurking in the rafters long enough to find the help he needed. Having found it, he wasn't going to waste any more time looking back.

The boy raced through the camp and Kira raced after. Sometimes she sidestepped people and things that got in her way, sometimes she didn't have that luxury. She heard more than one "Hey! Watch where you're going!" and "Talis Cedra, what kind of trouble are you in now?"

As if in answer, the boy shouted, "I didn't mean to take it, lady! Honest, I didn't!" He kept up a barrage of whiny please for clemency until he and Kira were out of the cramped precincts of the camp and well into the plowed lands. Once there, he stopped so abruptly that Major Kira ran right into him and knocked him sprawling.

"You mind telling me what that was all about?" she asked as she yanked the boy to his feet.

"Didn't want anyone else coming with us," he said, breathing hard. "No one would if they think it's just something between you and me." He wiped sweat from his forehead, leaving a brown smear. "Now we have to go quiet."

"Not so fast." Kira's hand closed on his shoulder. "I need to know what I'm walking into."

"You didn't, once. I told you: He took my sister."

"Who did?"

"Remis Jobar." The killing look was back in Cedra's eye. "He's got her out there, in one of the huts the reapers use to get out of the rain." He pointed out across the empty fields.

Major Kira shaded her eyes and gazed into the distance. She could just see a battered metal roof sticking up above the brow of a shallow depression in the land. "Are you sure?"

"I tracked him when he took her. Then I ran back to the infirmary and hid. I said I didn't want a whole mob, just you."

"How do you know he hasn't moved on?"

"He can't. He's not strong enough. And he's just realized that now he's got her, he doesn't know how to sell her for the best price. He's trying to make up his mind."

Kira regarded the boy thoughtfully. "It sounds to me as if your sister's not the only member of your family who's been touched by the Prophets."

Cedra gave her the same look children always give adults who have just said something stupider than usual. "You can make anyone think you're touched by the Prophets if you pay attention and play it right."

Kira did not chide the boy for his attitude. She knew from her own experience how quickly faith was eaten away by cynicism in the camps. All she said was "Don't let Vedek Torin hear you say things like that or when they take your sister to the Temple, you'll be left behind."

"Not me." He showed her a brave grin. "Dejana won't go anywhere without me, and I won't go anywhere without Dejana. If they want their *Nekor,* they've got to take us both."

Major Kira checked the setting on her phaser. "They'll

take you both; I guarantee it. What kind of weapons does Remis Jobar have with him?"

"A knife—not a real knife, something he made for himself out of a farm tool. It's clumsy, with a heavy handle."

"Anything else?"

"A big stick—a staff, I guess. He needs it to help him walk, but not that much. He used it to crack Brother Talissin's head when the monk tried to stop him."

"Not too bad," Kira muttered, preparing to advance on the hut. "If I can get a clear shot, I can stun him and—"

"And one of those." Cedra pointed at the phaser.

Kira sat down. "What? Are you *sure?*"

"I know what I saw," Cedra said. "And I remember."

Cedra remembered trailing after Gis while the monk made his rounds, extinguishing most of the infirmary lights for the night. The air was still, the silence broken only from time to time by the sound of Dejana's sporadic coughing.

"Do not fear, son," Brother Gis said kindly, patting Cedra's head. "She sounds better daily, and you know she will receive only the finest care when—"

"This is an *outrage.*" Talissin's angry face loomed pale and eerie in the dimness of the infirmary. He marched forward, shaking a bony finger. "Why is she still here, among these—these *common* people?"

"Perhaps because illness is no respecter of persons, my brother," Gis replied evenly. "Fortunately for us all, neither is sleep. Lower your voice before you wake her and the others."

"She should not be here," Talissin maintained, staring at the curtained cubicle where Dejana drowsed. "We should remove her, give up our own tent so that she need not lie here like—like—"

"Like any other sick child?" Gis asked.

"She is not like any other child; she is the *Nekor!* Do you not realize what this means? There are people in the capitol—*important* people—who will be grateful to us for having sheltered her, treated her well. They will provide us with all manner of things this camp needs desperately, solely because we were her attentive caretakers."

"Huh! Like you ever treated Dejana special before you found out who she is!" Cedra blurted.

Talissin's scowl was terrible. "Why, you impertinent—!"

"Let the boy be, my brother," Gis said. "He speaks the truth of his heart. The Prophets teach us never to fear the truth."

Another cough from Dejana's cubicle turned Talissin's ascetic face pale. "There! Do you hear that? She *must* be moved to better quarters."

"No, she must not," Gis replied. "What she must do is have an unbroken night's rest."

"Then I will stay here with her and keep watch." Talissin folded his hands inside the sleeves of his robe.

"I am assigned night duty," Gis said mildly. "And see, there is Ensign Kahrimanis to aid me." He nodded toward the back of the infirmary, where Dr. Bashir's assistant was stretched out on a spare pallet, snatching a catnap.

Talissin's chin rose sharply. "An unbeliever can not possibly attend the *Nekor* adequately. I ask you for the privilege of exchanging our assigned times of work in the infirmary. It is the keenest desire of my heart to spend as much time as possible in service to the child while she is still among us."

"Far be it from me to deny you your heart's desire." Gis shrugged. "Especially since I am not all that fond of night duty." He touched Cedra's shoulder. "You should also be in bed, child. Much awaits you tomorrow."

Cedra nodded and headed for the cubicle where

Dejana was at last sleeping untroubled by further coughing spells. Still, the child could not resist pausing before the smug-faced Talissin and remarking, "Dejana's asleep; she's not going to know if it was you or Brother Gis looking after her tonight."

Talissin huffed. "The *Nekor* will remember her servant," he said sententiously. Cedra had to dash into the sheet-hung cubicle, fist in mouth to hold back the laughter.

The night passed with little sleep. Dejana's cough returned. Cedra was worried and wakeful, but feigned sleep whenever Ensign Kahrimanis or Brother Talissin peered in.

The new day came heralded not by the dawn's light, but by a rising murmur of excitement from the camp. Word of the runabout's approach and landing slipped into the infirmary well before the sunlight penetrated that gloomy building. The place was astir as those patients well enough to venture out all swarmed from their beds to greet the marvel setting itself down on the outskirts of the camp.

Cedra stayed put, unwilling to leave Dejana's side. Through half-closed eyes the child observed Talissin trailing after the outrushing crowd as far as the infirmary doorway. Ensign Kahrimanis remained on duty, just across the aisle, caring for a child still too weak to rise from her pallet. "Some servant," Cedra muttered scornfully in the monk's direction.

And then, too fast for the child to react, a pair of work-worn hands pounced on Dejana, yanking the girl from her bed. Her cry of surprise and alarm shattered into renewed coughing.

Everything seemed to happen at once, and yet in Cedra's memory it all replayed itself in slow motion: Ensign Kahrimanis's shout, the flash of Remis Jobar's knife at Dejana's throat, the Bajoran's harsh command for Kahrimanis to throw down his phaser or see the girl die—all these memories spun themselves out like a bad dream.

Cedra remained frozen, too scared by what was happening to move. Dejana was small for her age. It was not difficult for Remis Jobar to hold her to him with the same arm controlling the knife while he used his other hand to grab Kahrimanis's discarded phaser and jam it into his belt. His walking staff, propped against one sheeted wall of the cubicle, fell to the ground, but he recovered it in an instant.

"Move," he commanded, gesturing with the staff for Kahrimanis to walk ahead of him. The man obeyed—he had no choice; the knife had not wavered an inch from Dejana's flesh. The girl moaned with terror.

Cedra watched them go, heard Talissin's momentary protest cut off by a sharp crack so loud that the child winced and murmured a prayer that the dour monk's devotion to Dejana had not ended in death.

"—and that was when you trailed them here?" Major Kira asked. Cedra nodded. "Smart boy. So he's got two hostages and a phaser." She weighed the situation. "A phaser he might not know how to use." She considered the risks of making that assumption. At last she stood up. "I think we'll do better if we talk to Remis Jobar."

"You're not gonna blast him?" Cedra sounded disappointed.

"Maybe later." One corner of her mouth twitched up as she patted him on the shoulder. "If you're good. Wait here."

Major Kira holstered her phaser, then proceeded to approach the hut cautiously. Since she had chosen parley over direct attack, she wanted to be in plain view when she hailed Remis Jobar. It wouldn't do to startle him. There was no telling how he would react. Even if he didn't know how to use a phaser, he was handy enough with knife and staff to do real damage to his hostages. She sidled her way down the slope until she could see the hut. It was an open-faced lean-to built into the side of the hill, but dug in deep enough so that the people inside were part of the darkness.

Kira cupped her hands to her mouth. "Remis Jobar!"

There was silence from the hut. Then: "Who's there?"

"I'm Major Kira Nerys. I've come for Talis Dejana and Ensign Kahrimanis. Let them go."

A wild cackle of laughter answered her demand. "Like that, eh? Give 'em up so I can be handed over to the Temple for killing a monk? Oh, yes! Straightaway!"

"Talissin is still alive!" Kira shouted. "You haven't killed anyone." *Not yet,* she thought. "You have nothing to fear from the Temple!"

"I'll say not!" came the defiant reply. The shadows inside the hut shifted. "Let them be scared of me for a change! I've got their miracle girl here. If they want her, they can come see me about it."

Kira took a deep breath. She knew the next step well enough: "What do you want, Remis Jobar?"

"I want out of this place, that's what! I want my own farm again, land that's mine! Here or elsewhere, I don't care. I want those fat old birds in the capitol to stop twiddling their thumbs long enough to remember that I'm *here.* Damn them all, if they'd done something for us early on, there wouldn't *be* these cursed camps. But they were living easy, and it made 'em squirm to think of folk like me and Cathlys, stuck away like old logs, so they 'forgot' we was there!" The dispossessed farmer took a step into the sunlight and shook his fist. *"I'll* give 'em lessons in memory now."

"I agree with you," Kira called. "You're right, you and the others have been overlooked too long. But why does the child have to suffer for it? Hasn't she gone through enough? Let her go!"

"The blazes I will!" He took another step into the light. "All the fuss over that girl's nothing; *nothing,* you hear me? Old mealy-mouth Talissin going on and on about how the Prophets meant for her to live through the fever—bah! She's alive this day because my sister *died* nursing her. Now she's going to be took off somewhere to live her days in comfort, and Cathlys left cold in the grave without a marker to say she ever lived at all. I won't have it! They'll pay me plenty if they want their precious *Nekor,* and they'll do right by honoring Cathlys for how she gave her life to save that brat's. Either that, or they can look for their *Nekor* in the same grave that holds my sister."

Major Kira heard him out, but her attention was split. While she listened to Remis Jobar recite his list of grievances, her mind was making its own calculations. *He must have them tied up in there,* she reasoned, *or he wouldn't turn his back on them. Unless . . .*

"Listen to me, Remis!" she called. "I don't represent the Temple or the provisional government, so I can't speak for them. I'm the Bajoran liaison officer from *Deep Space Nine* and you've got one of our crewmen in there. The Federation can be your ally in this, but not if you've harmed Ensign Kahrimanis."

Remis Jober spat. "I ain't harmed no one, not him nor the girl. *But that can change.*"

"Prove it! Let me hear them tell me they're all right."

"Hah! The girl I can carry out of the hut for you to see, but the other? You expect me to tote that big lump of a man?"

"Can't he walk for himself?"

"He walked far enough. I ain't untying him for you, that's sure. He might try something stupid and then I'd have to kill him . . . *and her.*"

"You wouldn't do that," Kira said, no longer shouting. "You're not a child-killer, Remis."

"I don't want to be! If I do—do what I've got to—it'll be on account of you and the rest pushed me to it. Don't try me, I warn you!"

"Let me talk to them, Remis," Kira persisted, still calm. "You don't need to drag Ensign Kahrimanis out of the hut. Do you see this insignia I'm wearing?" She pointed to her comm badge. "There's one almost like it on his uniform. You turn it on with a touch. If you've got his hands tied, you'll have to activate it for him. You'll hear my voice come from it, calling his name; that's when you turn it on. Understood?"

"I got it." The Bajoran retreated into the shelter of the hut, casting more than one wary look back at Major Kira.

Kira touched her comm badge. "Kira to Kahrimanis."

There was a pause that lengthened uncomfortably, then finally the response: "Kahrimanis here. He's got me and the kid tied up, Major, but we're all right."

"That's all I wanted to know. Kira out." She broke the connection and wondered whether Remis Jobar had done the same. "Remis!" she called.

The farmer's grizzled head poked out of the hut. "Proof enough for you?" he snarled. "Now you go back and tell 'em what I want. And you get your folks to bring one of them flyers to take me to my new land. Soon as I've got the soil under my feet, I'll let you have these two back—not before."

"Be reasonable, Remis," Major Kira said. "The longer you hold out, the worse you make it for yourself. Release them now and I'll plead your case myself. I know what it's like to have nothing, no one."

"I want my land," the farmer said stubbornly. "They want their *Nekor*. Even swap or nothing. You tell 'em that, back in the capitol. Not such a hard message to remember, eh?"

"What if they refuse? I don't believe you'd hurt a child, Remis Jobar."

"Believe what you want. What have I got to lose?"

"Say they give you a farm," Kira persisted. "Do you think you'll be allowed to work it in peace?"

"I don't care!" Remis Jobar's voice rose hysterically. "I just want what I lost! I want what they took from me!"

"It was the Cardassians who took it from you, not the Temple or the government."

"Then why won't they give me my own land back, now the Cardassians are gone?" He emerged from the hut, leaning on his staff, a bent and limping figure against the naked fields. "Dammit, not even the Cardassians kept us prisoner like this, tied to land that can hardly feed us! Our own folk left us here, out of sight, out of mind, shoved us into the dark like it was our grave! Look at me! You see me?" He threw his arms open wide.

"I see you," Major Kira replied evenly.

"Then you're the only Bajoran outside this valley who can. We're invisible. We're not there. But so long as I've got that girl, they've *got* to see me. They can't pretend we're—"

A phaser beam whined through the air, blasting Remis Jobar from his feet. The impact hit him squarely in the back, flinging him forward, face in the dirt. Major Kira drew her own phaser and crouched, ready. The blast had come from just over the hill where she'd left Cedra.

"Hold your fire, Major Kira." A tall, stocky Bajoran dressed in somber robes stepped into sight and presented a clear target on the hilltop above the hut. He raised his hands to show he carried no weapon, but Major Kira saw the phaser nestled in his sash. "I am Kejan Ulli. I represent the *Dessin-ka.*"

"As what? A hired assassin?" Kira shouted without thinking. She kept her phaser trained on him.

"I assure you, I am nothing of the sort. I was informed of the situation here and came to see if I could render any assistance."

"Informed how? By who?"

He glossed over the questions. "Our ambitious friend there is only stunned. He will see the error of his ways when he awakens. It has been written that the *Nekor* brings a sword, but I have always interpreted that to mean that she shall claim ultimate victory over those who doubt her powers. I did not feel it was necessary to serve her with unnecessary bloodshed."

Major Kira was on guard. Every mistrustful instinct in her was on full alarm when she looked at Kejan Ulli. He was too smooth, too plausible, his responses were too pat and answered nothing. Keeping an eye on him, she moved quickly to check the fallen Remis Jobar for signs of life. Her fingers found a pulse, and his breath warmed her hand.

"You see?" Kejan Ulli sounded as proud as if he had dragged the distraught farmer back from the brink of death instead of having nearly shoved him over. "Now, let us free the *Nekor* and—"

A small, lithe shape skidded down the slope under the startled eyes of Kejan Ulli and vanished into the hut. A breath later, Ensign Kahrimanis emerged, rubbing his wrists and blinking his eyes in the sunlight. He was followed by Talis Cedra, who carried a weeping Dejana on his back. When the ensign attempted to help the boy with his burden, Cedra pulled away, scowling. Clearly he was not about to let anyone else get near his sister.

Major Kira tossed Kahrimanis his phaser, taken from Remis Jobar's body. She glanced up at the hilltop. Kejan Ulli was on his knees, gazing raptly at Dejana.

Does he want to worship her or devour her? Major Kira touched her comm badge and hailed the runabout. "Kira to Munson. There's been a change. Assume low orbit immediately, three to beam up from these coordinates, myself and two children."

"Aye, sir." Munson was too good a crewman to question orders.

"Contact the station. Inform Commander Sisko that

I'm bringing the *Nekor* and her brother aboard; I'll explain everything when I get there. You'll have to return for Ensign Kahrimanis; he's taking care of an injured man."

"I'm on my way," Munson responded crisply.

"Good. Kira out." She saw Kejan Ulli rise to his feet and start down the slope toward them, but she knew she could rely on Munson to act quickly. Her trust was not misplaced.

A cry of protest escaped Kejan Ulli's lips as Major Kira, Talis Cedra, and Talis Dejana shimmered from sight just as he was about to reach them.

CHAPTER
10

LIEUTENANT DAX was the last to enter Commander Sisko's office, under the eyes of Kira, Odo, and O'Brien. "Sorry I'm late, sir. I've just come from the infirmary."

"How is the girl?" Sisko asked.

"A little cough and a few sniffles. She's more upset than ill."

"Can you blame her, after what she's been through, poor thing?" O'Brien commented.

"There is one problem," Dax went on.

"Yes?" Sisko did not look as if he was in the mood for any more problems.

"Her brother, Cedra; he won't leave."

"I'll see what I can do about that after this meeting," the commander said. He clasped his hands on the desktop. "I've called you here to brief you on a situation of some delicacy. You're all no doubt aware that Major Kira returned to us accompanied by two Bajoran children. Although I initially promised Vedek Torin complete secrecy, circumstances have changed. You need to

141

know who these children are and what they mean to the stability of Bajor if we are to accomplish our mission effectively."

"And what is our mission?" Odo asked stiffly.

"To protect them and to see that they are delivered to the Temple on Bajor as soon as possible."

"With respect, sir," the shapeshifter said, "if that is all we must do, why don't we simply put them back aboard the runabout and send them on their way?"

"Two reasons: First, the girl is sick. I realize it's only a mild cold, but in view of what's awaiting her, I'd feel better myself if the child were in top health before she begins her new life. Second, there has already been one attempted kidnapping. As long as she's under our protection, the chances for another are slim." His tone as good as added: *They had better be impossible.*

"Kidnapping!" O'Brien exclaimed. "Who is this child?"

"She's the *Nekor,* according to the *Dessin-ka,*" Major Kira provided, and went on to explain the whole matter of the Kai Opaka's last message and all it meant. "And they're expecting to see her presented in the Temple at the *Berajin* harvest festival," she concluded.

"Berajin . . ." O'Brien scratched his head.

"It's still a week and a half away," Dax said. "Before, when I was searching for her, I thought that was hardly enough time. Now it seems like far too much."

"Don't worry, Lieutenant," Odo said. "I'll oversee the child's security personally. I'll be sure to put my best people on the case at times when I am . . . indisposed." It was a nice way of saying that the shapeshifter had to spend part of each day in his naturally formless state. *Indisposed* sounded better than *in a bucket.*

"I have no doubt that Talis Dejana is in good hands with you, Constable," Sisko said. "However, while we are making sure that the security surrounding her is airtight, we must not lose sight of the fact that she is only eight years old. She's spent all her life on rural Bajor, and most of that in a refugee camp. She may be terrified by her new surroundings."

"Sir?" O'Brien spoke up.

"Yes, Chief?"

"Maybe Keiko could come by the infirmary and visit with her, bring Molly, you know, something like that. And after she's over her sniffles, she could come to the school and see the other kids."

Sisko turned to Odo. "Would that be a security risk, Constable?"

"Nothing I couldn't handle," the shapeshifter replied. "I believe your young ones are happiest in the company of their agemates. A happy child is more accommodating, and I can do my job best when the person I'm supposed to protect cooperates."

"For a moment there I was afraid Odo'd got a soft side," O'Brien whispered to Kira.

"Sir, after she's feeling better, where is she to stay?" Dax asked. "She can't live in the infirmary. As you said, she's only a child. She needs to know where she belongs."

"She could bunk with me, sir," Major Kira volunteered.

"She might feel more at home if she came to live with my family," O'Brien said. "Keiko wouldn't mind."

Sisko looked at Odo again, but before he could speak, the security chief said, "Yes, I can handle that situation, too, sir." He glanced at O'Brien and added, "Provided that your wife won't object to armed guards in the home."

"In it?" O'Brien objected.

"Cheek by jowl, if you prefer. I should think you'd welcome the protection. In view of what Major Kira has told us, this child is the target of every Bajoran with an ideological ax to grind. By taking her into your home, you'll be placing your family between those people and what they're after. It has been my experience that such persons are none too picky about how they deal with obstacles."

O'Brien was crestfallen. "Then I can't do it. I can't put Keiko and Molly in jeopardy. I'm sorry; I did want to help the child. . . ."

"We can settle the matter of where Talis Dejana will stay later," Sisko said. "Twenty-four hours in the infirmary won't do her any harm, particularly if your wife and daughter can pay her that visit, Chief."

"Gladly, sir." O'Brien nodded happily. "At least there's something we can do for her."

"As for her brother," Sisko went on, "he can stay in my quarters until we reach a decision about his sister. Jake won't mind sharing, I'm sure. That's settled, then. Now, about Dr. Bashir . . ." He was still looking at O'Brien, but his expression grew grave.

"Still no luck with the long-range sensors, sir." O'Brien spoke as if this state of affairs was a direct attack on his honor. To him, it was. "Near as we can guess, the problem's due to a badly done patch job in the station circuits, something slapped together by the Cardies when they were evacuating and left behind as good enough. Which it was *not*." O'Brien's gut feeling was that the shoddy patch job had been deliberate, but he decided to keep his suspicions to himself until he could prove them. "The linkage feedback's caused the same situation with the runabout sensors, although on a minor scale."

"Can we use the runabout sensors to locate Dr. Bashir?"

"I wouldn't bet his life on it. The station system's much more sophisticated—by comparison, that is, although it's all a load of Cardie—"

"How long will it take you to run down the weak spot in the circuitry?" Sisko interrupted.

"I can't tell. It's not in the sensor circuits proper,

according to diagnostics. We may need to run hands-on testing over every inch of the systems."

"How long will that take?"

"Working on it when we can——"

"Working on it constantly, Chief," Sisko corrected him. "We cannot afford to be unable to locate our medical officer. I know I told you to work on sensor repairs when you could; now I'm telling you to give that job top priority. Put as many men on it as you can spare, but I want the long-range sensors functioning and capable of pinpointing Dr. Bashir on the planet's surface."

"Yes, sir." Under his breath he muttered, "It *can* wait, it *can't* wait . . . I wish some people would make up their minds."

Sisko either did not hear or knew when to overlook his chief of operation's remarks. "Lieutenant Dax, I'd like you to escort Talis Cedra to meet me at the Replimat. I think that will be a less threatening environment where he and I can get acquainted. Jake is supposed to meet me there after class, too. The boys should get to know each other if they'll be living together." He sat back. "That's all, everyone. Dismissed. Oh, except for you, Major Kira."

As the others left the office, Sisko's chair swiveled to face his Bajoran liaison officer. "Major Kira, I need your help in finding Dr. Bashir. I want you to contact the appropriate authorities on Bajor. I want a full description of Dr. Bashir transmitted with instructions to detain him and notify us the moment he's found."

"With all due respect, sir, you make him sound like a criminal," Kira returned. "Is it fair to treat him like a fugitive from the law? In my opinion, he's to be commended. The Federation came to Bajor and talked about making things better, but all I see you doing is playing political games with the provisional government. Dr. Bashir is out there helping *people,* not politicians. He's dealing with a problem hands-on, and you want to call him off. I say you ought to follow his example, not stop him."

"Dr. Bashir is acting alone, with no more authority for his actions than a deliberate misinterpretation of orders and a blind conviction that he's doing the right thing," Sisko answered.

"Do you think what he's doing isn't right?" she challenged him.

"If Dr. Bashir were only responsible for himself, I'd be his biggest admirer," Sisko confessed. "As this station's medical officer, he also has a responsibility for the health and well-being of every person aboard DS9. When he accepted that post, he gave up the luxury of following whatever dream—no matter how noble—takes his fancy."

"What's wrong with independent action in a good cause?"

"Need I remind you, Major, that the reason your world is so politically fragmented is due to a host of Bajorans, each convinced he alone is doing the 'right' thing for Bajor?"

Kira's mouth shut tight. For a time she and Sisko exchanged hard stares. At last she said, "Whatever you think of his actions, Dr. Bashir's convinced they're right. When we do find him, will you be able to persuade him to give up the choice he's made?"

"I hope so," Sisko replied. He pushed back in his chair. "He's too good a man to lose, even to a dream."

Jake Sisko and his best friend, Quark's nephew Nog, walked along the Promenade, heading for the Replimat. "Why do we have to waste our time with this Bajoran?" Nog demanded, doing a little dance around the commander's son as they passed the various brightly lit shops and kiosks. "I'm not like you, hu-man! I don't have time to kill. My father expects me back at Quark's Place in an hour to help him clean the holosuites. I don't want to spend it nursemaiding some little nobody."

"I told you before, Nog," Jake said with the air of one who has gone over the same ground too many times already. "This is a favor for my dad. Cedra needs kids his own age. He's a refugee—"

"I know, I know! You'd be surprised how much I know. What, you think maybe I didn't *hear* you?" The Ferengi's sarcastic grimace showed off a double row of small, sharp teeth. It was unthinkable for anything to elude Nog's hearing; Ferengi males were almost literally all ears. ("The better to hear opportunity knocking," as Nog's lobe-proud uncle Quark was fond of saying.) "Refugee, *hunh!* That means he's even poorer than us." He fell into a sulk. Then a spark of hope touched his wrinkled face. "I don't suppose your father gave him some pocket money to share? As part of this *favor?*"

"I don't know; maybe."

"I'll bet he did. And poor—what's his name?"

"Cedra."

"Right. Poor Cedra probably never saw so much money before in his life. He won't know what to do with it. He'll be an easy mark for every sneak and swindler aboard DS9. Jake!" Nog planted himself right in front of young Sisko and seized his shoulders. "Do you realize what this means? We have to *help* the boy! Without our expert advice, he's in danger of squandering your father's generous gift. We wouldn't want that to happen."

"We wouldn't?" Jake said, trying not to snicker. He knew his friend too well.

Nog assumed a look of dramatic shock that would have made his uncle proud. "I'm surprised at you! Of course we wouldn't—we *couldn't* allow Cedra to be taken advantage of. It would be a violation of hospitality. We Ferengi have a universal reputation for being perfect hosts."

"Do you?"

"Absolutely." Nog's smile almost split his face. "Especially when our guests can foot the bill. Come on, I want to meet our new friend." He grabbed Jake's wrist and towed him rapidly down the Promenade.

Not too long after, Nog had ample reason to reevaluate his plans for Talis Cedra and any funds the Bajoran boy might command. He was lying facedown on the Promenade with Cedra pinning him to the floor at the time.

"Not the ears! Not the ears!" Nog wailed, wriggling and twitching in a desperate attempt to shield the most prized and sensitive portion of his anatomy. "Jake, make him let me up!"

Jake spread his hands and tried to look regretful. "I can't do that, Nog. It's between you and him. You told me to keep out of it."

"That was before this crazy fool knocked me down over a harmless little remark I—" He cast a nervous look up at Cedra. "Nothing personal," he said.

"You take back what you said about my sister and I'll let you up," Cedra growled. "Not before. You don't, and I'll fix it so you have to do all your listening through your puny, pathetic little *nose.*"

"I'm sorry, I'm sorry I ever doubted your sister, I'm sorry I ever called your sister a phony, I'm sorry I ever *heard* of your sister! Is that enough?" the Ferengi gibbered.

Cedra sat back on Nog's rump, his knees still pinning Nog's arms helpless. "Buy us all something tasty and I'll let you know."

Nog's eyes doubled in size. *"Buy?"*

Cedra leaned forward and got an uncomfortable grip on Nog's ears. "Buy."

A short while later, the three boys were ensconced under a high-legged table in one of the holosuites at Quark's Place. A picnic of delicacies, plundered from the establishment's stores, lay in ruins before them. Cedra wiped sugary syrup from his mouth and sighed, content. "That was delicious, Nog. Any more?"

"No." The Ferengi was sullen and grumpy. "And when my uncle finds out I took so many of them, I'll catch it."

"If you only took 'so many' that means there *are* more," Cedra reasoned. "Go back and get them."

"I won't," Nog maintained. "These are a delicacy— Taxman's Delights don't come cheap! I'm not putting my neck on the line any further."

"But Nog—" The Bajoran threw one arm around the Ferengi's shoulders. "I thought we were *friends.*" The arm tightened sharply into a choke hold.

"That's enough, Cedra." Jake yanked the Bajoran away from Nog. "It was one thing when you two were fighting on the Promenade—and you were lucky Constable Odo didn't catch you. Nog deserved it then."

"What did *I* do?" the Ferengi implored, awash in wounded innocence. "Why does everyone always blame me?"

"I think it was the part where you said Cedra's sister was the best con artist you'd ever heard of," Jake said mischievously.

"Stupid hu-man! That's a *compliment!*" Nog yelled. "Look, my family's been aboard DS9 for years, since before the Cardassians left, right?" Jake nodded; Cedra's face remained unreadable. "We know what it's like down on the surface. We hear plenty. You wouldn't call me a liar if I said there's hundreds of kids like you and your sister down there, would you?" he appealed to Cedra.

"It's the truth," the Bajoran said.

"You bet it is! *Hundreds* of 'em, and does anybody care? Does anyone even mention they're down there?"

"You've got to admit, Nog," Jake said, "the kind of people who come to Quark's Place aren't going to be talking about war orphans."

"Not just *them.*" Nog glowered at Jake. "Everyone. The shopkeepers, the maintenance crews, even the

Bajoran monks in the shrine, *none* of them said a word about the kids."

"Maybe not where you'd find out about it."

"Not me, but Uncle Quark?" Nog's triumphant laughter sounded like a bark. "If he didn't hear it, it was never said."

"It's all right," Cedra said calmly. "We're used to being ignored."

"Then get *un*used to it, Bajoran!" Nog responded. "I knew something was up as soon as you and your sister came aboard. Two orphans out of hundreds—why you? What made you two so special? Then I hear that it's not *you* anyone cares about, it's your sister."

"What did you hear about my sister, exactly?" There was an ominous note in Cedra's voice. Jake saw the boy's hands start to tighten into fists.

"Nothing." Nog popped the remains of a half-eaten Taxman's Delight into his mouth and chewed noisily. "Just that she was *so* special no one could know the reason *why* she was so special. My uncle sent me to the infirmary with a fruit basket for her—just a nice gesture of welcome. Constable Odo chased me halfway back to Quark's Place. It just seems funny to me. Like a big, fancy package, tied up with shiny paper and bows— who's to know if there's anything inside it but air?"

"You really *don't* like your ears, do you?" Cedra growled.

Nog looked unconcerned, but he put a little distance between himself and the Bajoran. "Did *I* say your sister was full of air? You take everything personally, that's your trouble. Back home, we've got a story about two brothers. One day, the younger one showed up with a bottle and told his older brother he'd captured a *gragol*—"

"A what?" Jake asked.

"A wish-spirit. I didn't say this was a *true* story. Shut up and let me finish. The older brother wanted to see proof. He told the younger brother to uncork the bottle and make the *gragol* grant him a wish, but the younger brother said that this was a very small *gragol* and it had only one wish left to grant. As soon as the bottle was uncorked you had to make the last wish fast or the *gragol* would vanish and you'd have nothing. So he convinced his older brother to buy the bottle from him—"

"—and it turned out to be just an empty bottle," Cedra finished the story for him. "Is that what you're saying? That my sister's as big a phony as the younger brother in that story?" He crouched, getting ready to throw himself onto Nog again.

The Ferengi made a guttural sound of disgust. "You don't know how to listen. No, that's *not* what happened. There really was a *gragol* in the bottle, but when the older brother opened it to make his wish he forgot one thing: Whenever he got excited, he always stuttered! The *gragol* flew away while he was still saying 'I w-w-wish I had a b-b-b-billion b-b-b-bars of g-g-gold-p-p-pressed latinum.' So he took the empty bottle and broke it over his younger brother's head, got his money back, and told everyone that his younger brother was a swindler—an *incompetent* swindler." It was obviously the ultimate Ferengi insult.

Cedra sat down and looked totally bewildered. "I don't get it."

"It's a Ferengi thing," Jake whispered to him. "I think it means that he's not insulting your sister unless he's sure it's safe. Just eat your cake and forget about it."

With a second wind, the three boys soon demolished what was left of the stolen feast. When crumbs and empty cups were all that remained, Nog said, "My father thinks I'm working in here. You two help me. If we get done fast, I'll show you something fun."

"Fun?" Cedra was interested already.

Nog's tiny eyes sparkled. "Ever seen a holosuite, Bajoran?"

"Come on, Nog, if we turn on this suite, we're all going to get it from your uncle *and* my dad," Jake protested.

"I'm not going to turn on *that* kind of program," Nog sneered.

"What kind?" Cedra was really interested now. Jake leaned over and whispered all he knew of the holosuite's potential delights. Cedra's eyes grew wider and wider the longer Jake spoke. "Naked?" he gasped. "Seven? In a pool full of *what?*"

"Anything you want." Nog folded his arms across his chest proudly. "My uncle Quark spared no expense on this system. It's easy to program and there are no limits. Look, I'll show you." He scampered over to a panel by the door and revealed a keypad. A few taps of his fingertips, a few commands spoken aloud, and a tall, statuesque, bejeweled, nearly naked Bajoran redhead was standing at his side, her arms draped around him in loving embrace. She bore more than a passing resemblance to Major Kira.

"Want one?" Nog offered, showing all his teeth.

Cedra's face went bright red and he turned away.

"Better cancel her, Nog," Jake cautioned. "We're not supposed to be fooling around with the holosuite controls."

"Coward." The Ferengi sneered, but he dispatched the redhead to invisibility. "Even if Uncle Quark did catch us, I was only trying to teach our new friend how to use a hologram projector. He *is* allowed to use the holosystems, isn't he?"

"The holosystems?" Cedra's color was back to normal and he was attentive once more.

"Like this place, only with different program options than the ones Quark's got," Jake explained. "There are hologram system ports in our classroom and in some of the shops, and Dad says Chief O'Brien's installed a small one in Ops, too, but they're nothing like this one."

"If they were, customers wouldn't pay us so much to get in here," Nog gloated.

Cedra studied the control panel on the wall. "Tell me more . . ." Jake and Nog did so gladly. The two friends found themselves vying to give the Bajoran as much information as they could. Something about Cedra's expression promised them a very rich return on their investment. Jake in particular thought he recognized it: it was the same gleeful look of mischievous anticipation he'd seen facing him in the mirror just before he went along with one of Nog's schemes.

Makes sense, I guess, he thought. *It gets kind of boring here, sometimes. Even getting in trouble's better than more of the same, and there's always the chance we won't get caught. Besides, I'll bet this is the first time in Cedra's life he's been able to just relax and have some fun. Look at him! He's thinking up something good right now; I'd bet on it.*

Then Cedra spoke, and as Jake listened he realized that his bet was about to pay off bigger than he'd ever dreamed.

"Miles! Thank goodness you're here!" Keiko cried, seizing her husband's arm and dragging him into the classroom.

"I came as soon as you called," he panted. "I was flat on my back halfway down an access channel when—" The words froze on his tongue.

There, in the middle of a classroom full of innocent children, stood a fully armed and armored Cardassian warrior. He strode between the desks, glowering at them fiercely. The ghastly face with its heavily pronounced ridges of bone and ropes of muscle looked familiar.

"Gul Dukat," O'Brien breathed, naming the former Cardassian commander of *Deep Space Nine.* "What the hell is he doing here?" He reached for his comm badge to summon help.

Keiko's hand closed over his, preventing him. "He's our astronomy lesson," she said. She didn't sound amused.

"He's what?" Before Miles could get an answer, the Cardassian lord stopped in front of a desk occupied by a very young Bajoran girl. He loomed above her like a wave about to come crashing down. Her eyes and mouth were three perfect circles of awe as she watched him raise his fists high above his head—

—and execute a dainty pirouette in place while a frilly pink tutu blossomed at his waist. Prancing and mincing on tiptoe, Gul Dukat sang a song declaring that he was just a little *kata*-bunny in the sunshine. The class rocked and howled with laughter.

"He was *supposed* to be a holographic projection of the wormhole," Keiko said grimly.

"Uh?" O'Brien was incapable of speech.

"Miles, this is *serious.*" She shook him. "I can't cancel the image or override the program. The children have gone wild. I want this stopped and then I want to know who's responsible for it."

"Oh." Miles was still staring at the twirling Cardassian. "Um . . . I'll fix it right away." He dashed out of the classroom before he, too, exploded with laughter.

Security Chief Odo paced slowly back and forth before the three boys awaiting their fate in his office. "A Bajoran couple, having rented one of *your* uncle's holosuites for a special occasion, is suddenly surrounded by Klingons singing opera," he announced, glaring at Nog.

Jake looked at the floor. Nog squirmed. Cedra remained standing tall, meeting Odo's eye steadily whenever the shapeshifter looked his way.

"A hardworking businessmen, on returning to his quarters, attempts to use his personal holoport to view a sporting event and is instead regaled with a sermon by a miniature monk who thwarts all attempts to have his program terminated," Odo continued. "The classroom holoport remains unusable. The complaints from some of the *other* holosuites at Quark's Place are not fit to repeat. There are *hyurin* dancing on the counter at Garak's tailor shop whenever he attempts to show a customer holograms of the latest styles . . ." He stopped pacing and faced the boys. "What do you have to say for yourselves?"

"He did it!" Nog exclaimed without hesitation, pointing at Cedra.

"Oh, he did, did he?" Odo's voice gave up nothing. He eyed Cedra. The Bajoran remained unmoved, although there was an almost imperceptible quiver at the corner of his mouth, and his nostrils flared with something that might have been suppressed laughter. "Nice try, Nog," the shapeshifter grated. "Talis Cedra is new here. Do you expect me to believe he could *recognize* a holosystem control, let alone know how to use one? Use one well enough so that all Chief O'Brien's efforts to fix the problem are blocked by a series of failsafe commands to counter his every attempt at entering the system?" Odo added. He shook his head. "You'll have to do better than that."

"I'm telling the truth, I swear!" the Ferengi shouted. "Ask my father if you don't believe me. Ask my uncle!"

"One Ferengi to vouch for another," Odo commented. "Of course. Why didn't I think of that."

"Probably because you've made up your mind already," Cedra stated.

"What did you say?" The constable gave him a sharp look.

"What you heard," Cedra replied calmly. "Unless it was something you didn't want to hear."

"Are you implying that I am not a reliable witness?" Odo's primitively molded face darkened.

Cedra was unruffled. "No more than you've implied

that I'm too stupid to learn how to use the holosystem. You never alter evidence, Constable; that's not in your nature. But sometimes—when the way things are doesn't fit the way your sense of justice says they ought to be—you're tempted, aren't you?"

Odo's shoulders stiffened. "So it *was* you."

"I told you!" Nog acted wounded. "I said he did it!"

"He said he *learned* to do it. The question remains: who was his teacher?" Odo regarded all three of the boys closely. "Unless you want me to believe you had access to hologram projectors at that refugee camp." This last was directed at Cedra alone.

"Maybe you should go there yourself and see what we have," Cedra answered. "It might help you learn that worse than not knowing where you come from, is knowing there's nowhere you can go."

For once, Odo had no acerbic comment to make. He stared at the small, scrawny Bajoran as if the two of them had suddenly had their positions reversed. *Now knowing where you come fro— How did he know?* The instant's qualm passed. *Rumors. This station is riddled with them. If he's been running around with Quark's nephew, he's had his head stuffed with every bit of gossip on the station by now, including all there is to know about me.*

"If you want to play games, I'm sure Commander Sisko will have some new ones to teach you when he arrives," the shapeshifter said.

"You sent for my father?" Jake was alarmed.

"I thought it might be in order," Odo said dryly. "He'll have a word or two to say about creating new problems for Chief O'Brien when he's got more vital repairs to make."

"You won't imprison us, will you?" For the first time, Odo saw concern on Cedra's face.

"I wasn't planning on it. Commander Sisko might order you confined to your quarters, but—"

"He can't! Dejana needs me! She's sick," Cedra cried.

"Your sister is getting the best of care. She ought to be out of the infirmary tomorrow."

"I can't be separated from her; I *won't* be!" Cedra's cheeks paled. "Constable, if I give you my word that I won't touch the hologram system again, if I help Chief O'Brien get it back to normal, will you tell Commander Sisko I cooperated with you?"

"I'll see what I can do." Even the normally impassive Odo was perturbed by the Bajoran child's agitation. "But I assure you, your sister is perfectly safe—"

"Not without *me!*" Cedra insisted. "She doesn't know what they'll want from her. What good is it to get her out of the camp if they tear her to pieces here?"

Nog nudged Jake and whispered, "Who wants to tear her to pieces?"

Jake shrugged. "I heard Dad talking with Lieutenant Dax and Ensign Kahrimanis about Talis Dejana, but—"

"Later," the Ferengi hissed. "I want to hear this."

"Calm yourself," Odo directed Cedra. "Your sister is safe."

Cedra shook his head. "Not until she's been presented at the Temple. Maybe not even then, but at least once the *Dessin-ka* have seen her, they'll be her protectors. *Please,* Constable, I can't be apart from her for long. I've always looked out for her . . ."

"Then it's time you allowed someone else to take over that job. You are young. I suggest you see if you can't find some way of enjoying your youth without setting the whole station on ear."

Cedra met Odo's gaze with a look that added years to the boy. "It's always easier to play, isn't it?" he said. "To do tricks for an audience and earn applause, that's cleaner than dealing with thieves and murderers, trying to see justice done. Yet we choose our work, no matter how hard, because it creates us in our own image."

Odo's brows met, or would have, if he had any. He had the unsettling feeling that the boy had just held up a mirror between them and made it vanish, all in an instant. "What did you say?"

A guileless smile replaced Cedra's sober expression. "I said I promise I'll be a good boy. *Please* let me see my sister?"

"Please, Constable." Jake joined his voice to Cedra's. "It wasn't all his fault. I'm the one who came up with the pink tutu for Gul Dukat, and Nog suggested the Klingon opera singers."

"Hey! I never did!" Nog objected. "You can't prove it!"

Odo took control. "Very well. Commander Sisko has better things to do than deal with you three. I'll release you on your word of honor—even you, Nog—but if I catch you tampering with the holosystem again—"

His threat was met by a chorus of effusive oaths as the boys swore up and down that they would sooner die, be dismembered, or get their earlobes clipped before they would *dream* of touching a projector after this. Odo didn't believe it for a minute, but he was satisfied for the time being. "Fine. Cedra, you report to Chief O'Brien. You two can go where you please."

In the corridor outside Odo's office, Cedra waved a quick farewell to his new friends and ran off to find Chief O'Brien. Jake turned to Nog, grinning.

"See? I told you he'd be all right."

The Ferengi snorted. "Almost got us arrested and you call that all right? Where's the profit in that?"

"Well, we *didn't* get arrested. We didn't even have to face my father. He talked Odo out of it for us."

"He is a very good talker," Nog admitted. He grew thoughtful. "What did your father say about Cedra's sister?"

Jake tried to recall. "He called her *something*—a Bajoran word I never heard before—but whatever it was, he made it real clear to Lieutenant Dax and Ensign Kahrimanis that they weren't supposed to repeat it.

Ensign Kahrimanis said not to worry, he'd had firsthand experience with how dangerous it could get when people knew who Talis Dejana was. So I guess it's okay if I forgot what Dad called her." He smiled, but Nog remained serious. Jake gave him a friendly shove. "Hey! Snap out of it. Let's go back to the Promenade and get some glop-on-a-stick or something. I don't want to do my homework yet."

"Find your Bajoran friend, if that's what you want," Nog snapped. "I have important business to look after." He stalked away, leaving a bewildered Jake behind.

"You finished with Chief O'Brien already?" Jake was surprised to find Cedra waiting for him when he returned to his quarters.

"They wouldn't let me stay in the infirmary. What's the matter?" Cedra was stretched out on Jake's bed fully clothed, staring at the ceiling. "Don't I belong here either?"

"No, you're welcome here, but I thought that if you were done helping fix the holosystem, you'd rather be having some more fun out—"

"That *fun* almost got me separated from my sister."

"Well, it was your idea," Jake mumbled.

"Oh, good; Nog's contagious," Cedra remarked.

"Huh?"

"Is avoiding responsibility the only thing you picked up from him?" Cedra inquired. "Or did you catch all the symptoms?" He rolled onto his stomach. "I think I've discovered a new disease—creeping *Ferengitis*. I feel just like Dr. Bashir."

Jake sat down at the foot of the bed. "Do you think they'll ever find him?"

"Who?"

"Dr. Bashir."

"Yes." Cedra chewed his thumb. "No." He rested his chin on his interlaced fingers. "Maybe. I don't know."

"Well, *that* covers it." Jake sounded disgusted.

"Leave me alone. I'm tired of having all the answers." Cedra flopped back to his original position and yawned. "I'm just plain tired. Let me sleep."

"Okay." Jake got up and fetched a set of pajamas. He dropped the wad of cloth on Cedra's head in jest. "Those ought to fit."

The Bajoran sat up and studied the pajamas with interest. "What's *this?*"

"Pajamas. Or I can find you a nightshirt if you want. What did you wear to sleep in on Bajor?"

"Whatever we had on," Cedra answered. "Or nothing, when the weather was warm."

"You can do that here, too, if you want. Just put on a robe if you get out of bed. Dad's kind of conservative."

"No, no." Cedra held up the pajamas and stroked the soft material appreciatively. "These are great."

Jake grinned. "Try them on."

Cedra went pale. "What?"

"Try them on. See if they fit."

"Now?" Cedra clutched the pajamas to his chest.

"You said you wanted to go to sleep. You've got to see if they're the right size. If not, I'll see if I can replicate something else." Jake sat down beside Cedra and took the pajama top. "Try the bottoms first. If those are too tight—" He made a pained face. "You know how *that* can feel."

Cedra jumped up. "Later. I'm not that tired anymore. Hey, how about we go find Nog and see if we can't get him to come up with some more of those Taxman's Delights?"

Jake was bewildered. "I thought you said you were tired."

"I'm *tired* of not eating." He playfully threw the pajama bottoms in Jake's face and dashed out of the room shouting, "Last one to find Nog's a *kata*-bunny!"

* * *

"A Bajoran word?" Quark repeated his nephew's scrap of news irritably. "A Bajoran word you don't even *know*? How in the name of all the Rules of Acquisition am I supposed to turn *that* into a profit?"

"But Uncle Quark, think!" Nog insisted. "It's something they think must be hidden! People only bother to hide things of great value."

A slow, snaggletoothed smile slowly spread itself across Quark's face. "Is that so? All the secrecy . . . hmmm . . ." He clapped Nog on the back and cackled. "You're right, boy! I'm proud of you. With a mind like that, you'll be able to buy and sell your own father at a profit someday soon."

"I'd rather sell you, Uncle." Nog was sincere. "You're worth more than my father."

"So I am, so I am," the adult Ferengi said complacently. "You stick with me, Nog. Tell me everything you know. Together we'll find the answer to this puzzle *and* a way to wring some profit out of it."

"Shared profit," Nog prompted.

"Shared profit," Quark agreed. Under his breath he added, "A five-percent share for you, ninety-five for me."

CHAPTER
11

DR. BASHIR reined his *verdanis* back from a lope to a walk
as they entered a scraggly grove of trees. He looked to left
and right, assaying the tale that stumps and slashed
branches told. Once upon a time this might have been a
forest, hugging the foothills, even stretching onward, up
into the mountains that flanked the Kaladrys Valley.
Now it was a remnant, pathetic, and soon it would not
even be that.

They were so proud of themselves in that camp, Julian
reflected, thinking of the place he and Tossi had just left.
*Always warm, they told me, with plenty of firewood, plenty
of brand-new timbered buildings, no need to reuse patchwork pieces of old structures . . .* He rested his hand on
the raw scar where a branch had grown. *No attempt at
replanting the wood; just harvesting the forest as if there
were no tomorrow.*

He sighed. He knew that that attitude was not entirely
their fault. It was hard enough for ordinary people to
think about tomorrow, but for refugees sometimes the

present was all that mattered. Perhaps he should go back and speak with the monks in charge, help them make the people see that present comfort would only mean future hardship—

"I can't," he said aloud. "I spent too much time there as it was, but there were so many fever cases—!" He slipped easily from the *verdanis*'s back and tied his mount to a branch that so far had been spared the camp's unchecked wood-harvesting efforts. "Good Tossi," he said, patting the creature's long, flexible neck.

He took down his pack, gave the *verdanis* its feedbag, and made camp. He had no tent, but the inhabitants of the second camp he'd visited had expressed their gratitude with the gift of a fine, weatherproof tarpaulin. With some rope and the aid of a few fortunately placed branches, it made a decent shelter. When he found himself in terrain that lacked branches, he turned the tarp into excellent ground cover, or else simply wrapped himself up in it against the chill of night.

Dr. Bashir soon had the tarp deployed to his liking. All he needed now was a campfire to cook his evening meal. He hesitated over gathering the scant supply of dead brush, thinking of the people he had left behind in the last camp. *They'll need it more than I.* Cold rations weren't appetizing, but he wound up nibbling them anyway.

Frontier living to go with frontier medicine, he thought, and enjoyed his private jest a little more than he enjoyed his meager meal.

When he had eaten, it was full night. The moons of Bajor cast a bright, silvery glow through the branches of the devastated woodland. Julian leaned his back against a tree and gazed up at the stars caught in a net of branches. His mind drifted in the calm of the night until he realized that one cluster of twinkling lights in the blackness was not made up of stars after all. He dropped his head to rest wearily on his updrawn knees and tried not to think of *Deep Space Nine*. Eventually he wrapped himself in a blanket and went to sleep.

"You! Get up!" A booted foot kicked his leg lightly but insistently. Julian's first groggy thought was that Commander Sisko had dispatched a search party for him and that they'd found him.

They can make me go back, but they can't make me stay, he thought. *I'll find a way, make them see that my work here's more important, leave Starfleet if I have to, only—*

The boot kicked him again, harder, and he awoke to realize that a search party from the station would never rouse him so roughly or stand there with a row of phasers leveled at his eyes.

"You heard me: Get up!" A tall, broad-chested Bajoran male gave him an extra kick for good measure. This one hurt. Dr. Bashir obeyed. There were too many of them for resistance to be more than a bad joke. He counted seven in all, all of them sturdy, hard-faced men whose clothing was much the worse for wear but whose weapons gleamed. One of them reached in swiftly to snatch Julian's phaser. He handed it over to the leader immediately.

"Is that the one?" another man asked his comrade.

"Idiot," came the reply. "How many Starfleet uniforms have *you* seen around here lately?"

"Huh! As if you even knew what a Starfleet uniform looked like before the boy described one!"

"Shut up, the two of you!" the tall one barked. He returned his attention to Julian. "Are you the healer?"

"I am Dr. Julian Bashir of Starfleet," he replied. *And you look like one of those bands of hill fighters I've heard about,* he thought. The camp he'd just left had had some highly unfavorable things to say about them, enumerating long lists of supplies stolen and draft animals "borrowed" in aid of a cause the raiders never bothered to explain. *At least they leave the children alone.* The last camp had been overrun with fever, but the infection had not yet had time to take many lives. The children there still had the care and supervision of enough concerned adults to make running away not seem so attractive.

"I am Borilak Selinn," the Bajoran said in turn. "We've heard of you. Come." He gestured with his weapon.

Julian turned to his campsite, only to have Borilak Selinn grab his arm and yank him away with a harsh "Where do you think you're going?"

Julian shrugged off the Bajoran's grasp. "I need to pack my things."

"They'll be brought along for you."

"Listen, you know I'm a healer. If you need my services, you'd better let me pack my own equipment. If you or your men break any of it, I'll be no good to you."

The Bajoran showed his teeth, broken and brown. "Then you'd better hope my men are careful, because if you're no use to us as a healer without your toys, you're no use to us at all."

Dr. Bashir had no choice but to follow. Two of Borilak's men fell into step behind him; the other four remained behind to secure the campsite. Julian dearly regretted having removed the biosample replicator and prayed it would survive whatever handling they gave it. He heard Tossi whicker and snort, and he knew he had probably seen the last of that untiring mount.

Borilak Selinn led the way into the hills. They took narrow paths, rocky and overgrown with thorny brush. Down into gullies and through stands of trees still growing wild and untouched by the comfort-hungry refugee camps they went, sometimes doubling back on their tracks. Dr. Bashir tried to keep himself oriented, calling to mind the careful traceries of Talis Cedra's amateur map. His efforts were not helped by the fact that it was still night, with dawn little more than a thin line of gray against the black. Once the marchers emerged from the upland woods onto a promontory that offered a breathtaking view of the Kaladrys Valley. The thin wash of a day's light shimmered over the meandering river, picking out roads, the ruins of towns, and in the distance an abandoned Cardassian outpost. Then the trail took another turn and the view was gone.

The path became steep, the trees thicker. Despite his excellent physical condition, Dr. Bashir's legs began to complain under the constant strain. He breathed more and more heavily, until just when he felt ready to give in and ask the Borilak Selinn for a rest, they emerged from the trees into a small clearing on the flank of the mountain.

"In the cave." Borilak Selinn took Julian's arm and steered him across the open ground toward a low stone arch. As Julian stumbled along, he noted the unmistakable signs of habitation everywhere. Here was neatly stacked wood and there the fragments of a broken clay water jug, the edges still wet and shiny. A tumble of poles and leather lashings might have been a drying rack for meat or laundry when set up. He tripped over what looked like a hank of rags. The toe of his boot flipped it over; the charcoal-drawn face of a child's doll smiled up at him.

Then the blackness of the cave swallowed him.

"Commander?"

A shadow fell across Benjamin Sisko's table at the Replimat. He looked up to see a stocky, plainly dressed Bajoran regarding him as happily as if he were an old friend, newly found.

"Do I know you?" Sisko asked, bemused.

"May I?" The Bajoran indicated the empty chair across from Sisko's. Benjamin nodded, still perplexed. The man sat down, his smile rigidly in place. "Forgive me if I am intruding, but I recognized you from your description and when I saw you sitting here I thought it might be better to conduct our business informally, rather than see you in your office. You must have many other official matters to look after, and what we must settle is really so simple that—"

"*Have* we business?" Sisko was no longer puzzled; he was annoyed.

The Bajoran gasped and snapped his fingers as if he had just remembered something that made him laugh. "I do beg your pardon, Commander! How foolish of me. I assumed that because I knew you, you must also know me!" He clicked his tongue indulgently over his own folly. "I am Kejan Ulli, a representative of the *Dessin-ka*. And by the way, if we have not yet commended your Major Kira for the way she so ably protected our beloved child, consider it done."

"Kejan Ulli . . ." The name was familiar. Sisko recalled it from Major Kira's report. Despite this man's air of joviality, he could be ruthless. "What is your business with me?"

"Why, the child, of course." Kejan Ulli acted surprised. "The *Nekor*."

"Talis Dejana will be presented to your people, as agreed, in the Temple at the festival of *Berajin*."

Kejan Ulli's smile grew harder. "*Berajin* is not so far off, and the child is here. Why must we delay? I will escort her to the Temple personally."

"I'm sorry, I can't allow that." Sisko was firm. "The Kai's message did not say that this child was to be found for the *Dessin-ka* alone. If I turn her over to you, there might be accusations of favoritism from among the other factions within the provisional government. If, however, she is conducted to the Temple by representatives of Starfleet, no one can make any such charges."

Now Kejan Ulli was not smiling. "You do not trust the *Dessin-ka*?"

"It's not a matter of trust. The child is my responsibility."

"Then I suppose you will refuse me even to see the *Nekor.*" Kejan Ulli bit the words off short.

"I never said that. You're welcome to visit her. Would now be convenient?"

"Very." It was a snarl.

Sisko stood up and had the Bajoran accompany him. When Kejan Ulli saw the infirmary sign, he balked.

"What is this?" he demanded. "Why is the *Nekor* kept here?"

"Talis Dejana has spent most of her life in a refugee camp. The infirmary is the best place for her to gain strength and to correct symptoms of malnutrition," Sisko explained. "She's receiving the best of care."

The Bajoran scowled. "We'll see." He strode past Sisko without apology and accosted the first aide he saw. "Where is the *Nekor?*" The crewman only stared. Kejan Ulli seized the man's arms and shook him, repeating the demand: "*Where is the* Nekor?"

Sisko pulled the Bajoran away. "You will not treat my crew in that manner," he directed, voice a powerful rumble. He hustled Kejan Ulli aside and added, "Hardly anyone here except for my most trusted crew members knows that Talis Dejana is the *Nekor,* as you call her. For security reasons, understand?"

Kejan Ulli tried to make light of it. "No harm done. As you said, *Berajin* is almost here. The *Nekor* will soon be among those capable of protecting her holy person without having to resort to such games. Now take me to her." He showed his teeth briefly. "Please."

Smoldering, Sisko conducted the *Dessin-ka* agent to Talis Dejana's bedside. In Dr. Bashir's absence, Lieutenant Dax had seen to the child's comfort personally, setting up a temporary cubicle in what was usually an open ward. Within the movable walls, Talis Cedra sat beside his sister's bed, a wary eye on the life-sign readings while the two of them talked. Commander Sisko frowned when he heard the girl's lighthearted giggles degenerate into a spasm of coughing, but it soon passed.

"Oh!" Cedra went on guard as soon as he spied Kejan Ulli standing at Commander Sisko's side. "What do *you* want?"

Kejan Ulli's false smile was back in place. He was hardly aware of Cedra's presence. His eyes shone as he stared wolfishly at Dejana. He took several steps toward her, hands outstretched, as if he intended to scoop her out of the bed. The little girl cringed and groped for Cedra's hand. Sisko saw Cedra's brown fingers squeeze reassurance into Dejana. That one clasp worked wonders: the child sat up straight and met Kejan Ulli's officious advance with a look that made the grown Bajoran hesitate and pull back before he dared touch the girl.

"Commander Sisko, why is this one here?" Dejana inquired, her hard stare never swerving from Kejan Ulli.

"He's Kejan Ulli, a representative of the *Dessin-ka,*" Sisko replied. "He has my permission to visit you."

"But he does not have *my* permission," the child stated.

Kejan Ulli fell to one knee at the foot of the bed. "Holy one, have I your permission?" he implored.

Dejana's eyes flickered toward Cedra. The boy said, "As you wish," although the girl had said nothing. He moved smoothly away from the bed to stand beside Commander Sisko. Dejana beckoned Kejan Ulli, who needed no second invitation. He hastened to take the spot that Cedra had vacated.

"You are not a patient man, Kejan Ulli," Dejana said with the same remarkable self-possession Sisko remembered from his interviews with the Kai Opaka. It was all the more remarkable coming from one so young.

Is this the same child I saw less than a minute ago, so scared of Kejan Ulli? he wondered. The transformation was astounding.

Meanwhile, it was the *Dessin-ka* agent's turn to squirm. "Holy one, it is only because I am so eager to serve you."

"You would serve me better if you showed more respect for your brothers. You fired at Remis Jobar when there was no need."

"I only stunned him," the Bajoran said, some of the fawning reverence freezing out of his voice.

"That is not what you intended to do, at first," the girl replied. The words had a perceptible effect. Kejan Ulli pulled back, his face fighting to conceal shock.

"I never—"

"You did." Dejana was calm. "But by good fortune you turn—were turned from your intention. You may thank the Prophets for that. I would not have had a murderer among my chosen attendants."

"Your chosen—?" All suspicion vanished from Kejan Ulli's expression when he heard Dejana's words. "You were nowhere near when I felt the Prophets' inspiration, telling me to show mercy to the one who stole you away. How could you know, unless you truly are—? Oh, this is better than I hoped!"

"Don't get so excited," Cedra drawled. *"I* was the one who told you you'd do better to switch your phaser to stun."

Kejan Ulli glowered at the boy, but Dejana said, *"He* knows you were the one who told him, silly! He also knows that it was the Prophets speaking *through* you." Cedra snorted. Dejana turned to Kejan Ulli. "My brother's like that. Don't pay any attention to him. I think he's jealous."

Sisko thought he saw the girl stick out her tongue at her brother, just like a normal child her age. Suddenly a fresh attack of coughing shook her body. She sank back against her pillows under the horrified eyes of the *Dessin-ka* agent.

"What is the matter with her?" he demanded of Sisko.

"It's a cold, one that's taking a little longer than usual for her to shake off, according to my science officer. That's why we've kept her here, so that she can be well cared for."

"Is that so? Then why is she not constantly attended by a healer?"

"It's only a *cold*," Sisko stressed. "She'll be fully recovered in plenty of time for *Berajin*."

"I will see to that," Kejan Ulli stated. "My report will recommend the immediate dispatch of three healers for the *Nekor's* exclusive service."

"*Dessin-ka* healers, I assume?" Sisko asked. Kejan Ulli's smirk as good as said *What else?* "Impossible. Talis Dejana is not the property of the *Dessin-ka*. The Kai's letter—"

"We are well aware of the Kai's letter. There are many within the provisional government who are already busy trying to lay claim to the holy one's attention and patronage, even if it entails denying that she is the *Nekor*, of blessed prophecy. We of the *Dessin-ka* will not stoop to their level. However, we also will not stand by and allow the holy one to suffer needlessly simply because Starfleet and the Federation are incapable of giving her the care she requires." With a condescending look, he spread his hands and addressed Commander Sisko: "A child is sick and we offer help; in mercy's name, can you forbid us?"

"If that's your only motive, I can't forbid it," Sisko said. Then, as the smile of victory was still forming on Kejan Ulli's lips, he added, "I will inform the provisional government that the *Dessin-ka* have generously offered to dispatch three healers to work with the sick children still in the refugee camps on Bajor."

Kejan Ulli's objection was intercepted by Dejana, who recovered enough from her coughing spell to clasp his hand and hoarsely say, "You will be blessed for this." The cough took her again. Cedra dashed out and returned in the blink of an eye with a female nurse, who gave the girl an injection that silenced her cough.

"She needs to sleep now, sir," she informed Sisko.

The commander and the *Dessin-ka* agent left Cedra helping the nurse make Dejana more comfortable. Sisko considered the reports he'd had about the boy. It was as if there were two Cedras sharing one skin. Word had reached Sisko from the infirmary staff that when Cedra was not visiting his sister, he lingered to observe how other patients were treated.

"He's so quiet, we'd never know he was there," one aide said. "Except eventually he always has some comment to make about the way we're taking care of this case or that. I've let him help out a few times. From what I hear, he's a troublemaker, but you'd never know it to see how he behaves here."

A troublemaker, yes. Sisko deplored the boy's escapades with the station holosystem. It was bad enough that his son Jake ran around with Nog, but with Talis Cedra in the pack, the mischief the three of them got into had taken a distinctly creative turn. *And yet . . .*

"Very clever, Commander." Kejan Ulli brought Sisko sharply back to the present. "Naturally we will obey the *Nekor's* wishes concerning the healers, but that does not mean we will tolerate the holy one abiding in the midst of unbelievers any longer than need be."

"Kejan Ulli, no matter what you think, we are not holding the *Nekor* here to keep her away from you, or anyone," Sisko said, trying to be patient. "The decision to have her remain aboard *Deep Space Nine* was made for the child's sake alone, because of her health."

"Am I to take your word for that?"

"I hope you will."

"As if I had a choice." Kejan Ulli gave him a venomous look. "Of course you have the authority to decide where the holy one stays until her presentation at the Temple. I, on the other hand, have a certain amount of authority as well." He reached into the bosom of his robe and produced a folded document, which he presented for Sisko's perusal. "On that authority, granted to me by the elders of the *Dessin-ka,* I ask that the child known as Talis Dejana be brought to the Temple on the eve of *Nis Thamar,* four days from now."

"The agreement was that she would be brought to the Temple for the festival of *Berajin,"* Sisko protested hotly. "I don't care who authorized you to make such unreasonable demands, I will only honor the arrangements made with the provisional government—arrangements made with the full knowledge and consent of the *Dessin-ka."*

"You are a man of honor, Commander." Kejan Ulli did not make it sound like a compliment. "But you are not a man of knowledge. According to the beliefs of my people, the festival of *Berajin* begins on the eve of *Nis Thamar."* He tucked the authorization document away again. "And I am entirely within my rights to request that the presentation of the *Nekor* take place then without violating the previously made agreement."

"And you'll insist on this, even if the child hasn't recovered her health?"

"Really, Commander," Kejan Ulli sneered. "You sidestepped *my* offer of medical assistance so artfully, I thought your people could work miracles. The eve of *Nis Thamar:* we shall expect the *Nekor* to be there, and in good health, or we will see to it that the Federation answers for the consequences." He was gone in a swirl of somber robes.

"Get out, Vung," Quark said, slamming a drink down on the bar. "This is your last one. You wouldn't even have this one if I didn't have that Bajoran bartender on duty. He doesn't know you, but I do. Drink up and get out."

"Why? What have I done?" The other Ferengi tried to

meet Quark's angry dismissal with the same look of wounded innocence Quark himself favored when dealing with Odo or Major Kira. There was just something about this Ferengi's face that made such an expression impossible.

"Word travels fast," Quark replied. "When my brother Rom told me he'd seen you aboard DS9, I hoped it was just a bad dream. Then you turn up *here.*"

"Just passing through in the course of business," Vung said, resting his elbows on the bar and steepling his stubby fingertips. The threadbare, shabby clothing he wore did not make him look like the typically successful Ferengi businessperson. "I'm bound for the wormhole. I've come into possession of a nifty little gadget—a surefire big seller—that no one's licensed to manufacture in the Gamma Quadrant . . . yet. Maybe I can cut you in. Interested?" His chummy smile revealed more than a few missing teeth.

"I don't need a cut of your kind of business," Quark responded.

"Oh, come, come! You're forgetting the eighth Rule of Acquisition: Only a fool passes up a business opportunity."

"Then there ought to be a Rule Eight-and-a-half: Only an idiot takes a business opportunity *you* offer."

Vung shrugged. "Have it your way. My ship leaves within twenty-four hours. I won't bother you again. But I *will* finish this." He held up his glass, made a mocking gesture of toasting Quark's health, and sipped it slowly; *very* slowly.

Quark showed his teeth in frustration and removed himself far enough from Vung to be able to keep an eye on him without appearing to associate with him. The other Ferengi noticed, understood, and sipped his drink even more slowly, savoring Quark's displeasure.

It was while Quark was eyeing Vung and polishing the

same glass for the twentieth time that he felt a tapping at his elbow. "Uncle Quark?" It was Nog.

"What do you want?" Quark demanded, never taking his eyes from Vung.

"I just wanted to— Who is that?" Now Nog's eyes followed his uncle's hostile stare.

"No one any decent Ferengi would ever associate with willingly," Quark snapped. "None of your business."

This reply only served to fascinate Nog even more. "Why? What did he do?" His voice dropped dramatically as he added, "Give someone a refund?"

Quark grabbed his nephew by the scruff of the neck and hustled him away. "If you must know, *that* is Vung. Remember the name: there are certain quarters where it's considered a dirty word. That—that *person* was once a trader second only to the Grand Nagus himself! What a touch, what a touch he had! The deals that fell into his lap, the bars of gold-pressed latinum he amassed, the females of all species who—"

"That's" why I shouldn't have anything to do with him?" Nog was nonplussed.

Quark paused long enough to wipe the corners of his mouth. He addressed Nog in the strictest tones: "Don't be as big a fool as your father, boy! If Vung had gained all that through skill, I'd sell you *and* Rom wholesale just to hear one lesson in salesmanship from his lips. But it wasn't skill; it was *luck.* The lobeless wonder said he had a fortune-token, a lucky talisman that he'd bought from a wandering Andorian tradesman. Paid *full price* for it!"

Nog made a face, appalled to hear of such obscenity. "And that's what did it for him?" He glanced at Vung, who was still nursing his drink. The outcast Ferengi grinned at the boy, who looked sharply away. "Some lousy piece of junk jewelry?"

"Junk?" Quark repeated. "Only let me get my hands on that kind of 'junk'! The point is, it *worked.* So Vung

said and everyone saw the proof. Until the day he was
waylaid by a Cygnetan dancing girl. She tried to steal the
charm from around his neck while he slept."

"Did he cut her throat, Uncle Quark?" Nog wore a
cheerful, bloodthirsty grin.

"Him? He slept right through it. She stole the talisman
and got away clean. But she didn't get the chain it hung
from, and *that* was Vung's real undoing." Quark sighed.
"The luck was in the whole necklace, chain and charm
together. One without the other is worthless—worse
than worthless!"

"Worse than worthless? Why? How?"

"First, he lost his fortune. Then, when he tried to
acquire another, he had the longest run of twisted luck
you ever saw. Good things still fell into his lap, but they
somehow managed to slither right out again. Sometimes
they bit him first. Luck smiles on him a dozen ways, and
each and every smile spits right in his eye. Sometimes
other people get a taste of his misfortunes if they stand
too close." Quark shivered. "He knows it's the charmless
chain doing it to him, but does he foist it off on some
unsuspecting customer? Oh no! He holds on to it in
hopes of one day finding the fortune-token again. Until
then, he's a living jinx—a jinx with the best bad luck in
the universe!" Quark's gaze flickered from Nog to Vung
and back. "So say what you've got to say and make it
snappy. I want him out of my place before he decides to
try his 'luck' at Dabo."

"Uncle Quark, I found out what the word is!" Nog said
excitedly. "The word that says why Talis Dejana's so
special: *Nekor.*"

"*Nekor . . .*" Quark tried out the sound of the word on
his tongue. "What does it mean?"

Nog beamed. "Profit."

Quark motioned for the boy to lower his voice. "How
did you find this out? The girl's brother?"

Nog made a face. "Him? Huh! You'd get more out of a

Vulcan in a holosuite. You know how you sent me to the infirmary with that fruit basket? Well, I went back there on my own with another one."

"Odo didn't chase you off again?"

A bark of laughter shook Nog's small body. "He's busy overseeing the holosystem repair project. We've got Cedra to thank for all I learned. One of Constable Odo's lieutenants was on duty instead. I told him I was a good friend of the girl's brother and I had a gift for her from him."

"And he let you in?"

"No," Nog admitted. "He took the fruit basket in."

"Another fruit basket? This is coming out of your share," Quark said, shaking a finger under Nog's snub nose.

"Even if that fruit basket paid for the information? When the guard went into the infirmary, a Bajoran male came bustling up, waving his hands and squawking about how *dare* they leave the *Nekor's* doorway unguarded and what sort of incompetents has the Federation assigned to the welfare of the holy one?"

"Holy . . ." Quark's eyes sparkled with speculation. "Good, good. These Bajorans take their religion seriously. People always pay more for anything they think is serious. And you found out what *Nekor* means?"

Nog looked insulted. "I used the classroom computer!"

"Well, well. Who said education doesn't pay?" Quark mused.

"You did."

Quark cuffed his nephew. "I know that! I was just testing you. And what *does* it mean?"

Nog opened his mouth to speak, but uttered a yelp of dismay instead. "Uncle Quark! He's getting away without paying!" The boy pointed at Vung's fast-retreating back.

"Ah, let him go. Good riddance. The price of a drink's

cheap enough to be rid of him. Anyway," he added as an afterthought, "I'll find out which vessel he's booked passage on and have the captain reimburse me and put it on Vung's shipboard bill. Now, you were saying about the *Nekor* . . . ?"

Commander Sisko was wakened from a restless sleep by the alarm raised at his door. He scarcely had time to vault out of bed and throw a robe on before his quarters were flooded with Major Kira, Security Chief Odo, a monk from the station shrine, and a wildly gesturing, shouting Kejan Ulli.

"My apologies, Commander, but—" Odo began.

"—vanished!" Kejan Ulli cried. "There's no sign—"

"Kejan Ulli, please," Major Kira said, trying unsuccessfully to calm him. "No ship has left the station since the last time Nurse Guerette checked on her. No one had access to any of the runabouts either. She *has* to be here."

"Who—?" Commander Sisko asked, trying to sort sense from chaos.

A bleary-eyed Jake and Cedra came stumbling into the already crowded room just as Kejan Ulli exclaimed, "The *Nekor,* may the Prophets strike her kidnapper down! They have stolen the *Nekor!*"

Cedra stared, stricken, then burst into wild sobs and fled.

CHAPTER
12

"THAT'S THE LAST OF THEM," Major Kira said, her voice barely concealing the frustration she felt as she reported on the search efforts to Commander Sisko. "She's not aboard any of the ships in the docking ring."

Sisko said nothing, but his anger showed on his face. He paced from post to post in Ops, hearing similarly fruitless reports from other personnel and fighting the urge to slam his fist into the bulkhead. "What about the life-sign scans?" He touched his comm badge. "Chief O'Brien, *report.*"

Miles O'Brien's voice filled Ops. "We're running them now, sir, a full sweep of the station. Nothing."

"You're sure you have the correct codes for Talis Dejana?"

"Absolutely, sir. We're even running variant readings, from the infirmary records, just to make sure. Sometimes we seem to get a reading, but then it vanishes before we can pinpoint it."

"The sensors are working?"

"Aye, sir. For a job at this distance, there never was any trouble with them. It was only on making long-distance readings, and for that, it looks like Ensign McCormick's licked the problem. A test or two and we can commence the search for Dr. Bashir."

"Save that. We *must* find the child."

"Aye, sir," O'Brien repeated. "I'll report any developments immediately. O'Brien out."

"Nothing, Commander?" Kejan Ulli stepped forward.

"How did you get in here?" Sisko wanted to know. "You're not cleared for access to Ops."

Major Kira cleared her throat. "I gave him clearance, sir," she murmured. Before Sisko could say anything, she added, "He was threatening to return to Bajor and tell the *Dessin-ka* that the whole business of the *Nekor* was just a lie concocted by competing factions within the provisional government. The *Dessin-ka* aren't known for their tolerance of lies."

"But it isn't a lie," Sisko objected.

"They'd demand immediate proof of that. Could we give it to them?" Major Kira pointed out. "It's better to appease Kejan Ulli and keep the *Dessin-ka*'s support."

"A sop." Sisko rubbed his chin. "I can't say I like it."

"I'll take full responsibility, sir," Kira said. "I can't afford your morals. If there's a way to keep the peace on Bajor, I'll take it."

"Just see to it that he doesn't get in the way."

It was an empty hope. Kejan Ulli attached himself to Sisko at once and laid down a barrage of questions: "What measures are you taking to locate the *Nekor?* How many crewmen have you assigned to handle this emergency? Where are your security forces? Why didn't they do something to prevent this disaster?"

"Ensign Tolland is in the infirmary with a concussion he got while guarding Talis Dejana," Sisko snapped. "He was struck from behind."

"With such alert personnel, I'm surprised no one

kidnapped the *Nekor* earlier than this," Kejan Ulli sneered.

Sisko's teeth clamped together. "Officer Tolland is one of Odo's best men. He claims that he didn't see his assailant."

"A likely story." The *Dessin-ka* agent folded his arms. "You believed it, of course."

"I believed it." Odo made his presence known. He had just entered Ops. "One thing I demand of my officers above all others is absolute truthfulness."

"Which you always receive, no doubt." Kejan Ulli's lip curled.

Odo regarded him dispassionately. "How fortunate for us all that your doubts have no effect on the truth."

"What have you learned, Odo?" Major Kira skillfully interposed her question between the shapeshifter and the *Dessin-ka* agent to prevent any further clashes.

"We have initiated a level-by-level search of the station as a backup procedure to Chief O'Brien's sensor scans. I am myself about to requestion a prime suspect in this matter."

"Who? Who is this suspect?" Kejan Ulli insisted. "Take me to him. I'll have the truth soon enough."

"Yes, I've heard of your methods." Odo refused to be swayed. "This is a matter for Security. You'll be kept informed as necessary." He turned on his heel and left.

"Three guesses who Odo's prime suspect is," Kira murmured for Sisko's ears alone.

"The child is worth a lot to a lot of different people," Sisko returned. "Can you think of anyone more likely to want a piece of that?"

"You again? Can't you think of anyone else to bother except an honest businessman?" Quark whined. "Go harass Garak if you want to look busy. That Cardassian knows more than he lets on."

"Garak has been questioned, along with the other merchants on the Promenade," Odo said, leaning across the bar until his ill-defined nose was less than an inch away from Quark's wrinkled one. "None of them complained. All of them cooperated completely."

"Oh, and just because I'm the only one with enough lobes to stand up for my rights and not *cringe* before almighty Security, I'm automatically a suspect, is that it?"

"Pardon me, Quark. I was so busy listening to you whimper and wail about a few simple questions that I missed the part where you stood up for your rights." Quark tried to turn away, but Odo's arm shot out and twirled the Ferengi into an about-face that brought them back nose-to-nose. "Now, you listen to me: I'm only telling you this because we are such good friends," Odo said in a voice that reeked of anything but friendship. "It's a warning."

"A w-w-warning?" Quark quavered.

"My top man was seriously injured while guarding Talis Dejana. Somehow, someone managed to sneak up behind him, unseen, and hit him in the head hard enough to give him a severe concussion. That much is common knowledge. However, when I went to visit him in the infirmary, he told me that just before the blow that struck him down, he happened to see something peculiar."

"Peculiar, eh?" Quark's voice was a peep.

"A shadow."

"A shadow? Whose—?"

"Whose," Odo repeated. "That is the question. There was nothing there to cast it. A shadow of a shadow, Ensign Tolland called it. It was very faint, even though the lighting at his post was so bright, but Tolland saw it well enough to say what *might* have cast it." Odo sat back on the barstool. "Has anyone ever told you that you Ferengi have a very distinctive outline?"

Quark slapped the bar. "That's hearsay, not proof!"

"Oh, I never said it proved a thing. But then, I'm not the sort to go jumping to conclusions. I was the first Officer Tolland told about the shadow; I doubt I'm the last." He let the meaning of this sink in.

Quark became edgy. "But I didn't—I have witnesses —I'd never—"

"I wouldn't go that far," Odo commented.

"You mean to say someone will hear Tolland's wild story and blame *me?*"

"You do maintain the highest profile of any Ferengi aboard *Deep Space Nine,*" Odo said. "And you have a certain reputation."

"Blast my reputation to the pits!" Quark cried. "All I need is for one Bajoran fanatic to decide I'm the one who stole their cursed *Nekor.* Then when I can't produce her, who knows what nasty little treat the all-meddling Prophets will 'inspire' him to give me!"

"What did you call the missing child?" Odo asked almost too casually.

Quark's expression as good as said *Oops,* but he tried to put a good front on it. "Nothing, nothing, a little pet name my nephew said the girl's brother has for her. You know these children, heh, heh."

"I see." Odo stood up. "By whatever name, the girl must be found, and soon. If I were you, friend Quark, I'd be doing what I could to help the search, not hinder it. Before Ensign Tolland has the chance to speak with too many others about that shadow."

Major Kira was grabbing a quick bite when Vedek Torin presented himself before her. Modestly he cleared his throat and said, "The peace of the Prophets be with you."

"And with you," she replied automatically. His face told a troubling story. "What's wrong?" she asked, hunger forgotten.

"It is—it is a delicate affair, Major. I did not know whether I should bring it to Commander Sisko's attention."

"What is it?"

"As I was—meditating in the shrine, I thought I heard a strange sound nearby, like the whimper of a frightened child."

"Dejana," Kira breathed. "But we searched the shrine."

The vedek agreed that this was so. "Yet it sounded so *real*. I was on my feet in an instant, trying to determine from which direction the sound had come. I heard nothing. I convinced myself that it had just been my imagination, but when I settled down again, I found this." He handed her a flimsy slip of paper.

Major Kira read it and her expression hardened. "I wondered how long it would be before this happened. It's a ransom note."

"With respect, Major, it is not." The vedek shook his head ever so slightly. "Read it again."

Major Kira did so, this time aloud: " 'If you're interested in the girl, you're not alone. Let's talk about what it's worth to you. Leave your reply where you found this note. You have four hours.' " She looked at Vedek Torin. "Printout from a handcomp, no way to trace it. If this isn't a ransom note, what is it?"

"It is an invitation to bid for the child."

No matter how deep Major Kira's doubts ran, they were soon dispelled. On reporting this development to Commander Sisko, her information was greeted as old news.

"There are representatives of a dozen Bajoran political and religious splinter groups aboard DS9," Sisko said. "Every one of them has been approached in the same manner by our mysterious kidnapper: a secluded part of the station, a lone person to discover a note that's suddenly there, and the words always the same. Kejan

Ulli is the only one who says no one has approached him."

"I don't believe that for a minute," said Major Kira.

"I don't either. He may be hoping to make a preemptive bid and secure the *Nekor* for the *Dessin-ka* this way."

"It looks like the kidnapper wants to start a bidding war for the girl." Her look promised war of a different kind. "If he's willing to sell her to whoever offers the best price, what's to stop the Cardassians from doing it? If that child falls into their hands—"

"There are no Cardassians aboard DS9 at the moment," Sisko said. "Except Garak."

"Ah, Commander Sisko! So good of you to drop by." Garak rushed forward to greet his callers. "And the lovely Major Kira. This *is* an honor." He reached out as if to take her hand. She pulled it away. "Yes, an honor," he repeated, unruffled. "And an unlooked-for convenience. I was just about to close up shop and come looking for you."

"For me?" Sisko was taken aback.

"You know, it's the strangest thing." Garak assumed a thoughtful pose. "I was just going over some fabric samples when what do I find in the binder but—you'll never guess—a *letter*. More of a note, really, and not directed to me at all. I don't know why—"

"Let's see it," Major Kira snapped, her hand thrust out as fast as it had been jerked away before.

"I can refuse you nothing," the urbane clothier replied, and produced a flimsy that was the essential twin of the one Vedek Torin had found. "You see, it asks me to bring this to the attention of Commander Sisko," said Garak, peering over Sisko's and Kira's shoulders while trying to squeeze his way between them.

"To me, as a representative of the Federation," Sisko corrected him. He crumpled the paper. "Of all the gall."

"Ferengi are well stocked in that department," Garak

remarked. Sisko and Kira stared at him; he raised his hands in disclaimer. "Only a rumor, only a rumor. I can't vouch for it at all. This is *such* a deplorable business. That poor child." He clicked his tongue.

"I'm sure you deplore it enough to come right out and tell us whether you received a second note from the kidnapper," Kira said.

"A second—? Now, why would I?"

"The kidnapper's not particular about who he deals with. Commander Sisko represents the Federation. Who do you represent, Garak?"

"No one but myself, dear lady, and some of the finest fashion designers this side of the wormhole. Politics is bad for business." He waggled a chiding finger at her. "You'd best be careful, Major. You're starting to sound like my good friend, Dr. Bashir. By the way"—an able tailor, Garak altered his expression from puckish to sincerely concerned—"any word from him?"

"You'll be the seventy-third to know," Major Kira gritted.

"Four hours." Commander Sisko spread out his fistful of flimsies on Odo's desk like a hand of cards. "They all agree on that."

Odo picked up one of the printouts and examined it. "They all tell the recipients to leave their bids in the same place they found these messages as well. I can have my people cover the pickup points. Are these all of them?"

"I don't know. There's reason to think that not everyone who was approached has come forward. More than a few possible buyers would sooner have the child become their personal bargaining chip rather than see justice done."

"That is their error," Odo said grimly. "If we don't know where all the pickup points are, we can't conduct an effective stakeout."

Sisko concurred. "The kidnapper knows he can't keep the girl hidden forever. If he gets just one good offer, he'll make the sale and run. I can't keep the station sealed off forever, either. If the captain of one of the ships currently docked here decides to leave without clearance, we can intercept his craft with our tractor beams. If they all lose patience, we can't hold so many."

"Is that a possibility?"

"I've had several meetings with at least five of the ship's captains. They want to know what's going on. They have schedules to meet, rendezvous to keep. I've put them off as much as I can without actually telling them about the *Nekor*. All we need are more potential buyers."

"The best way to prevent that," said Odo, "is to apprehend the seller."

Not long after making this observation, he and Commander Sisko bent over a collection of glittering handcomps while their Ferengi owner jigged nervously from foot to foot, trying to get a glimpse of his property.

"Hey, be careful with those!" Quark protested. "They're not cheap, you know. Top of the line, that's all I use in Quark's Place. If you break anything—"

"If you don't shut up, I'll start by breaking your neck," Odo grumbled.

"Why did you want to see all my handcomps anyway?" Suspicion touched the Ferengi's mind. "Is it because of that kidnapping?"

"Shouldn't you be telling us?" Odo remarked.

Quark bridled; then his eye lit on the fan of flimsies on Odo's desktop. Weasel-fast and weasel-slick, he pounced on them before the shapeshifter could stop him. "What are these?" he exclaimed, holding them up to read. "Oh, ho! Now I see what you're after." He tossed the papers over his shoulder disdainfully. "You're wasting your time. None of *my* handcomps would print out these messages. They're the product of a machine so old, so

cheap, that no Ferengi with an ounce of self-respect
would use—use—" He slapped his own face as realization came. "Why, that overbought, undersold, son of
a—*Vung!*"

"Yes?" Vung said, glancing up from his meal at the
Replimat to see a ring of faces. Sisko, Odo, Quark, and
Kira glowered down at him. "Can I help you good
people?"

Quark seized Vung by the collar of his jacket and
hauled him to his feet. "Any last words before I shove
you into an airlock?"

Vung kicked and struggled, but Quark's grip was firm.
The taller Ferengi began to twist, sending Vung into a fit
of choking and gibbering. "You—you—you—*you'll
never find her if you kill me!*" he gasped.

Sisko intervened, breaking Quark's grip only to lay
hold of Vung himself. "Where is she?" he demanded.

"That—that depends." Vung made a great show of
brushing off the commander's hold as if it were dust. Free
to breathe once more, he regained his confidence rapidly.
"Are you asking as a serious buyer, or are you just
browsing?"

"Now look, you—!" Quark lunged for Vung again.
The shabby Ferengi flung himself out of reach, behind
Sisko.

"Ah, ah, ah!" he cautioned. "You won't get anywhere
that way. For once all the tiles are coming up with my
number on them. I'm not letting *this* opportunity get
away from me."

"Then how about if *this* gets away from you?" Quark
reached over and yanked the chain around Vung's neck.
A weak link snapped and the necklace came off in
Quark's fist. Vung uttered a cry of anguish and tried to
recover the chain, but Quark held it well out of his reach.
"Feel more like talking now?"

"If you don't give me that back, I'll *never* tell where the girl is!" Vung cried. "She can't move, she can't speak, and if I don't take care of her, she can't eat or drink. Without me, you couldn't find her unless you tripped over her." He looked smug enough to be believed.

"Give him his necklace back, Quark," Sisko directed.

"But—"

"Now." Reluctantly, Quark complied. Vung pocketed the broken chain with a condescending sniff. "All right, Vung," Sisko went on. "Take us to the child before anything happens to her and I give you my word, your case will be tried in a Federation court."

"Is that supposed to be an inducement to give up a fortune?" Vung asked.

"Idiot," Quark muttered. "The alternative's a Bajoran trial. What do you think the sentence will be for the fool who stole their *Nekor?*"

"A little less than the sentence on the moron who told me what's so valuable about a *Nekor* in the first place." Vung grinned at Quark. "Right, *partner?*"

"How dare you! I had nothing to do with this!"

"How will you prove that?"

"The girl knows who stole her."

"The girl isn't here." Vung's smile widened. "Could I interest you in a nice combination deal, old friend? A fat financial stake and safe passage to the Gamma Quadrant for me, an exonerating witness for you. I'll send you full instructions for locating the girl once my ship is well away. Interested?"

"He is *not,*" Odo said.

"Now, let's not be hasty, Constable," Quark temporized. To Vung he said, "How *reasonable* a stake did you have in mind?"

"Five hundred bars of gold-pressed latinum," Vung replied without blinking.

Quark clutched his chest and staggered backward,

right into the arms of his nephew Nog. The young Ferengi was accompanied by Jake and Cedra. "Uncle Quark, what's going on here?" he asked.

"That—that—that—" Quark wheezed, flapping his hand weakly at Vung. "That Romulan bloodsponge wants five hundred bars of gold-pressed latinum from me or he won't tell where he's hidden that blasted girl-child!"

Kira and Odo flanked the recalcitrant Vung. "You've had your fun with Quark," Odo said. "Now take us to Talis Dejana."

Vung folded his arms and said nothing.

"Damn you, if your moneygrubbing ways destroy Bajor, I'll—" Major Kira's hand rose, but a smaller hand closed around her wrist before she could strike the closemouthed Ferengi.

"There's no need," Cedra said quietly. He turned to Vung and held the startled Ferengi by the shoulders, bringing his face near enough to brush cheeks. He took a deep breath, then released his hold. "I thought so," he informed the puzzled observers. "Please come with me."

Commander Sisko found himself trotting after the young Bajoran, Major Kira and Jake behind him. Quark was still recuperating from shock, Nog in attendance, and Odo remained to take Vung into custody. The four of them threaded a strange dance through the corridors and levels of *Deep Space Nine,* coming to a halt at last in a dark corner of a disused runabout repair station.

"But we searched here!" Major Kira protested. "We searched everywhere."

Cedra ignored her objections. He was kneeling in the corner, whispering words of comfort. The darkness shifted, then shimmered and thinned as the bound and gagged body of Talis Dejana appeared.

"Here, hold this," Cedra ordered, shoving an unfamiliar object no larger than a comm badge into Sisko's hands. "That's why you couldn't see her when you searched in here." He removed the girl's gag and hugged her close, then began to work on freeing her hands and feet.

"But the sensors—!" Major Kira said.

Commander Sisko turned the object over and over in his hands. "A cloaking device?" he marvelled aloud. "So small, and yet . . ."

"How did you find her?" Kira asked Cedra.

The boy glanced up. "My sister's scent was on the Ferengi, but it was her smell mixed with the smell of this place. Jake showed me all around the station, so I recognized the scent. Once we were in here, she was easy to find."

"But that's not—" Kira began.

She did not get the chance to finish her thought. The object in Commander Sisko's hand started to hum. The hum rose to a low, menacing whine. Cedra sat up straight from his ongoing task of releasing Dejana from her bonds. "Get rid of it!" he shouted. "I didn't know the release code! Throw it away! Hurry!"

Major Kira snatched the device from Sisko's hands and threw it into a thickly walled container used to hold suspected unstable materials. Sisko scooped the still-bound Dejana from the floor and ran, the others after him. They were barely out of the repair bay when an explosion rocked the area.

"If the holy one has been found, why can't I see her?" Kejan Ulli demanded.

"The child has been through an ordeal," Vedek Torin said, standing beside Commander Sisko in the neutral territory of the shrine. "She needs her rest."

"An ordeal that need never have happened if you Federation people could do your jobs," the *Dessin-ka* agent accused, pointing a finger at Sisko.

"You can't blame Officer Tolland for not defending the *Nekor* against an enemy he couldn't see," Sisko responded. "The kidnapper somehow got hold of a miniature cloaking device. It shielded the wearer from detection, even by sensors. After the kidnapper had the child, he tranquilized her and transferred the device to her. He carried her right out of the infirmary with no one seeing a thing. He kept moving the child from one out-of-the-way hiding place to another. When he needed to present his demands, he risked leaving her hidden but uncloaked while he used the device on himself. That was why Chief O'Brien's sensor scans were so spotty. Once all the notes were delivered, he moved her one last time and left the device on her."

Kejan Ulli was unmollified. "Still you refuse to divulge the criminal's identity."

"He's in custody aboard a starship, in transit to the nearest Federation outpost, where he'll stand trial. The *Nekor* is safe. That should be enough for you."

"And where did he get that device, eh?"

"We don't know. He refused to say." *Leave it to a Ferengi to hold on to salable information,* Sisko thought. *Chief O'Brien almost went into mourning when he found out we had our hands on a piece of technology that powerful and we lost it. He couldn't tell much from the fragments, except that some of the components were Romulan-made.* "It self-destructed when Talis Dejana's brother detached it."

"How convenient."

Sisko's brows drew together. "What are you implying?"

"It would make your mission here so much easier if the *Nekor* remained in Federation hands, under Federation influence," Kejan Ulli said smoothly. "She would be your puppet, if not your hostage. No need to woo Bajoran sympathy when you can take it."

"The Federation doesn't take hostages," Sisko said

through clenched teeth. "And we don't try to rule member worlds through puppet leaders."

"Why should I trust you or your Federation?"

"We've given you our word: You will see the child when we agreed—in three days, on the eve of *Nis Thamar*. Can't the *Dessin-ka* wait even that long?"

"We can wait," Kejan Ulli returned. "Unless some other faction persuades the all-powerful Federation that the holy one should be their exclusive charge!"

"I can promise you, the Federation doesn't traffic in influence peddling," Sisko declared, but he saw the skepticism in Kejan Ulli's eyes even as he spoke.

"Might I say a word?" Vedek Torin said. He addressed Kejan Ulli. "If you cannot visit the child, no other representative of any Bajoran sect shall. I offer you this promise as a gesture of goodwill. I have the authority to control all travel permissions for those in orders who answer to the Temple. The keepers of the shrine must remain here, of course, but I will lay the strictest sanctions on them to keep themselves apart from the girl. When she is presented in the Temple, she shall come to us free of any influence."

"Any Bajoran influence." Kejan Ulli stared meaningly at Commander Sisko. "Well . . . it's better than nothing. Agreed."

"We shall depart at once," Vedek Torin said, happy to have kept the peace.

Commander Sisko strolled along the Promenade on his way back from the runabout pad. He felt at ease for the first time in a while. Having seen the last of Kejan Ulli had a lot to do with it.

He was browsing over a display of native Bajoran crafts when he heard ragged panting and the sound of running feet come up behind him. He turned just as Talis Cedra clutched his arm. Tears streamed down the boy's face.

"Commander, come! Come quickly!" he gasped, tugging at Sisko's arm.

"What's the matter, Cedra?" Visions of a prank gone wrong, of Jake in trouble on account of the mischievous Bajoran boy, flashed through his mind.

"No, no!" the boy said, shaking his head violently. "It's my sister! It's Dejana! She's dying!"

CHAPTER
13

"BELEM?" Dr. Bashir leaned over the feverish boy. "Belem, can you hear me?"

Belem's eyelids fluttered, but he did not seem to understand what was going on around him. He groaned, tossing his head from side to side, and muttered a stream of gibberish that ended in a series of escalating cries. His arms and legs flailed the air. Dr. Bashir tried to hold him down before his wild gyrations struck the cavern walls. There were enough scrapes on the boy's hands and arms to testify that these attacks were no new thing.

There had been more abrasions streaking Belem's skin when Borilak Selinn first brought Dr. Bashir into the hill fighters' cave stronghold. In the rocky chamber designated for the care of the sick and wounded, Belem's bedroll was set far apart from the rest. It was a shock to find the boy there, but not half so great as the shock of his condition. It took Dr. Bashir more than a second glance before he recognized his former assistant.

The old woman in charge of nursing the patients gave

195

Dr. Bashir a guilty stare when he stooped to examine Belem. Julian was willing to bet all he had that the crone kept the boy's care to a minimum. He couldn't blame her; fear of contagion was a phenomenon as mindless as it was universal.

All that Borilak Selinn said was "He named you," and left Dr. Bashir to his work. Days had passed since then, and the only change Julian noted was that more bedrolls appeared near Belem's; the fever was spreading. He dealt with these cases as they came in, and there was a notable improvement in the patients. Only Belem resisted treatment and grew worse.

Belem's convulsions subsided but did not vanish. Dr. Bashir took advantage of this lull to heal the new scrapes. The soft hiss of antiseptic and sealant was almost inaudible, yet it was loud enough to make Belem's eyes fly open abruptly. "Serpents!" he yelled. "Yellow-rings! They're crawling all over me! I feel their tongues!" He lashed out, knocking Dr. Bashir's instrument across the cavern.

Julian tried to immobilize the boy and got a fist in the eye for his troubles. Belem's skin was clammy, sweat streaming from every pore, and a thin, rancid smell rose from his soaked bedclothes. In all the cases of camp fever Dr. Bashir had treated, he had never encountered such violent symptoms. Every illness had its own rank perfume; this was different and he didn't know why.

A hand bearing a damp compress passed between Dr. Bashir and the boy. From the other side of Belem's bedroll, a doe-eyed young Bajoran woman stroked the cloth over the boy's brow. At the cooling touch, Belem's thrashing died down. His hollow chest heaved rapidly. Little by little, Julian withdrew his restraining hold. He sat back on his haunches, one hand to his injured eye. He met the young woman's gaze across the boy's body.

"No change, healer?" she asked.

Dr. Bashir rested his hands on his thighs and shook his head. "Nothing. I've given him the vaccine, but he doesn't seem to be responding to it."

The woman nodded. "I have heard of your miracle, healer. In the camps they called you blessed. Here too it works its magic. The others to whom you gave it all recover quickly." She looked at Belem and sighed.

"I'm not doing any more than my job," Bashir said. He too looked at Belem, who had fallen into a fitful doze. "And apparently, I'm not even doing that." He slammed a fist into his palm. "Why doesn't it *work* on him? Even if they damaged the bioreplicator, I still have fresh vaccine loaded in my injectors. I made a point of reloading them before leaving the last camp. I cured the others with shots from the same batch I used on Belem. Why isn't *he* getting well?"

The woman reached out to lay a soft, capable hand on Dr. Bashir's arm. "The Prophets have granted you knowledge and compassion, but they have not made you more than you are. Do not seek to drive yourself beyond the limits they have decreed. Come." She stood up and offered him her hand. "He is resting now. You should eat while you can, and I should get you something to put on that eye."

Bashir glanced at Belem again. The boy was breathing regularly, with a disquieting wheeze, but at least he was not suffering delirium for the moment. "That's a good idea," he admitted. Her answering smile lit the darkness of the cavern as he got to his feet and accepted her handclasp.

It was a gesture of necessity rather than friendship, although he wished it were the other way around. Whenever he left the precincts of the infirmary, he was always taken by the hand and guided through the underground labyrinth that was Borilak Selinn's domain. The twisting passageways with their multiply branching tunnels had an exotic beauty that fascinated Dr. Bashir. Luminous stone columns and frozen waterfalls of ageless rock, slick with the eternal drip of seeping water, all made him think of the tales of lost fairylands he had read when very young.

Fairyland . . . he mused, gazing at the bowed head of his lovely guide. *And a princess of the Fair Folk to lead me.*

Then he remembered the whole of those stories: The mortal who stumbled into the enchanted underground realm never returned to the light of day again, or only returned to die.

If I tried to find my way out of here by myself, I would die, Dr. Bashir thought. *Borilak Selinn took care to lead me up, down, and sideways all the way in, and I'm never allowed to explore. I sleep in a rocky niche overlooking their infirmary and that old hag brings me anything I need.* He smiled as a turn in the path took them past a glowing oil lamp that illuminated the young woman's delicate face. *Almost anything. If you're taking charge of things in the infirmary so Mother can have a day off, I hope she gets to take a permanent vacation.*

Dr. Bashir's guide led him to a grotto that he had visited only once before. She paused on the way to pick up the makings of a meal in a naturally cold larder among the rocks. The hill fighters' food was crude and scant rations, but Dr. Bashir was relieved to discover that their water supply was an underground spring of remarkable purity. He and the woman sat beside the gurgling pool of water, under a bower of glistening yellow stone. His teeth fought a losing battle with the strips of dried meat she gave him, and the bread was even harder than what he'd tasted at the first refugee camp. She hid her giggles behind her hand as he struggled to work a chewable piece loose.

"You must be hungry," she said. "You aren't even waiting for the broth." She hurried away and was back swiftly, carrying two steaming bowls. Expertly she shredded his portion of dried meat into the bowl of hot broth, then broke off bits of bread and added them as well before handing the whole thing back to a sheepish Julian.

"Well . . . I *am* hungry," he admitted. He ate; it tasted good. He recalled the days when his father would brag to his diplomat associates about young Julian's taste for only the finest cuisine. The right words from his father's lips transformed picky eating into a virtue, but using the right words was all part of a diplomat's task. Julian wondered what his father would say if he could see him now, eagerly sopping up a brigand's brew.

At least he couldn't fault me the company, he thought, gazing at the Bajoran woman. She ate daintily, without fuss. *Take her out of that tattered shirt and trousers, put her in a fashionable gown, and she could grace any embassy's table.*

"I want to thank you for helping me with Belem," he said softly. "I should have thought of that remedy myself, but—"

"You want to think of everything," she replied; her words carried no criticism. "That is the fire in your *pagh*. Like all fires, it transforms dull wood into a gift of light, heat, beauty, but it also can consume." She bent her head over the bowl in her lap. A webwork of innumerable black braids encircled her head like a gleaming crown. "Keep the light, healer. Turn back from the devouring flame."

He dared to slip his fingertips beneath her chin and make her look into his eyes. "My name is Julian," he told her.

She smiled and did not resist his touch. "You are wise, Julian. If you are called only Healer, you will think that is all you must be." Gently she pushed his hand away. "I am Borilak Jalika."

"The troll-king had a beautiful daughter," Julian murmured to himself. To Jalika's inquiring glance he responded, "Nothing. I was just thinking of an old story."

Embarrassed at being caught in one of his fancies, he changed the subject: "Are you Borilak Selinn's daughter, or—?" *Not his wife!* he prayed.

"Yes, I am his daughter." She reached into her pocket and produced a clean, folded cloth. "And now let us see whether my remedy will also work on your eye."

"I'm sorry our paths haven't crossed earlier," he said as she applied the compress to his face. "You have a natural instinct for healing."

She laughed. "You think you flatter me, but you speak truer than you know. I have more than instinct: I was trained in the Temple. I was to have entered a healing order, but my father sent word that he needed me more." She set the compress down and looked wistful. "I should have been Vedek Jalika by now."

"Didn't you just tell me that what we're called can imprison us?" Julian asked. He wished there were some way he could get her to reapply the cold cloth. The touch of her fingers on his face filled him with longing.

"You are clever." Her lashes were thick and sooty, bright eyes captivating him with a sideways glance. "Father warned me about clever men."

Julian raised one hand as if taking an oath. "I swear I'll be as dense as a rock if you'll like me better for it."

"You have brought healing to us," she answered. "How could I not like you?"

Julian's face fell. He had been hoping for a different sort of declaration. "I didn't have much choice in the matter," he said. "Your father and his men brought me here. I ought to be on the road, bringing the fever vaccine to other camps."

"You are here because Belem asked for you," Jalika told him. "When he was well, he used to help me take care of our sick. He spoke of you often and he told me how you mended his leg. He respected my skills as a healer, but he made it very plain that I was nowhere near as talented as you."

"I'll have to have a few words with him about courtesy when he gets better," Julian joked. *If he gets better.* He didn't care to admit it, but he had his doubts about that.

"He said that you were seeking a cure for the fever that was ravaging his old home. He was certain you'd find it; there was nothing you could not do, according to him. Soon after Belem joined us, we began to get word of a man—a man who wore the uniform of Starfleet—who traveled from camp to camp curing the sick, conquering the fever, bringing help and then disappearing. Belem heard the descriptions and said it was you. My father was impressed."

"Impressed enough to have me kidnapped," Julian remarked.

The crystals adorning Jalika's earring tinkled as she shook her head. "He would never have done it for that reason alone. The camps needed you more; I was enough to look after our people's health. Then Belem fell ill. At first he swore it was not the camp fever. He had already had it, he said, and he recovered on his own. Is that possible?"

"Yes; I've seen several cases like that in my travels. There doesn't seem to be any common factor for cases of spontaneous recovery—not age, not sex, not even previous physical condition. The initial case I saw was a little girl, eight years old, in the first camp I visited."

"Maybe Belem will cast off the sickness on his own this time, too." Jalika tried to sound hopeful. "May the Prophets will it." She sighed. "My father refused to believe it was not the camp fever. He had heard reports of how devastating that could be, and he wanted it out of our midst as soon as possible. He recalled how highly Belem praised you, and he had word of your accomplishments. Do you wonder that he set out to find you and bring you here?"

"I wonder what he thinks of my accomplishments

now," Dr. Bashir said somberly. He picked up his empty bowl and stood. "I'd better get back to Belem."

Jalika rose to her feet, took his bowl from him, and stacked it on top of hers. "I'll take you. You'd never be able to find your own way."

As they wandered back through the twists and turns of the caverns, Julian asked, "You still haven't answered my question: Why haven't I seen you before this? If you worked as a healer, why aren't you in the infirmary now?"

"Father," came the terse reply. "He fears for my health. He claims that old Merab Jis can manage the infirmary without me." A half-smile came to her lips. "He did not forbid me to *visit* the infirmary, only to work there. And today he is away."

"Where has he gone?" Julian asked.

"Down out of the mountains. We need fresh supplies." Her voice was strained. Julian could guess at the methods Berilak Selinn and his followers used to obtain supplies, and he could tell that this knowledge was a source of deep shame to the man's lovely daughter.

"When he returns, I want you to tell him something for me," Dr. Bashir said. "The same injection that cures victims of camp fever also protects against contracting the disease in the first place. If he'll give me space where I can set up my equipment, I can manufacture enough vaccine to immunize all of you. That's what I've been doing in the camps."

"If there were no more danger of infection, Father would have to let me return to my work. Oh, *would* you?" Jalika's clasped her hands, beseeching.

"No reason why I wouldn't. If everyone here is immunized, then perhaps I can convince your father that he has no further need of me."

"But . . . Belem—"

Julian's hands closed tightly over Jalika's. "I promise you I won't abandon him."

"You will heal him, Julian." Jalika's eyes shone. "I know you will heal him."

"I don't see how he did it," Major Kira said to Lieutenant Dax, resting her hand on the back of the Trill's seat in Ops. "I do *not* see how Cedra managed to find his sister while she was hidden by that miniature cloaking device."

"I thought he explained all that," Dax replied. "Her scent—"

Kira snorted. "If there ever was a Bajoran who could follow a scent trail that subtle, that stale, for that far, we wouldn't need to breed *tokkas* to track fugitive criminals."

"I've seen stranger things," Dax said.

"I'll bet you have."

"So you think it was another of Cedra's pranks?"

Major Kira took a deep breath. "How can I think of it as a prank when it saved his sister's life—and so much more? Why should I care if the boy lied to us? He found Dejana, that's the only thing that ought to count. But it still leaves me with a funny feeling . . ." She twisted up her mouth. "Why do I feel so guilty for suspecting Cedra of trickery?"

"Probably because the boy's so distraught right now. He and his sister are as close as twins."

"When you go through so much with another person, it makes you grow closer, even if you're not related to start with. Sometimes it gets to the point where you don't know how you'll survive if anything should happen to your—your other half." Major Kira spoke as if inspired by memory, not theory—a memory at once personal and painful. She shook off her ghosts and asked Dax, "Any sign the girl's getting better?"

"No. The opposite's truer, sad to say. I've taken biosamples from the child, run tests, and come up with no answers."

"You're baffled?" Kira was amazed. "You mean there's no information you've gathered from any of your lives that can help?"

"I was always drawn to science, but that doesn't mean I concentrated on medicine. If I had, I'd be Dr. Dax. I never wanted to limit my studies by specialization." She gave Kira a rueful smile. "For all of my precious scientific knowledge, it was Dr. Bashir who found the cure for the camp fever."

"It's Dr. Bashir who should be here now," Kira muttered.

"I thought you were the one who was so proud of him for taking his medicine to the people?"

"There are people who need him here, too. If anything happens to the *Nekor*—" She didn't want to think of that eventuality. "I thought the child only had a cold. What happened?"

"I thought the same; all the signs pointed that way. As near as I can tell, in its first stages the illness she's contracted mimics the symptoms of the common cold. Then, when Dejana's resistance was lowered by all she went through during Vung's kidnap attempt, the disease bloomed."

"The disease?" Kira echoed. "Doesn't it have a name?"

"If I had a name to attach to it, I'd have a treatment. I've run all the data through the computer and come up blank. The symptoms she's showing now could belong to any one of dozens of illnesses, but the microorganisms in her blood don't match any of them. I ordered her put on wide-spectrum antibiotics and antivirals, but it's only a stopgap." Dax looked her Bajoran friend full in the face. "I'm afraid we're losing her."

"We *can't* lose her." If passion could cure Dejana, Major Kira's would do so in an instant.

"Agreed. But we can't save her; not without help. There must be medical personnel on Bajor who—"

Kira threw up her hands. "Impossible. Vedek Torin's kept his word to Kejan Ulli even better than promised: There's to be no commerce between DS9 and Bajor until the eve of *Nis Thamar*. No one's objected because it's less than two days away." She shuddered and repeated, "Less than two days."

Dax stood up. "We need Dr. Bashir."

"How did you ever manage this, Jalika?" Dr. Bashir stood on the outthrust crag overlooking the Kaladrys Valley and let the cool evening wind scour his face. It felt good to breathe air that did not reek of dampness and stone. "How did you ever convince your father to let me out?"

The Bajoran woman looked up from the thicket of scrub where she knelt beside a small reed basket, her lips curving up sweetly. "It was simple, Julian. I told him that if your Federation medicine alone could not heal Belem, perhaps it might work better coupled with some of the herb lore I learned while in the Temple. I have his permission to teach you the healing uses of our Bajoran plants."

He could not resist returning that enchanting smile. "Alone?"

"Does that surprise you?"

"No guards," he pointed out.

"What need do we have for guards?" she replied with a casual toss of her head. "None of father's men are interested in herb lore or healing, and they have enough to do elsewhere. Besides, I don't need nursemaids."

Julian squatted on his heels. "Isn't your father afraid I might try to escape?"

Jalika moved a few feet to one side, her back to Julian. "On foot? Without equipment, supplies, even a map? You would be very easy to catch."

He recognized that what she said was true. He had known it from the moment she came to him with the offer of a brief respite from the caverns. Still, he felt like teasing her, if only to make her pay some attention to him. He wondered if there was some way he could work his prowess as a Starfleet Medical prodigy into the conversation. Failing that, he urgently needed to impress her somehow.

"I could—" he said, rising soundlessly and beginning to edge toward her. "I could find my way. I've grown familiar with the hill country, and only a fool wouldn't know you reach a valley by going *down* a mountain. Once I'm down there again, I know the territory. I could find my way to a friendly camp. They know I'm their ally."

"Ally," the woman repeated with a little laugh. "Their legend, you mean."

"They would provide me with whatever I needed—if it was theirs to give," he said. His talk was all air, and he knew it. Despite the easy confidence with which he outlined his grand plan of escape, he knew that there was more to finding a way out of these mountains than merely tumbling downslope like a rockslide. Still, he had to make her believe he was the equal of his own legend. "They'd even give me a new *verdanis*. I could gallop away in a cloud of—"

"Aren't you afraid that I'll tell all this to my father?" Jalika responded, still not turning around. Her hands grubbed in the rocky soil, uprooting a brambly green shoot and laying it in her basket. "Then he'll never let you out of the caverns again."

Julian crept nearer, his feet making no sound. Not even a pebble was dislodged as he came nearer and nearer to the apparently preoccupied young woman. "Then perhaps I shouldn't return to the caverns at all," he murmured. He rested his hand on the trunk of a wind-twisted tree. "And perhaps, when I go, I should make sure that your father doesn't try to follow—"

The beam of energy sang through the air, shearing off a dusty green twig just inches from his fingertips. "Pick that up, will you, healer?" Jalika requested demurely, placing the phaser back in her belt. "If you brew the needles with *hasva* root it stops fever visions."

"Does it." Julian fetched the twig, a wary eye on Jalika. "It certainly cut down *my* illusions." He brought her the twig and maintained a rigid silence for the rest of their time on the mountainside.

The light was mostly gone from the sky by the time she led him back into the caverns. The guards on duty and the other folk who shared the underground warren observed the two of them closely, but said nothing. He noticed that this time, she conducted him back to the infirmary by a route so direct it would be simple to retrace.

The old woman, Merab Jis, came bustling up to greet them with her wide, almost toothless smile. "The Prophets praise your name, healer," she enthused, her gnarled hands shaking. "Hardly a bed remains occupied here, and no new sickness comes in."

"No more will," Julian responded. "No camp fever cases, at any rate." He patted the old woman's shoulder and said, "You were a very great help to me, taking the inoculation first in front of all the others."

Merab became as flustered as a maiden. "Oh, healer, I did nothing!"

"You were *very brave*," Julian insisted. "Half the struggle with a vaccine is getting the patients to take it."

"Some of these men, yes." Merab sniffed. "All talk about how bold they are, but not a one would let you tend to them until they saw *me* receive the treatment with no harm done."

"Precisely what I've been saying." Julian had become far better friends with the old woman since Jalika's appearance. He wasn't sure whether Merab hoped to impress her leader's daughter by cultivating the healer or whether he himself was working it the other way around. He stole a peek at Jalika, who was surveying the nearly empty infirmary and paying no attention to either of them.

"Borilak Selinn himself was here to inspect our efforts," Merab continued, "and he was pleased. That is—" She cast an uneasy glance toward Belem's place apart.

"Soon we will give my father no cause for displeasure, Merab," Jalika reassured the crone, showing her the contents of her basket. "Bring me some freshly boiling water—draw it from the spring itself, mind!—and we will see if that may do some good."

The old woman bobbed her head and scuttled away. Jalika led the way to the cozy side cavern where Julian had set up his equipment. Here she appropriated a mortar and proceeded to strip the needles from the twig she had so dramatically harvested. "You only need to bruise the needles," she explained while she worked. "Just enough to encourage the release of the aromatic oils. If you crush them, too much of the essence is lost. Here." She passed Julian the mortar and pestle. "I need to prepare the *hasva* root."

He watched her as she cleaned and slivered the spidery root end of the shoot she had dug from the mountain earth. She worked with a cool, professional expertise that even Selok of Vulcan might have approved of. The thought of his old teacher passing judgment on this flower-faced Bajoran woman twisted Julian's mouth into a peculiar mix of skepticism and amusement.

Jalika caught him staring at her that way. "What is it, healer?" she asked. "Am I doing something wrong?"

"That's not for me to say," he replied. "After all, you're the one in charge now."

"In that case, why have you stopped working?" She nodded toward the idle pestle in his hand.

"Oh . . . I was just thinking of someone I used to know."

"Someone—special to you?"

"You might say that."

"Ah." Her lashes lowered. She chopped the root more briskly.

"I was thinking that he'd like you . . . as far as it's possible for a Vulcan to *like* anyone."

"He?" she repeated, raising her eyes suddenly, then looking away before Julian could read their expression. "I thought—I thought that when you said you were thinking of someone *special,* you meant . . ." Her voice trailed off.

He understood. "No." He worked the pestle carefully, mashing the needles just enough so that a clean, heady fragrance filled the small cave. "There's no one like that—no one special—for me."

She made a sound of acknowledgment.

"And you?" he asked.

"None." The slivers and threads of *hasva* root were chopped almost to dust under the edge of her knife. "When we enter the Temple to study healing, we make a promise: Until we have mastered the art with hands, heart, and *pagh,* we must regard all others equally as vessels to receive healing or sources to teach us. There is no room for anything else in our lives."

"Good Lord, that's Starfleet Medical!" Julian blurted. Then he added, "My training was like that, too. At first, that is. No time for any sort of social life, just study, study, study—although I *was* very good at it," he said hastily, seeing his chance and pouncing on it. "Did you know I was second in my class? If I only hadn't incorrectly identified a postganglionic—"

"Why must that matter to us here?" Jalika asked quietly.

Julian stood slack-jawed. Her soft words stung like a slap across the face. His mouth snapped shut. "I suppose it doesn't makes a difference," he said curtly. "Except when I'm trying to make a damned fool of myself. Now *there's* a function of the postganglionic nerve we never covered."

Meticulously she brushed the powdered root into a small wooden bowl and set it aside before taking the mortar from his hands. "You are no fool, healer."

"Kind of you to say so," he said stiffly. "Even if only to spare my feelings. You needn't bother; I've been put in my place by other beautiful women before this."

"Beautiful?" Her lips scarcely moved over the word.

"Here is the water!" Merab Jis bustled in, carrying a steaming pot. She set it down on the table between them. "What else shall I do?"

"That is all for now, thank you," Jalika replied.

"Well, if I'm not needed here, I think I'll go have a little nap. You *will* call on me if I'm wanted, won't you, healer?" she simpered at Julian.

He called up a smile just for her. "You know I will." After he was sure she was gone, he addressed Jalika once more: "Listen, I'm sorry if I've embarrassed you. Before, when we were outside gathering plant samples, you gave me the message loud and clear."

"What message?"

He pointed at her belt where the phaser was partly visible. "I have been known to take *no* for an answer. You might have to slam my head against the wall a few times, but I do catch on. Ask Lieutenant Dax, if you ever have the chance to meet her."

"Who is Lieutenant Dax? Is she also . . . beautiful?"

"Lieutenant Dax is . . . unique."

"You are fond of her." Jalika's face was unreadable.

"We're friends. Or so she's stressed." He couldn't help chuckling. "I suppose a fondness for beautiful women is my worst fault, if you'd call it a fault at all."

"I would." Her vehemence startled him. "If their beauty is all that draws you to them, then with respect, healer, it is a fault indeed."

Julian lost all pretense of good humor. "Is that what they taught you in the Temple along with healing? How to sit in judgment on others?"

Borilak Selinn's daughter took a precise portion of the powdered *hasva* root and added it to the broken needles. "They teach us to judge ourselves and others by the measure of the Prophets. For them there are no externals, only deeds done and their causes. You must see both, healer. To weigh the deed without the cause is to open the eyes to darkness."

"I think it's not too hard to see why you used that phaser out there," Julian said, his eyes hard. "Maybe you should open your eyes as well and understand how I really see you. You *are* beautiful, Jalika—I can't deny it and I can't help how it makes me feel—but I see more than beauty when I look at you. When I work, it's like the way you described your Temple studies: There are no beautiful women, no distractions, only the patients who need me. When you came to help me with Belem and the others, all that entered my mind was gratitude and admiration for your skill and kindness. Now, because I've behaved like an idiot—*again*—I'm afraid I'll drive you away. Please don't go. I need you here. If I promise not to bother you anymore, will you—?"

She looked away from him sharply, her face hidden by a tumble of tiny braids that had come loose from their securing pins.

"What have I done wrong now?" Julian asked.

"I am the one who has done wrong," she replied, her voice thick. "You are right: I should listen to my own lectures. I have not judged you by what you truly are, but by my own measure." One hand clasped the wooden bowl, the other let the boiling water trickle over the mixed herbs.

Jalika watched the fragrant steam rise. "As soon as I heard that Father had brought you here, I wanted to observe you, to see how you worked your miracles, and whether I could pick up some secret to add to my own knowledge. When Father was busy elsewhere, I stole to a gallery overlooking the infirmary. I saw you at work, and at first the work was all I saw. I came back many times."

"Jalika, look at me," he urged. At first she would not, but gradually she complied. "You said that *at first* the work was all you saw. Did that—did that change?"

"I—" she began.

He laid a finger to her lips. "The truth. Please."

"To begin, I came because I was curious. All the stories I had heard about you, your kindness, your devotion—I did not think they could be true. I returned because the stories *were* true and—and—" The dim light of the cave and the wisps of steam could not hide the color rising to her face.

"Thank you." Julian took her hand away from the bowl and raised it to his cheek. "You needn't say any more."

"I am ashamed," she said, shaking her head. "I returned because it stirred my heart to see you. On the mountainside, I wanted to do something—something *different*—something that would make you notice me as more than just the one who helps you here. I wanted you to know that I can be strong, that I can be as—as *unique* as your Lieutenant Dax." She bowed her head. "And I wanted you to know that for me, you too are . . . beautiful."

He drew her nearer. "And you are more than beautiful to me," he breathed. "More than I hoped, more than I knew a woman could ever—oh, *much* more." His fingers traced the soft curve of her cheek and he kissed her.

Jalika was the first to break the embrace. She looked into the wooden bowl as if trying to read the future in its swirling depths. "This is a dream. The Prophets guide you when you heal, Julian. With their help, you will cure Belem. And then . . . you will leave us."

"If I do leave, it will be the hardest thing I've ever done. But would you want me to stay if it meant Belem would never get well?"

"You could stay on after Belem was well." She melted back into his arms. "I could ask my father never to let you go."

His arms slipped around her slender waist. "You know it would be wrong to keep me here. I must go. There are other camps, other places where the children need my help."

"I know." A sigh tore from her body. He pressed his cheek to her hair and inhaled its sweet, spicy perfume.

"I can come back," he whispered. "I can, and I will."

In the commander's office, Benjamin Sisko heard Lieutenant Dax's strong personal recommendation for dispatching a search party to the surface of Bajor. Major Kira stood attentively nearby.

"I'm ahead of you, Dax," he replied. "With the long-range sensors back on-line, a search won't be necessary. Chief O'Brien can locate the doctor through his individual life-sign readings. We'll have him back aboard and working on Talis Dejana's case before the day is out. In fact, I've already dispatched a runabout to bring him in. Chief O'Brien is running the scan from Ops and I was about to meet him there. Would you care to join me?"

Kira and Dax accepted the invitation with enthusiasm. The three of them were heading for Ops when they passed the entrance to the schoolroom just in time to hear a resounding crash.

"What the—?" Sisko bolted into the class and found Talis Cedra and Jake in the center of a ring of smashed school equipment. The other children huddled in a crowd around Keiko. Jake had his arms encircling Cedra, trying to hold the Bajoran back. It was no easy task. Cedra kicked, squirmed, and struggled madly, spewing curses. Another Bajoran boy lay on his back in the middle of the disaster area, his nose bloody, face bruised, and the start of a black eye already visible.

Commander Sisko took hold of Cedra's arm, relieving Jake. "What's the meaning of this?"

"Thank goodness you came, Commander," Keiko O'Brien said, coming forward. "Cedra has been difficult since his sister fell ill, but I tried to take the situation into account. This was the last straw."

"What happened here?"

"A fight over nothing. Rys Kalben's handcomp was malfunctioning, so he asked Cedra if he could borrow his. He reached for it without waiting for an answer. That was what set the boy off."

"It's *my* handcomp!" Cedra shouted, trying to writhe free of Sisko's grip. "Everything that's ever mine gets taken away, and I'm sick of it! And no one cares. *No one!* Not even now, when my sister's being taken away from me too." He swung a fist at Sisko, who bent away from the blow and easily avoided it. Cedra began to cry.

Sisko put his arms around the sobbing child. "We do care, Cedra," he said. "We're going to take care of your sister. We've got the means to bring back Dr. Bashir; he'll help her, you'll see."

Cedra wiped his nose on the back of his hand. "I want to come," he announced.

Sisko saw no harm in it. In view of the recent uproar, Keiko decided that an early dismissal might not be a bad idea, so Jake too was free to accompany his father to Ops.

"Do you have a reading on him, Chief?" Sisko asked as soon as they entered the room.

"That I do," O'Brien replied, directing his commander to see for himself. "Give the word and he'll be here as soon as I relay the readings to McCormick aboard the *Rio.*"

Sisko looked at the sensor readings. His smile faded. "What's this fluctuation?"

"Minor, sir. For some reason, Dr. Bashir appears to have gotten himself well below the surface of the planet with a good-sized thickness of rock between him and the open air, don't ask me why."

"That won't affect retrieval, will it?" Sisko asked.

O'Brien shook his head emphatically. "Not a bit, sir, but it is why we're relying on the station sensors instead of the runabout's system. They're more sophisticated and accurate."

"Very well, then; proceed."

O'Brien hailed the *Rio*. "McCormick, lock on to Dr. Bashir's life-sign coordinates."

"Got him, sir," came McCormick's voice.

"Energize."

There was a pause that lengthened uncomfortably. Then McCormick's voice came again: "It's no good, sir. I can't retrieve him."

"Why the hell not?" O'Brien barked. "Is it the transporter or the sensors that's kicking up now?"

"Neither, sir. The sensor relay works perfectly; so does the transporter. The trouble is when we try to use 'em both at the same time. I lock on to Dr. Bashir's life-sign readings, but when I try to energize the transporter, the signal slips. Do you think maybe it was something we did to the system while we were repairing the sensors?"

O'Brien smacked his hand down hard on the control panel. "Blasted Cardie piece of—! And blast *me* for a brainless idiot. Why didn't I think to check that?" He turned to Commander Sisko.

"Can't you locate Dr. Bashir, disengage the sensors, and retrieve him from his last known coordinates?"

"I wouldn't care to risk that, sir," O'Brien said. "You might get him, pretty as you please. If he's sleeping or standing still there'd be no question. But what if he moves between location and transportation?"

Cedra nudged Jake. "What could happen then?"

"Either we'd miss him altogether or else only the part

of him left at the old coordinates would be transported," Jake whispered. "So if he took a step but one foot was still—"

"Yuck."

"If the difficulty's with the relayed sensor signal, have McCormick use the runabout's own sensor system," Sisko directed.

O'Brien held a short conference with his man aboard the *Rio*. "No good, sir. The runabout's system would work like a charm if Dr. Bashir were on the surface of the planet, but since he's chosen to burrow in like that—" He snorted. "What the devil ever possessed the man . . ."

"How long will it take you to correct this problem?" Sisko asked.

O'Brien looked unhappy. "Too long, sir." He knew of Talis Dejana's condition and his heart ached for the child.

"But there *is* no problem," Cedra piped up suddenly. "We don't need to worry. Dr. Bashir is coming back." Four puzzled faces stared at him. Cedra only smiled.

In a cold cavern on Bajor, Belem took a breath, released it, and died.

CHAPTER
14

JALIKA THREADED HER WAY over the stepping-stones bridging an underground stream. She found Julian, as she knew she would, under a spray of rock the shape and color of a willow's trailing curtain of branches.

"He is looking for you," she said.

Julian raised his head. His eyes were red and the marks of tears were still evident on his face. "Why didn't you bring him here with you?"

She settled herself beside him on a cold outcropping of stone. "This place is mine. I choose who shares it." She took his hand. "Are you prepared?"

"I have nothing to hide, nothing to be ashamed of. Why must I prepare?"

"He will make terrible accusations against you."

A humorless smile curved Dr. Bashir's lips. "Is that necessary? Can't he simply order my execution?"

"Here such decisions of life or death must be made with the agreement of all. So the Prophets have taught us. Father leads by consent. He never tires of telling me that

217

his powers of persuasion won him his place and keep it for him. It is true; I have seen it to be true. He has yet to ask something of our people that they have refused him." Her fingers dug into Dr. Bashir's flesh. "Julian, I am afraid for you."

He kissed her lightly on the cheek. "Don't be." He stood and stretched until his hands brushed the damp, shiny curve of pale green stone overhead. "Let's go."

Jalika conducted Dr. Bashir to a part of the caverns he had never seen before. Here there were higher, wider, more open spaces in the rock, huge chambers hollowed by the hand of nature from the living mountain. Cressets of oil burned in metal holders, but in some places the stone itself gave off an eerie glow that provided light enough for human sight. Dr. Bashir thought he could have gazed on so much beauty forever.

"Up here," Jalika said, turning aside from the great hall of stone yawning before them. She took him up a winding way where rocky inclines lay slippery underfoot in spite of scatterings of dirt laid down for traction. Where the water ran most heavily, the dirt quickly melted into mud, making the way even more treacherous than before. A pickax had bitten handholds out of the walls, and Dr. Bashir clung to them gratefully. Jalika's graceful form seemed to dance up the narrow ramp ahead of him, her tiny feet sure as if they moved over carpet instead of slick stone.

They emerged on a platform high above the floor of the huge cavern chamber. It was a natural balcony, though without railings or any barrier to keep an incautious visitor from missing a step and plummeting from the little lip of rock to the stone so far below. Dr. Bashir did not suffer from a fear of heights, but even he felt better standing with the wall to his back, as far from the edge of the precipice as he could get.

Borilak Selinn had no such need for security. The hill fighter chief stood between two of his burliest warriors, a pace from the edge. Jalika's father was no longer dressed in the utilitarian shirt and trousers he and all the cavern dwellers favored; now he wore robes, faded and old yet steeped in an air of grim formality. His escorts, too, were clad in ceremonial garb and the phasers at their sides were accompanied by swords. Such weapons would be useless in the confines of the cavern tunnels; their purpose was to impress, not defend. Looking at those three awaiting him, Dr. Bashir could not deny the gravity of his situation.

A low rumble came from the chamber beneath the stone balcony. Dr. Bashir took a few tentative steps nearer the brink and saw the hall filling with people. When the influx dwindled to a trickle, Borilak Selinn faced the massed crowd and raised both hands high for silence.

Dr. Bashir did not understand a word of the hill fighter chief's first speech to his followers. The intonation was Bajoran, but the words were alien. For the first time he regretted that he no longer wore his comm badge, with its accompanying translation capabilities.

"It is the old tongue," Jalika said softly. "Father was a scholar in the capitol, before the Cardassians killed his family. He too was supposed to have entered service in the Temple. Instead he joined the Resistance."

"Couldn't he have returned to his studies after the Cardassians were expelled?" Bashir asked, still listening to Borilak Selinn's oration. He was almost certain he could understand some of the antiquated words now. The Bajoran way of saying *treachery* had changed remarkably little between the old tongue and the new.

"He wanted to," Jalika said. "But when the provisional government was established, he felt betrayed. There are interests now represented in the council that dealt willingly with the Cardassians. He wants the government purified, for the sake of all those who died during the occupation."

"Your father is a man of ideals," Julian commented.

"Someone should tell him that he'd accomplish more to advance his cause if he borrowed a little practicality. If he shuns the provisional government completely, he misses the chance to affect it. He hasn't enough followers to overthrow it directly and he knows it, or he wouldn't be lurking in the hills. If his knowledge and powers of persuasion are half as impressive as you say, he ought to bring them to the capitol and put them to work where they might do much good."

Jalika sighed. "He does not believe that his efforts can achieve anything indirectly."

"Ah." Julian felt a passing qualm—nothing he could put a reason behind. Before he could ponder it, Borilak Selinn finished his formal opening exhortation and returned to the common language.

"The healer Bashir is accused of the death of our brother, Borilak Belem," he said. The words broke over Bashir's head like a thunderclap.

"Borilak—?" he whispered to Jalika. "But Belem had no family name . . ."

"Father knew. He gave him ours when the boy joined us." Her hand stole into his. "He had no son, Julian."

Her father saw her take the doctor's hand. His scowl was terrifying and his tone grew even more fierce. "Who here does not know the trust and duty of a healer?" he demanded of his followers. "That his gifts be shared without prejudice or measure among all who come to him for aid. You have all witnessed the effects of this man's gifts. The fever of which we heard, the fever which we so feared sought us out in spite of our seclusion. Many of you burned with it, many of you would have died of it." He wheeled to point a finger at Dr. Bashir. "You know this man! You knew him long before he came among us. The same tales that came from the camps where our brethren suffer—the tales of the wasting fever without a cure—these tales soon changed from cries of despair to prayers of hope because of this man!"

"Whose case is your father pleading?" Julian whispered to Jalika. "He sounds like he's taken my side."

"Wait," Jalika said, miserable.

"How did Commander Sisko ever get talked into this?" Odo muttered as he and Major Kira climbed the mountain slope, scrambling to keep up with Cedra. "This is not the place for a child."

"Cedra disagreed," the liaison officer responded. "He can be very convincing when he wants to be. Commander Sisko started out against the boy coming with us; then before you knew it, he gave his approval. He had to: Cedra's plan for bringing Dr. Bashir back once we find him won't work without Cedra."

Odo snorted. "Why do we need any sort of plan in the first place? Once we find the doctor, you deliver Commander Sisko's orders for his return. Unless you think he'll disobey a direct command?"

"He's too good a Starfleet officer for that." Kira pushed her way through the bush. "And he's too good a doctor. When he hears we need him back aboard to save Talis Dejana's life, he'll come; that's not the problem. It's making sure he stays put once he's healed her."

"You don't expect him to do that?"

"No, to be honest, I don't. You've never seen a refugee camp, Odo. You've never seen the children who are forced to live there. Neither had Dr. Bashir. Lieutenant Dax told me all about how shocked he was, and how he threw himself into his work—one man trying to right the biggest injustice he'd ever seen. If that was you, would you be able to turn your back on a job that was less than half-finished?"

"Yet you say he would never disobey orders," Odo reminded her.

"Have you noticed, Odo? There's no order so direct, so specific, that a determined person can't reinterpret it to suit his own purposes." She gave him a meaningful look.

221

Odo became uneasy. "That was—it was vital to solving the case. Besides, it was a single incident that happened long ago. I did not disobey—"

"Sure you didn't." Kira's smile was there and gone. "But you do see what I mean about Dr. Bashir." Odo grumped something unintelligible and continued to toil up the slope.

"Anyway," Kira went on, "it doesn't look like our doctor's in a situation where we can just walk in, give him his orders, and walk out again. There are reports of political splinter groups in this area—former Resistance fighters who don't support the provisional government. No one's exactly sure of their affiliations. The council treats them all as potential subversives."

"With a warm welcome like that waiting for them I'm surprised they don't come streaming out of the hills" was Odo's acerbic comment. "And where do they stand on the question of Bajor joining the Federation?"

"I don't know."

"Wonderful."

"Hurry up," Cedra hissed from above. "What's taking you two so long?" The boy clung to a small tree growing out of the mountainside at a crazy angle. "We haven't got *time.*"

Major Kira caught hold of one of the tree's lower branches and hauled herself up behind the trunk to catch her breath. She turned to give a hand to Odo, but he was nowhere to be seen. The shapeshifter had come up with his own solution to the unfriendly terrain. A nimble-footed *hyurin* scurried past Major Kira and Cedra, leaving them to follow it through the trees into a small clearing slightly higher up the hillside. There it stopped and shot back into the familiar form of Odo.

"I don't know why I didn't think of doing that sooner," he remarked. To Major Kira he said, "Are we almost there?"

"Yes, we are," Cedra replied. Neither one of the adults paid any attention to him.

Kira took a reading on her tricorder, sweeping the territory ahead. "There's an entrance to a series of caverns about a hundred meters in that direction. That's where the sensors picked up Dr. Bashir's life signs. No wonder Chief O'Brien said it looked like the man was under several layers of rock. All we have to do is locate Dr. Bashir inside the caverns, get a comm badge on him, and signal the runabout. The transporter aboard the *Ganges* is programmed to home in on the comm signals without having to use the long-range sensors to spot us."

"How simple. And all we have to do to reach Dr. Bashir is explain to any of the cavern residents that we mean them no harm, we've just come looking for a friend."

"Odo, you know that's where Cedra's plan comes in. Sometimes your cynical attitude gets a bit old," Kira said.

"*I* would like to get old, too," the shapeshifter replied.

Cedra made an impatient sound. The Bajoran boy had climbed one of the trees and was sitting on a branch, swinging his legs. "Nothing bad's going to happen. Didn't you *listen* when I explained it all to Commander Sisko?"

"I was too busy asking myself what possessed him to consent to this ludicrous arrangement," Odo said. "I suppose it didn't hurt to have his son take your side," he added grudgingly.

"It's a good plan and he would have approved it with or without Jake's support," Cedra snapped. He dropped lightly from the tree. "Commander Sisko wouldn't approve a plan—any plan—if he didn't think it would work. Not when something so important depends on it working. You know how he always thinks things through."

I do, Kira thought. *But how do you? You've hardly known him a week.* She itched with the same peculiar feeling she'd gotten when Talis Cedra explained how he'd located his sister by scent alone.

"More of that invaluable Starfleet training in action," Odo drawled.

"I like Starfleet," Cedra remarked casually. "Commander Sisko said I'd make a good recruit. Maybe I'll do that, join up, go to the Academy"—he gave Odo an arch look—"and come back to DS9 as your new commander."

"I can hardly wait," Odo said through his teeth.

"In the meantime, you do your part and I'll show you how well I do mine."

"All right. Sit down over there where there's some light." As Cedra obediently sat on a nearby boulder and Major Kira kept watch, Odo unpacked a small box from his belt.

"This must be a change for you," Kira said, glancing over Odo's shoulder as the shapeshifter deployed the assorted jars, tubes, and pencils of a makeup kit. "I hope you're as good at changing someone else's looks as you are your own," she joked.

"There have been *many* times during my tenure aboard the station when I needed more than one member of Security to work undercover," Odo replied testily. He gave Cedra's skin an unwholesome pallor, then darkened the circles under the boy's eyes and created deep hollows under his cheekbones. "All we require is for him to look ill. That's a simple transformation." He studied Cedra critically. "I've done my best. See that you can act as sick as you look."

Cedra grinned. "Don't worry about my acting talents, Constable."

"He looks *awful,*" Kira said, impressed.

"Thank you," said Odo. As a last touch, he tucked a comm badge between the layers of the deliberately tattered and filthy clothes Cedra wore. "That one's yours. You remember what to do with it?"

Cedra made a face as if to say he'd remember long after Odo had forgotten. "Lose it and I get left behind. I'm ready."

Major Kira checked her tricorder. "There are four sentries, two in plain sight near the cave mouth, two on patrol." She and Odo set their phasers on stun, in case some mischance let the patrolling guards stumble upon them before they could use the sensor warnings to evade them. "That seems to be all. Funny . . . Most of the life-sign readings are coming from one central area inside the caverns. Dr. Bashir's there too." She shrugged. "We can use luck like that. Do you have the comm badge for Dr. Bashir, Cedra?"

The boy nodded; he showed her the glittering Starfleet insignia before hiding it under his rags. "One for him, one for me."

"Then good luck." She stooped and gave the child a hasty kiss.

"Don't smear the makeup," said Odo.

Dr. Bashir felt as if his legs had turned to jelly. Jalika was right—her father was an excellent orator. From an opening that seemed to do nothing but praise Dr. Bashir's medical triumphs among the hill fighters, he skillfully forged those same words of praise into a sword that was pointed right at Julian's heart.

"He has saved so many!" Borilak Selinn cried. "Why, then, could he not save one? One boy—little more than a child—a child who suffered from the same fever he cured so many times before!"

"But it *wasn't* the same fever," Julian muttered. "It would have responded to the vaccine if it were."

"My friends—" The Bajoran's tone softened from rant to purr. "—I know what you ask now. You ask *why* he would do such a thing. To kill a child—! All we have heard before of this Federation healer speaks of his selflessness, his compassion, of the countless children who owe him their lives. Why does Borilak Belem owe him his death?"

A murmur of speculation rose from the cavern floor to meet the question. Borilak Selinn allowed it to die down before he went on.

"You might as well ask yourselves why you are here, dwelling in caves, undergoing hardship, living far from even the most basic comforts. Why have you made this choice? Because you are people of honor. Because you did not fight—your loved ones did not die at the hands of the Cardassians—to have everything you hold dear destroyed by the perfidious and subtle agents of the so-called provisional government!" This time a roar of approval went up from the crowd below.

"Who is this man, this *healer?*" Borilak Selinn demanded. "Who is he, really? He wears the uniform of Starfleet—the same Starfleet that woos and coddles the very leaders who are taking Bajor down the path of ruin. What do these Starfleet people care for true Bajorans? All that they want is to have guaranteed access to the wormhole, and they'll pact with whoever can give it to them. Justice can hang, righteousness can perish for all they care. The provisional government offers them the wormhole and in exchange they give the provisional government their souls."

"My God," Julian said, the muscles of his jaw tightening. "What a pack of lies." He started forward, but Jalika held him back.

"You may not speak yet. If you try, Father's attendants will stop you. If there is even the smallest show of a struggle, they will use it to their advantage and see that you fall to your death. To the others, it will look like an accident." She twined her arm through his. "Do not give him what he wants, Julian. Your turn to speak will come."

Dr. Bashir bit his lip and said nothing.

"Where did this healer come from?" Borilak Selinn continued. "From the same camp as Borilak Belem! You all know this is true: the boy spoke of his past freely. *He* had nothing to hide. Perhaps that was what this man feared—that Belem's honest nature would compel him to reveal the true reason for the healer Bashir's presence in our midst."

"This is too much! You *brought* me here by force, dammit!" Dr. Bashir exploded, despite Jalika's attempts to quiet him. "You're filling your followers' ears with fairy tales and the one person who can testify against you is dead!"

One of Borilak Selinn's men moved forward and backhanded Julian across the face so hard the doctor staggered dangerously near the lip of the rocky shelf. The man's smile was calculating as he raised his hand for a second blow, strong enough to finish matters.

"No!" Jalika cried, leaping between Bashir and her father's henchman. She seized Julian in her arms and brought him away from the edge, holding his assailant at bay with a ferocious glare.

"See that he shuts up, then," the man said, and returned to his post at Borilak Selinn's side.

"I warned you," Jalika whispered to Julian while he blinked away stars and examined his throbbing jaw gingerly.

Borilak Selinn was smiling as if someone had just given him a gift. "You see, my friends?" he told his people. "A man who fears the words of honest men, *that* is this healer. Who knows what poor Belem learned of the man's true purpose here? Much evil may be done under cover of good deeds. Perhaps the boy knew nothing—did he deserve to die for what the healer *thought* he knew? Perhaps he knew everything, but refused to believe it because he felt that he was in the healer's debt. His loyalty did not save him. Borilak

Belem trusted the healer Bashir. To trust him was to trust Starfleet; to trust Starfleet was to trust the provisional government; to trust them was to die." He turned his back on the crowd, signaling that he had said all he needed to say, for the moment. The mob below cheered wildly.

Jalika nudged Julian. "Now it is your turn."

Still somewhat stunned, Dr. Bashir walked carefully to the edge of the stone shelf and gazed down. He saw hate and suspicion on every upturned face. *No matter what I say, they won't believe me,* he realized. *Borilak Selinn has fixed it so they* can't *believe me. The only thing my speech will earn me is a few more minutes of life.* He looked back at Jalika. She glimmered like a dream in the cavern light. *I have to try.*

"I did not kill Belem," he said. The simple declaration brought hoots and jeers from the chamber floor. "If I did want him dead, why would I do it so crudely? I could have healed him, been safely on my way, only to have him die through some—some—" He shrugged. "I don't know, some delayed release poison I'd left behind in his blood."

"How do we know that you didn't do that, too?" someone called from below.

"Yes, the injections he gave us!" someone else agreed. "How do we know what they'll really do to us, given time?"

Bad move, Julian, Dr. Bashir thought as the crowd seized on his words and warped them out of all recognition. *Stupid move. Maybe I should just take one little step now and put an end to this before I put my foot in my mouth up to the knee.* The thought of stepping off the ledge was not even half-serious, but judging from some of the things Borilak Selinn's followers were now shouting, he knew that taking that one small step might spare him a far longer, far more painful death.

"Let him speak!"

Jalika's voice, normally so soft and gentle, rang out through the hall and stunned the mob to silence. "Is *this* how you honor our laws? He has the right to be heard." A few diehards muttered excuses for the outburst, but most of the people did not say another word.

Jalika stared hard at her father. "I ask for the right of testimony," she said. Her tone made it clear that she would not accept a negative reply. Her father sullenly waved her his consent.

She walked proudly to the brim of the precipice and took Julian's hand where all the people could see. "I have been your healer. I was trained as a healer in the holy Temple. There I was taught that the Prophets offer vision and revelation, but we must seek our own answers within them and within ourselves. Is there a certainty except that no certainty exists? We are not the Prophets. Our answers are sometimes flawed."

She squeezed Julian's hand. "When I was your sole healer, there were times when my patients died. Why did no one speak of *my* dark motives? When Borilak Belem fell ill, I did not know how to heal him. Why was I not accused of murder for the same crime as Dr. Bashir? He and I are both healers. Why can't you accept the simple fact that no healer can cure all the ills we must endure?"

"How do you compare yourself to him?" a strident voice piped up. At least one of Dr. Bashir's foes had regained the courage to interrupt. "You're one of us! He's an outsider, he's Starfleet, he's—"

"Healer!" The call echoed from the mouth of one of the tunnels that fed into the vast hall. A man came running in at a clumsy lope. He held the limp body of a child in his arms. "Healer, this boy came staggering out of the woods and collapsed at our feet. He looks like he's from one of the camps. He's moaning with pain and he's had convulsions at least three times on the way here."

"Bring him up," Borilak Selinn directed. "My daughter will heal him."

As the man sought the spiral passageway up to the ledge, Jalika said loudly enough for all to hear, "Are you sure I should, Father? What if he has the camp fever? You forbade me to care for Belem as soon as you suspected what his illness was. You were afraid I would catch it too."

"You *can't* catch it now," Borilak Selinn snapped. "You were inoculated by—" He stopped, but it was too late.

"—by the healer Bashir," Jalika concluded in triumph. "So you *do* trust his remedies enough to let me touch a fever victim?" The crowd below heard, and the murmuring began again just as the guard emerged onto the platform. He laid the child down at Jalika's feet. "No," she said. "I trust Dr. Bashir, too." She stepped aside and addressed the crowd: "May the Prophets show us this man's innocence through the life or death of this child."

Julian approached the body cautiously, reaching for his diagnostic instrument as he knelt to perform his examination. The child lay with one arm thrown across his face. Dr. Bashir moved it away and raised the silvery wand to begin his work.

"Boo!" shouted Cedra, bolting upright and slapping the comm badge onto Julian's chest. It tilted at a lopsided angle, but it clung securely. With a whoop of glee, Cedra touched his own hidden comm badge. *"Now!"*

Borilak Selinn's men almost ran over the edge of the stone gallery as they rushed forward to try seizing two quickly fading transporter-stolen phantoms.

CHAPTER
15

"CONGRATULATIONS, CEDRA," Commander Sisko said. "Even Odo's admitted to me that your plan came off without a hitch. You can be proud of yourself; you're a fine actor."

"Thanks, but I don't think that's what I want to be when I grow up," Cedra replied with a smile.

"Plenty of time to decide that. You know, I wasn't joking when I suggested you consider a career in Starfleet someday."

All at once the boy was solemn. "My place is on Bajor."

"Your place is wherever you're happy." Sisko patted the boy's back. He looked troubled. "I wish I knew if Dr. Bashir still thinks his place is here."

"Is it?"

"That will be up to him. I couldn't bring myself to give him more than a slap on the wrist for his escapades on the surface. I can't deny the good he's done in the camps on Bajor, but I'm afraid we'll lose him to the camps again once he cures your sister."

Cedra's face was disturbingly adult as he said, "You don't need to lie to me, Commander. I know lies. You want to say *if* he cures Dejana."

"No, Cedra; I believe it will be *when,* not *if.*"

The boy cocked his head and gave Sisko a searching look. "You do." He appeared to think over this revelation. "And you truly believe Dr. Bashir is the man who can do it. They teach us that the Prophets reward faith."

"I respect your beliefs, Cedra, whether or not I share them."

"Then tell me more of what *you* believe about Dr. Bashir."

It was a strange request, but Commander Sisko answered it. "I believe that it would be a loss to DS9 and to Bajor if Dr. Bashir finds an excuse to return to the camps. Excuse? He wouldn't need one; he'd only have to resign his commission in Starfleet and go. But working like that he can only treat one individual at a time. Working here, gaining experience, reputation, expertise, he could become a voice of influence that could make the provisional government finally take serious relief action and eliminate the camps altogether."

"Is that all?" Cedra meant it as a serious question.

"Well . . . I'd also hate to lose him as a crewman; I respect him as a doctor and I like him, too. I admit he was a little irritating when he first came here, but he *is* brilliant, and since he's returned from Bajor I've noticed a change in him." Sisko ran a thumb along his jawline. "I think he's grown up."

Cedra poked his head around the corner of an open doorway and observed Bashir working over a microscanner. "Did you find it yet?" he asked.

The doctor's head jerked up from his work. "Oh, hullo, Cedra. Come in." He sat back on his stool. "I've just begun reviewing the samples Lieutenant Dax took from your sister since her arrival on DS9. I'm trying to see if there's any progressive physiological difference between the time she got here and the time she fell ill. Funny—I expected to see an escalating number of white blood cells to combat the infection, but instead it looks like her *red* cell count is up. If only I weren't so tired . . ."

Cedra came in and took a perch on a second stool at the lab bench. Drumming his feet against the legs he said, "I wish I was you."

"Do you." Dr. Bashir's face was too drawn and weary to reflect much amusement, but he tried. "And why is that?"

"Because when I get in trouble here, everyone yells at me, especially Odo."

"Odo doesn't *yell;* he freezes. Very loudly."

"Whatever." The boy shrugged. "But if I was you, I could get away with all kinds of stuff and no one would say a word."

"What kind of 'stuff' do you think I've gotten away with?" Now Dr. Bashir was not even trying to smile.

"Running away."

"I did not *run away.* I told you what I was going to do and why when we were both still back on Bajor. As I recall, you not only approved of my intentions, you helped me." Bashir turned from the boy to his microscanner. "I never thought I'd have to explain myself to a child," he said bitterly, head bent over the viewer.

The illuminated sample under the scanner suddenly went black. Bashir looked up to see Cedra with a finger cutting off the power source. "Isn't it time you explained yourself to yourself, then?" He folded his hands on the table. "How can you see what's wrong with my sister when all your ghosts get in the way?"

"What kind of nonsense—?"

"It's not. Everyone has them—ghosts. Every time we make a change, we make more of them. Don't you feel them holding you back, not letting you think clearly?

How can you help but feel tired when you're carrying such a weight of them?"

"All I know is that if you don't stop interfering with my work, your sister will suffer for it. Cedra, we don't have *time* here. I can't identify her illness; neither could Lieutenant Dax. I never saw anything like this in the camps."

"Yes you did." Cedra spoke with all the authority of Selok. "But he died."

Ghosts . . . Dr. Bashir closed his eyes and Belem's face appeared, smiling and happy, proudly showing off his mended foot to the other children. He heard the boy's voice, brimming with joy, thanking him for the miracle. The words of thanks faded into the rattling sound of Belem's last breath in the cold caverns.

"Do you remember the caverns, Dr. Bashir?" Cedra asked. "I saw them when the guard carried me through. So many passageways, so many choices. If you turn right, you come to a pit, turn left and there's a wall of solid stone, take the center way and a smooth path lies before you—until the ground shakes and new pits open, new walls rise."

"I don't underst—" Julian shook his head helplessly.

"Don't you see?" He lunged forward and grabbed Bashir's face, his fingertips closing tightly on the doctor's ears. "You can't carry Belem's death on your soul—it isn't yours to bear. Share it with the Cardassians who destroyed his home, the Bajorans who insisted that he wasn't whole because he'd lost his family name. Share it with Brother Talissin, who took your gift of healing Belem's twisted foot and turned it into blame when he ran off. Share it with Borilak Selinn and his followers who cling to the darkness because they're too stubborn to see how their visions might change in a new light."

Julian winced as Cedra's grip pinched his ears painfully. "Don't turn from the light too, healer," Cedra said, quiet strength filling his voice. "We can't afford to lose you."

As Dr. Bashir gazed into Cedra's eyes, a dizzying sensation overcame him. The walls around him melted like mists at sunrise. He felt as if he were falling through vast realms of space, only to come to a jarring halt when his heels struck rock. Once again he was in Borilak Selinn's domain, perched on the lip of the stone ledge high above the cavern floor. Jalika was in his arms, her warmth shielding him, the perfume of her skin and hair enfolding him like wings.

Suddenly she gave a little cry and slipped from his arms, her feet scrabbling at the edge of the drop, then skidding off entirely. She plunged from his embrace, her screams echoing from the vaulted roof. He grabbed for her hand, caught it, but felt himself being dragged down with her. He was slammed onto his stomach flat against the rocky shelf, one arm pulled half out of its socket by Jalika's weight, the other groping for any kind of handhold that would let him brace himself enough to haul her back to safety. He found none.

Then he heard the other cries. He looked to left and right and saw that the ledge had stretched itself into a gallery that encircled the entire perimeter of the great cavern. Hundreds, thousands of Bajoran children clung to the slick rocky lip, sobbing and screaming for help. Acid filled his mouth; there was no way he could save them all. He did not even know if he could save the woman he loved.

Julian . . .

The air in front of him shimmered. Lieutenant Dax was there, floating above the abyss. Commander Sisko stood with her, and Major Kira, and Chief O'Brien, and even dour Odo. Their hands were cupped, a white glow shining through their fingers. Together they opened their hands, releasing the light. Five spheres of brilliance like five stars flew up to join above their heads. The whole cave was illuminated with the dazzle of a hundred bolts of lightning. Then the light dimmed, hardened into a slowly spinning image of *Deep Space Nine*.

But the image was incomplete. A massive portion of the station was torn away, leaving a gaping hole that turned it from a graceful child of space into a wounded monstrosity.

Julian, look.

Dr. Bashir felt warmth fill his empty hand. A white light danced in his palm. The hand that held Jalika from death was also glowing. Without knowing how he knew, Julian realized that if the lights in his keeping were not brought together, if he did not send them out to complete the crippled image of the station, the children would perish.

But if he moved to bring his hands together, Jalika would fall.

Help us, Julian.

The children's mouths formed the words, but the sound came from Kira, Odo, Sisko, O'Brien, Dax. The voices of the children of Bajor, pleading for rescue, came from the lips of his crewmates aboard DS9.

Help us . . .

He gave Jalika one last look. All his heart went out to her with it. Her smile forgave him. *For the children, Julian* . . . He felt her fingers release their hold on his hand even before he let her go. She plummeted into the darkness.

Through tears, he brought his glowing hands together. A star leaped from the joining of the lights and shot across the void to the station. An explosion of radiance welcomed it home. When it faded, Dax and the others were gone; the station was whole once more.

And then Dr. Bashir saw countless silver threads spinning out from the body of *Deep Space Nine*. They whipped through the murk, bridging space, each reaching out to touch a Bajoran child. The threads were thin as gossamer, stronger than twisted ropes of steel. They coiled beneath the children's feet and lifted them up, away from the ledge, safe from the gulf beneath. As the silver threads carried them higher and farther away, Julian recognized faces he had known in the camps, faces that once regarded him with dead eyes. All that had changed: the children no longer wailed with fear, and their faces shone joyfully, the faces of children whose childhood has been reborn. Julian's heart lifted. He stretched out his hands to the children, stepped toward them, onto empty air—

—and woke with a start as his head knocked against the top of the lab bench. He was alone.

"I could have sworn—" He shook his head, baffled, and went back to work.

"Good, you've come! I think I've found it," Dr. Bashir said to Lieutenant Dax as she entered the infirmary.

"You don't sound so sure of it," she said.

He ran his fingers through his hair. "I was so tired, I wasn't even sure of my own name anymore. I actually nodded off, slept for hours, had the strangest dream— Never mind that, I'm fine now. Look in here." He moved aside so that she could use the microscanner.

"Blood from Talis Dejana. What's so special about it?" she asked, studying the sample.

"Can you tell when this sample was taken?"

"Of course not. All the samples I took from her looked identical."

"When you looked at them like this, yes." He touched the microscanner controls. "Try it now."

Dax pulled back involuntarily as the sudden rush of supermagnification made one of Dejana's red blood cells appear to race right at her face.

"What do you see?" Dr. Bashir asked.

"A red blood cell."

"No, that's what you *expect* to see. Look at it more closely; really *look*. Don't just accept it according to your preconceptions."

"All right, all right," Dax said with good humor. She adjusted the controls. "Hey!"

"There." Julian was satisfied.

"That structure inside the cell looks like—but it can't be—not in a red blood cell."

"If it *is*, why can't it be?" He pressed his face close to hers and spoke with the intent delight of a true scientist on the verge of discovery: "What is it, Jadzia? Tell me what it looks like to you."

She sat up straight and met his eyes. "A mitochondrion."

"Yes!" he crowed, seizing her hands and pulling her from the stool to join him in an exultant circle dance. "Yes, yes, *yes!*"

"But—" she gasped, her breath whirled out of her by Julian's antics. She broke away from him so that she could speak, leaving him still dancing in the middle of the floor. "But red blood cells don't have mitochondria; not human red blood cells, not Bajoran. They don't need them. They're manufactured in the bone marrow. Mitochondria are only found in cells that reproduce themselves."

He stopped his wild reel cold and seized her shoulders. "Exactly! Therefore, if Bajoran red blood cells do *not* have mitochrondria but this Bajoran red blood cell appears to *have* a mitochondrion, what must we conclude, my dear Lieutenant Dax?"

"That—that—" A smile of astonishment and delight illuminated her face. "That we've got our eye on the most skillful microscopic mimic in the universe."

"At the least." Julian flung himself back to the

microscanner. "I wish I had a sample of Belem's blood to confirm this, but I'm almost positive about what's going on here. Some victims of camp fever seemed to recover from the illness spontaneously. What really happened, though, is that the microorganism found something inhospitable in the host's body and made a strategic retreat. The illness became dormant—I think we'll find that the length of dormancy varies from subject to subject. It used this period of dormancy to mutate and adapt itself into a better, stronger, more effective form. Only then would it reassert its presence in the host." He laughed. "I think I'll get a monograph out of this."

"So you're planning to stay with us long enough to have your research on the case published?" It was a serious question sheathed in the disguise of a joke.

"Planning to stay—? Where else would I want to—?" Comprehension struck: "Ohhhhh. No, Jadzia; I don't regret a moment of my time in the camps, but I think that now I can serve the children better where I am. Perhaps Major Kira can arrange for me to have a few words with members of the council. I want to take what I saw, what I learned, and use it to convince the provisional government that disbanding the camps and resettling the children into proper homes must become their top priority." One corner of his mouth twitched in a half-smile. "Of course I'll make it sound as if the entire project will be in their own best interest."

"You, a politician?" Dax teased.

"And why not? I was raised in the diplomatic corps. Publishing my findings on this micromimic won't hurt either. A theory like this will be talked about, and so will I. I really would prefer it if the first council member I approach doesn't hear my name, make a face, and say, 'Dr. *who?*'" He assumed a mock-serious air and added, "You'd be surprised how many people don't know that I got the second highest marks at Starfleet Medical."

"Noooooo." Dax *tsk*ed. "You know, Julian, that's a rather big theory to hang on samples from a single subject. Shouldn't you—?"

"You're right; of course you're right. Where's Major Kira? Find her. Have her go to Bajor, to the camps. She has to gather samples from other fever victims who recovered without treatment."

"Julian, have we time for this?"

"No, we haven't, but it's something we must *try* to do. If she returns with the samples quickly, all the better, but you and I won't be twiddling our thumbs waiting for her to come back. I'm nearly certain this is our enemy's new mask. We've torn it away; now we can take this fight into the open again. Jadzia, I'm going to recommend an analogous antibody-based treatment for Dejana—"

"—and you want me to design the antibody this time as well?" she finished for him. "I can do that, only—how do you know that this version of the virus will respond to the same sort of treatment that controlled it in its original form?"

"I don't know that, Jadzia," Dr. Bashir said. "But it's all we have time to try."

"Cedra, let me *go,*" Major Kira yelled, disengaging her arm from the Bajoran boy's insistent hold. "I'm on a mission at Dr. Bashir's request. He needs data to help him find a cure for your sister."

"No one's telling me *anything,*" Cedra wailed. "I'm not even allowed in the infirmary anymore! I thought that once Dr. Bashir felt better, he could cure her right away! I don't know what's going on and nobody cares!"

Kira was about to yell at Cedra a second time to let her go; then she saw the child's stricken look. The hard words caught in her throat. Instead of pushing him away, she hugged the boy tight and stroked his hair. "Dr. Bashir will find the answer, *cheli,*" she murmured. "Don't be afraid."

"But *when* will he find it?" Cedra moaned. "She's so sick!"

"Soon, *cheli,* soon," Kira said soothingly. Her thoughts were less tranquil. *It had better be soon. The eve of Nis Thamar falls with tomorrow's sunset. The Dessinka are hungry for an excuse to leave the provisional government. They're a military sect—many of their leaders feel that if the government falls, they're convinced they could rally enough support to seize power easily. The only thing stopping an outright coup is their blessed sense of honor.*

Aloud she said, "You need time to calm down. Let me take you to the shrine. It's where I always go when things seem to be getting too much for me to handle."

Cedra did not protest as Major Kira brought him into the scented confines of the Bajoran shrine. She found him a small niche with a pillow on the floor and a curtain of tinkling crystal strands across the archway. A candle flickered before an abstract image of gold-flecked blue stone whose spiral, tapering shape led the eye upward in a dance to silent music. "Everything will be all right, you'll see," she whispered in his ear before she stole away.

Cedra sat cross-legged on the cushion and tried to focus on the statue. Tranquillity was elusive. Troubling thoughts of Dejana intervened, growing to nightmarish proportions with each passing minute. Cedra's hands clenched and unclenched and the Bajoran child's breath came more and more rapidly.

"Is it such a hard road you seek to travel, little one?" At the words, Cedra's eyes opened to behold a white-bearded monk standing in front of the statue.

"How did you—?" Cedra glanced back over one shoulder. The beaded curtain that sounded a melodious alarm at the slightest movement was not even swaying.

"Am *I* to tell *you* that the unseen door opens to greater possibilities than the door one can see?" the monk asked.

241

"Tell me your pain, child. The distress of your soul jangles louder than a thousand crystal curtains."

"I don't know what I'm doing here," Cedra said. "I want to be in the infirmary with my sister, but they won't let me."

"Ah." The monk nodded sagely. His eyes were the clear frosty blue of a winter sky.

"I can leave, if I'm in the way." Cedra started to get up, but the monk's hand gently urged him back down onto the cushion. In a rustle of robes, the monk joined the child on the floor.

"You must learn two things, little one: First that when we walk our own ordained paths with honesty, we can never be a stumbling block in the paths of others." He fell silent.

Cedra waited politely for the monk's other revelation. It did not come. He began to fidget until he finally demanded, "What's the second thing I need to learn?"

The monk smiled. "Patience."

Cedra tried to give the monk a look fit to kill, but too many tears were suddenly in his eyes. He sprang to his feet and started for the doorway. In one impossibly quick move, the monk was there before him, blocking the way.

"I apologize. Jests have always been a weakness of mine. I think that I jested myself all the way out of the Temple to this distant outpost of our faith. So many people refuse to believe that the Prophets may also instruct us through laughter." He sighed. "Now speak with me, child. Your sister in the infirmary—how sick is she?"

Cedra lowered his eyes. "She could die."

The monk's hand hovered over Cedra's dark hair. "My brethren in the Temple might tell you now that all of us must die someday. They would counsel tranquillity and setting your spirit in order so that if the worst should come, your *pagh* would not be overly disrupted." He shook his head. "I do not give such counsel. I see a fighter under my hand. A fighter opens every door and if no way of escape is revealed he takes an ax and chops out his own."

Cedra looked at the monk directly. "You don't like your brethren very much, do you?"

"Likes and dislikes . . . we are supposed to be above them. There's a fresh jest for you! Still, no matter what I think of my brothers in the Temple, I am forced to admit that they possess certain skills I envy. Our way is not merely a way of words, little one—it is also a way of action. I have only the ability to heal spirits, but there are monks in the Temple who have merged the healing of the body with the healing of the *pagh*. What they can do goes far beyond the results of medical technology, even the technology of the Federation. They work miracles, child, *miracles!*"

"My sister needs a miracle," Cedra said. "Can you help me? Tell me the name of the best Temple healer and I'll ask Commander Sisko to send for—"

The monk shook his head again, emphatically. "He will send for no one, and no one will come. An agreement has been made: None from Bajor with any interest in the child some call *Nekor* may come here until she has been conducted to the Temple."

"But how can they take her there when she's so sick? A Temple healer would fix everything. It's a *stupid* agreement."

"Those who required that such an agreement be made care more for what your sister represents than for who she truly is. They will protect their share in the symbol, not the child. If she lives, they will do their best to turn her to their own purposes. If she dies, she will still give them what they want."

"*Could* one of the healer-monks save Dejana?" the boy insisted.

"How to know? To travel here, against the express directive of one's superior, would mean the end of one's safe and simple life within the Temple."

"Nothing will be safe *or* simple if they let Dejana die! The whole planet could be thrown into war."

The monk made a gesture casting aside all blame. "Some only see as far as their own comforts and desires, and no farther."

Cedra was no longer on the point of tears. He was shaking with rage. "A healer who won't come because he's afraid for *himself?* Dr. Bashir was never like that. Someone who holds back his gifts because he doesn't want to have his comfortable life disturbed? That's *selfish!*"

"And if he were to send another healer in his place?" the monk asked casually. "Not a skilled healer, a healer in name only, would that do?"

"No!" Cedra stamped his foot. "That would make it worse! Anyone he treated would be depending on him to be a true healer, but he wouldn't be able to help them at all. He might hurt them instead. It would be—it would be—"

"The plan of a selfish man?" the monk inquired. "Or the work of a frightened child?"

All the blood left Cedra's cheeks. His hand rose to his lips to silence his own words. The awful look of guilt that filled his eyes turned swiftly to a grimace of fury. *"I hate you!"* he screamed at the monk, and ran from the shrine.

"I know," the monk said to the wildly swinging threads of crystal across the doorway. "I have that effect on many people." He raised his hand and the sparkling strands hung straight and still. He bent to blow out the candle, and vanished into the shadows.

CHAPTER
16

DR. BASHIR stepped away from Dejana's bed and turned to Commander Sisko and Lieutenant Dax. "That's it," he said.

Sisko came near the bed and looked down at the girl. Dejana's hair was a damp tangle, her face the color of cheese. She tossed her head from side to side, mumbling the way Jake sometimes did when his nightmares grew too vivid and took him back to the time of his mother's death. Sisko wondered what sort of visions the fever had called up to disturb this unlucky child's much-needed rest. She had lost a mother, too, and a father, and a whole way of life.

He looked back at Bashir. "What now?"

Dr. Bashir was washing his hands. "Now we wait," he said.

Sisko's eyes went back to Dejana. Her eyelids fluttered and her lips, cracked and dry, continued to mouth unintelligible syllables. He laid his hand on her forehead and stroked away the clinging wisps and tendrils of hair.

Sometimes the touch of his hand freed Jake from the grasp of nightmare. Jake was not Dejana; Sisko felt the heat devouring her alive before she groaned and wrenched her head aside. He fetched some water in a cup and ran a moistened finger over her lips.

"Sir—" Dr. Bashir was at his elbow. "We don't yet know whether this virus can live in human hosts as well as Bajorans. Perhaps you'd better—"

"You were exposed to it more times and more closely than anyone," Sisko said. "Have you felt any ill effects?"

"No, and neither has Ensign Kahrimanis," Bashir admitted. "Lieutenant Dax's physiology is another story altogether, of course. But we're in the realm of many unknowns here. Some microorganisms are choosy about their hosts, some are adaptable enough to cross any borders. If humans can contract this from Bajorans, we have no idea about how long the incubation period might be or how it would manifest itself at first. Dax tells me that Dejana's second bout with the fever began with the symptoms of the common cold."

"Talk about adaptable," Dax remarked.

"This is serious, Doctor," Sisko said. "You're telling me that we may have brought a highly contagious, adaptable, potentially fatal disease aboard DS9."

Dr. Bashir held up his hand. "I've already organized an inoculation program for all Bajoran residents of the station. As for members of other races, I don't think there's much danger. Talis Dejana's political and medical isolation worked in our favor there."

"Isolation?" Sisko frowned. "Not while Vung had her. That blasted Ferengi moved the child from one hidden spot to another aboard this station. We don't even know half the places he kept her while she was cloaked. How many people passed right by her and never knew?"

"How many of them have reboarded their starships and moved on?" Dax added. "Vung too."

Sisko closed his eyes and took a deep breath. "All right," he said, stretching out his hands to push away the ever-mounting possibility of a potential interplanetary epidemic. "We'll deal with this later. For the moment, our only concern is here, one case, one child."

"If this antibody works at all like the first, we ought to see a change fairly soon," Dax said.

"I don't know if we can rely on that," Dr. Bashir said. "Remember, we're dealing with a version of the virus that's gone an extra evolutionary step. It may be harder to kill than the previous generation. And I want a sure kill. If the antibody only drives the disease into a second period of dormancy, this child will know it later. No half measures, no future surprises; I want to give her back her life."

"She'll be closely monitored once she's taken to the Temple," Dax said. "The Bajoran monks who belong to the healing orders are excellent physicians, in their way."

"The Temple . . . how long until she has to be delivered there?" Bashir asked.

"How long before she can be safely moved?" Commander Sisko countered.

"The eve of *Nis Thamar*," Dax replied with crisp practicality. "How many hours until sunset over the Temple precincts?"

"No," said Sisko. "If there's any danger to moving this girl, she stays where she is. I'll meet with the *Dessin-ka* personally to arrange a compromise. They must be made to see that it's better to put off the *Nekor*'s presentation at the Temple if it means seeing her healthy and alive. I refuse to risk a child's life to meet an artificial deadline."

"And what if that child's life buys peace or war for Bajor?" Kejan Ulli stepped into the infirmary and strode past Sisko, Dax, and Bashir to stand at the foot of Dejana's bed. "So here she is. May the Prophets have mercy on you for what you have done to her."

"What are you doing here?" Sisko demanded. "You're in violation of the accord."

"The same accord you were just proposing to ignore

yourself," the *Dessin-ka* agent reminded him. "I do not belong to any of the formal religious orders. So long as I did not come here with my sole purpose to see the *Nekor,* I am not breaking the letter of the accord. Besides, she does not look at all susceptible to political influences now. Her death will be on you."

"She's not going to die!" Dr. Bashir cried.

"Why not? Because it would put the Federation at a disadvantage if she did?" He took a step toward Dr. Bashir. "I don't believe we've had the pleasure."

Bashir regarded the heavyset Bajoran askance. "I'm Dr. Julian Bashir, the station medical officer."

"Not *the* Dr. Bashir!" Kejan Ulli's delight was spread on too thickly to be real. "Why, you're a legend. Reports arrive at the capitol daily describing your work in the refugee camps of the Kaladrys Valley. It's been having quite an interesting effect on the political situation. Some folk are starting to realize that our people's distress didn't magically end with the departure of the Cardassians. They're beginning to remember that while the council enjoys comfort, there are Bajorans whose only comfort is a half-filled belly and the thought that they won't have to live forever. This is making the government distinctly *un*comfortable. My compliments, sir." He showed a wolfish leer.

"That was never my intent," Dr. Bashir replied hotly.

"No matter. You still have my admiration, and my thanks. You have not only caused the government to lose face, but your prolonged stay on Bajor kept you from being here to monitor the *Nekor's* health. When she dies, it will be a double blow to the provisional government and the Federation."

"You'd like that, wouldn't you." Commander Sisko didn't need to frame it as a question. "The only reason you've been concerned about her health is how badly it will reflect on the Federation if she dies. And yet Major Kira tells me that the *Dessin-ka* prefer to fight their political battles head-on, out in the open. They pride themselves on their honesty. So much subtlety doesn't ring true for them. Who are you really, Kejan Ulli? Whom do you really serve?"

The Bajoran's teeth sparkled. "Well done, Commander Sisko. I *am* a member of the *Dessin-ka,* you know; most of us are members of one sect or another. The funny thing about a group that puts such a high premium on honesty is how gullible they can be. They may not trust outsiders wholeheartedly, but they believe that everyone within their sect is trustworthy because only the *Dessin-ka* can be trusted. Circular reasoning like that provides a wonderful hiding place for my little group. Circular—ha!" He chuckled over a private joke. "We are just as much in favor of a strong military as the *Dessin-ka,* yet we find them a little—how to say it?—*timid* about their ultimate goals. They see their group as the only one pure enough to rule Bajor wisely. Once they have the power to rule, others may keep their own beliefs so long as they also keep the laws." He sniffed. "Milk-and-water politics! We believe that if Bajor is to be ruled well at all, the world itself must first be made pure."

"In your own image of purity, of course," Sisko muttered.

"There is no other. Is not The Circle the purest of forms?" He traced the symbol on the air.

"The circle . . ." Sisko sensed that Kejan Ulli was speaking of more significant matters than geometry.

"You will hear more of us, I promise. We have patience, Commander; we take our small victories where we may for the moment, but someday . . . We're already quite well placed in influential positions within the sects. I had hoped to take charge of the *Nekor*'s upbringing once she was presented in the Temple. If it meant entering orders, so be it; the *Dessin-ka* would think I did it for them!" He relished the irony of it. "Think of how well we might have spread our message from her lips! But her death will be useful for us too. For one thing, it will do much to turn Bajor away from the Federation, just as the Federation might have done its best to turn Bajor away from The Circle and our truth."

"The *Dessin-ka* won't turn from the Federation after they hear how you've been using them."

Kejan Ulli's laugh rang out sharp and loud in the infirmary. "And you'll expect them to *believe* you? An outsider's word against that of one of their own?"

"Commander Sisko isn't the only witness," Dr. Bashir said. "Lieutenant Dax and I—"

"Outsiders all." Kejan Ulli was unconcerned. "To the *Dessin-ka,* my word is my bond; yours are only noise and wind. Let the child live or die; my people will win either way."

"Damn," Julian muttered so that only Lieutenant Dax could hear him. "I wish Major Kira were here. The testimony of a Bajoran might do what ours can't."

"I think our friend Kejan made sure that Kira wasn't here before he opened up like that," Dax whispered back. "He is the thorough sort."

"I'll be going now," Kejan Ulli said. "I'm aboard *Deep Space Nine* for strictly business reasons and I have an appointment to keep with one of your local businessmen. It shouldn't take long. I want to be back in the capitol in time for the presentation of the *Nekor."* He curved his lips meaningfully around this last sentence and turned to leave.

He was almost bowled from his feet as the infirmary door opened and Cedra came barreling in. "Where's my sister? I want to see—" He stopped short and stared in horror at Dejana. "No," he breathed, his voice shaking. "No, she can't be dead."

"She isn't dead, son," Commander Sisko reassured him, one arm around the boy's shoulders. "Dr. Bashir has just given her an injection that should—that will heal her."

"No!" Cedra cast off Commander Sisko's arm under the highly interested eye of Kejan Ulli. "Dr. Bashir can't do this alone. We have to send to Bajor, to the Temple, for a healer!"

"Admirable faith," Kejan Ulli said, once more wearing the mask of the *Nekor's* devoted servant. "A shadow of the holy one's power has fallen over you, lad. The Prophets speak through your lips."

"I'm speaking!" Cedra shouted. "I'm speaking for myself and for Dejana. I won't let you play games with her life anymore! If a Bajoran Temple healer can save her, then *send* for one. But you won't, because all you care about is keeping this faction happy or not getting that faction mad. To the depths with all of them!"

"Cedra, you're upset," Dax said, trying to soothe him. "You can't help Dejana now. Dr. Bashir has done everything in his power. Come with me; we'll wait elsewhere." The Trill reached out to guide the boy away from his sister's sickbed.

"Ouch!"

Cedra leaped away as Lieutenant Dax held up a bleeding hand for all to see. "He bit me," she commented as if observing a new scientific phenomenon. Dr. Bashir stepped in quickly to treat the wound.

"Cedra, you must leave," Commander Sisko said severely. He tried to catch the boy by the back of his shirt, but Cedra danced out of range, dodging around the side of Dejana's bed.

"Stop that!" Dr. Bashir cried. "You'll knock a life-support feed loose." He, too, joined the hunt, only to have the child duck under his arm and come up on the other side with a mouthful of skin-frying curses. Kejan Ulli's dry, superior snickering filled the room.

His laughter died abruptly when Cedra snatched up an instrument from a nearby tray, sprang across the room, and jabbed it at his heart.

"You impertinent little—" Kejan Ulli brought his hand back for a heavy blow.

"Don't!" Dr. Bashir shouted. It was impossible to say which of the Bajorans he meant. Both froze.

"Listen to him," Cedra gritted. "He knows what this is." He shifted the angle of the wand. "And he knows what it can do."

"So do you, apparently," Kejan Ulli remarked coldly. "Would you care to enlighten me?"

"It's a surgical probe," Dr. Bashir said. "The boy saw me use it several times in the camp infirmary. It can make an incision of any depth and cut off excessive bleeding as it goes."

"Which means that when I cut out your heart, at least you won't bleed to death," Cedra informed Kejan Ulli.

"Child, why threaten me?" the man wheedled, his entire demeanor undergoing a radical change. "I am your friend, your advocate. I join my voice to yours in demanding the services of a Temple healer for your sister."

"You're a damned liar," Cedra returned. "You're no one's friend but your own." He glared at the others. "Just like all of you!"

"Cedra, put that down," Dr. Bashir said. He took a step toward the boy. Cedra pulled back, eyes on the doctor, pressing the blunt tip of the probe deeper into Kejan Ulli's chest. "Think: Does it matter *why* any of us try to save your sister's life as long as her life is saved?"

The probe withdrew a fraction of an inch. Cedra's lower lip trembled. "I used to think that," he said. "I thought that she and I had to get out of that camp, find a safe life, a *good* life, and it didn't matter what we had to do to get it. She's so small, so weak—do you know how many times she got sick on the road to the camp? I healed her, then. I used wild herbs, the way my father taught me on the farm. They worked enough to give her the strength to stay on the road until we reached the camp. But what if something happened to destroy the camp? What if something happened to me? She'd just be another kid in the mob, unwanted, alone. She couldn't survive on her own. I had to be sure she'd always have someone who wanted to take care of her—who *needed* to make sure she was all right—in case I couldn't do it someday. But I was wrong. What good is it if someone cares for her only because he can *use* her? What happens to her when she isn't useful anymore? I wish I'd never eavesdropped! I wish I'd never heard of the *Nekor!* I wish—" His voice broke.

Dr. Bashir stepped in and took the probe from Cedra's unresisting hand. The boy wheeled about and flung himself into the doctor's arms, sobbing. "Don't judge all of your people by the measure of one man," Bashir said. "Dejana is special to many who will look after her and serve her selflessly."

Cedra looked him in the eye. "What about the others? What about the ones like *him?*" He jabbed a finger at Kejan Ulli, who flinched and drew the edge of his robes away from the child. "How do we know which ones we can trust?"

"Trust whoever you like," Kejan Ulli growled. "Trust Starfleet, for all I care. They are no better than I. All they see when they look at your sister is a way to keep the provisional government on its shaky legs a while longer and the way through the wormhole free."

"If that were so, Kejan Ulli, why did Commander Sisko just say he refused to let the girl be moved if it would endanger her?" Dax asked quietly. "When I reminded him of the deadline, he said it didn't matter. In his eyes, her life is more important than a hundred political factions' demands."

Cedra came slowly toward Commander Sisko. "You said that?"

"Lieutenant Dax is an old friend of mine," Sisko replied. "Even so, she wouldn't lie for me."

"Then if you care so much about Dejana's health, *will* you send to the Temple for a healer?"

"Cedra, we've told you: Dr. Bashir has done everything possible. A Temple healer wouldn't—"

"*Send!*" Cedra screamed. "Send now, because if my sister dies, I swear you'll never have your *Nekor!*"

"Rather an obvious conclusion, don't you think?" Now that he was out of harm's way, Kejan Ulli had recovered his aplomb.

With perfect accuracy, Cedra spat right in his eye. "There's your *obvious,*" he said. "Dejana isn't the *Nekor!*"

"That's impossible," Kejan Ulli said harshly. "All the reports, all the proof—"

Cedra gave a bitter laugh. "Oh, it was so easy to fool you all! You saw what you wanted to see. I coached her, and she was perfect. I knew just what to have her do to convince you."

"The boy is jealous of his own sister," Kejan Ulli said. "Such ranting!"

"This isn't simple jealousy," Commander Sisko said. He approached the boy. "How did you know what would convince us that Dejana was the *Nekor?*"

"Nothing was simpler," Cedra said. "The tricky part was making you see all the signs in her without letting you see them in me first."

"In you?"

"She's not the *Nekor;* I am."

"May the Prophets grant that your Federation technology has a cure for madness," Kejan Ulli muttered.

Cedra gave him a hard look. "Your true loyalties will be discovered," he said. "The *Dessin-ka* trust each other's honor, but that does not mean their eyes are closed to treachery from within. There. Is *that* madness?"

"Why, you little eavesdropping—!" Kejan Ulli lunged for the boy, but Dr. Bashir stepped in front of him, jabbed his elbow back into the Bajoran's belly, spun to face him, slipped a foot behind his leg, and gave him a gentle tap in the center of his breastbone. Kejan Ulli tumbled backward onto the infirmary floor, curled up like a shrimp, and gasping for breath.

"I don't think you learned that by eavesdropping, Cedra," Dr. Bashir said calmly.

"I didn't," the boy replied with pride. "There are things I *know.*"

"We're just beginning to learn about Bajoran mystics," Sisko said. "There are more than a few people in service to the Temple who have gifts like yours. Some of them are still children. That doesn't make any of them the *Nekor.* The Kai Opaka's letter spoke of a healer to come. It didn't give us much to go on, but it was clear on one thing: The healer must be a girl."

Cedra tipped back his head and let loose a howl of utter frustration. "The accord said Bajoran monks must not come to the station! The Kai's letter said the healer must be a girl! The *Nekor* must be brought to the Temple by the eve of *Nis Thamar!* Must, must, *must!* Why don't you open your eyes?"

"Cedra, calm down," Sisko said firmly. He tried to take the boy's hand, only to have his own slapped away violently.

"Listen to me, Commander," Cedra said, leveling a finger at Sisko. "If my sister lives, we can go on pretending she's the *Nekor* and everyone will be happy. I'll see to it that she plays her part in the masquerade and does nothing to upset the peace of Bajor. But if she dies"—he let the words sink in—"if she dies, then I won't have any reason left to go on pretending she's the one they're after. I'll come forward and admit to being what I am. And then I'll do more: I'll find a way to escape this station, go back to Bajor, and give myself—body and soul—to any faction there that's willing to work against the Federation and against a peaceful Bajor!"

"How can you say that when you've seen what war has done to your own life?" Sisko asked. He spoke evenly, without anger. He could see that the child's wild talk came from fear and helplessness in the face of Dejana's plight.

"Let them learn what war is," Cedra shot back. "Let the council learn, let the people learn who turned their backs on us and pretended that the camps weren't there! If they had tried to help us, Dejana and I wouldn't have been so desperate to escape the camp any way we could. Let them all learn!"

"You're playing a dangerous game, Cedra," Lieutenant Dax counseled. "Suppose you do convince people that in spite of what the Kai Opaka's last letter says, the promised healer is a boy—what makes you think the leaders of Bajor would let you take them down the path to war? If you throw your support behind one political faction, the others won't just stand idly by. You'll be a symbol, a powerful symbol that each of them will want for their own purposes, and they'll fight for possession. There will be war, but you'll be the battlefield."

"Then I'll have to choose the right allies," Cedra said. "Strong and ruthless enough to protect me from the rest. Even if it means siding with something like *him*." He nodded at Kejan Ulli, who was huffing as he hauled himself to his feet, holding his middle.

"When dogs squabble over a bone, whichever dog wins, the bone still loses," Dax said. "Be fair to yourself, Cedra. You have gifts—I've seen them—but you have no training. In the Temple, or anywhere you could receive the proper instruction, you would learn to use the full range of your talents. If you cast all that aside for the sake of revenge, what will you be? A symbol—a hollow one—and never the promised healer you claim you are."

"As if—as if that—that *charlatan* could convince anyone that he is the *Nekor!*" Kejan Ulli panted, clinging to the edge of a countertop.

"Who are you"—Cedra spoke so that each word was impossible to ignore—"to tell me what I could and couldn't be when not one of you has seen what I really am?"

The child walked across the infirmary floor and lay down on an unoccupied bed. "Dr. Bashir, take the readings," came the soft plea.

Puzzled, Julian complied, initializing the unit. His eyes skimmed across the usual life-sign readouts. All seemed normal. He was about to voice his bewilderment with Cedra's request when he recalled the child's earlier demand:

Why don't you open your eyes?

He followed the readouts across a second time, until his gaze fell upon the line detailing the subject's reproductive capabilities. It was hardly a datum he checked often, in the ordinary course of a cursory examination, but now—

His eyes widened at what he saw. "Good Lord . . ." he breathed. He looked to Commander Sisko. "I never thought I'd have to say this outside of a maternity case but . . ." A wry smile touched his lips. "Congratulations; it's a girl."

Cedra grinned up at him. "I still won't wear a dress and you can't make me."

"Cedara!" All eyes turned to see Dejana sitting up in her bed with a look of childish outrage on her face. "You *told!*"

CHAPTER
17

THE FRAGRANCE OF a myriad alien herbs and flowers
sweetened the dusk in the small Temple garden. Commander Sisko walked paths of crushed stone whose
random twists and wanderings allowed the mind to
wander as well, bringing the seeker after peace closer to
the moment of discovery. Chips of rose, white, and gold
gravel winked up at him by the light of slender torches
carried in the hands of Temple folk who also walked the
garden paths as the daylight slipped away. Their voices
rose and fell in chant and song as they greeted the coming
dark and welcomed the eve of *Nis Thamar*.

Sisko gazed across the garden to the Temple, its golden
domes still burnished by the last violet glow of sunset.
We found her, my friend, he thought, the face of the Kai
Opaka rising in his mind. *I wish you could be here to see
the healer of your vision. I think you'd like her.* He
imagined that the Kai heard, and smiled.

In the center of the garden was a pool of still waters
where silver and black fish swam. Here a ring of

torchbearing Temple folk stood unmoving, their lights painting the surface of the pool with flame. Secular Bajorans, those in the habits of the Temple orders, and some in Starfleet uniforms, all mingled among the torchbearers, waiting. Sisko took special notice of a group of five somber-faced Bajorans dressed in the same robes that Kejan Ulli favored. The last Sisko had seen of the double agent was his rapidly retreating back as he ran from the infirmary.

I couldn't even send Odo after him, he thought. *He hadn't actually* done *anything wrong—not yet. And he was right: The* Dessin-ka *wouldn't believe any accusations an outsider made against one of their own.* Sisko's eyes searched the central area of the garden. *At least he isn't here.*

The sun was entirely below the horizon. At that precise moment, the songs of the wandering torchbearers stopped abruptly. They crept from the far corners of the garden to fill the spaces between their immobile brethren around the pool. The massed torches transformed the water into the glory of a miniature sun.

And as Sisko and the others watched, the waters of the pool began to drain away. The black and silver fish whisked from sight as the shimmering sandy bottom rose up, dry as if it had been lifted from the heart of the desert. The sand itself fell away with the soft pattering sound of rain as the bottom of the pool opened into sections like the petals of a waterlily. Within the blossoming flower of sand and stone Talis Cedara stood alone. The still air of the newborn night was moved by the softly exhaled breaths of wonder from the mouths of all who witnessed her appearance in their midst.

Cedra—Cedara—looks beautiful, Sisko thought, still trying to get himself in the habit of calling the child by her right name. *It's hard to believe that's the same hellion who was tearing through the station with Jake and Nog, biting Lieutenant Dax, wreaking havoc with the holoports, bloodying that Bajoran boy's nose—*

He watched as two vedeks stepped up to the edge of the pool and mounted the ramp made by one unfurled stone petal to join Cedara on her platform. One was his old acquaintance Vedek Torin, the other an unknown. *She's like a queen, receiving their homage—elegant, imperial. She's every inch the child of prophecy.*

Vedek Torin raised his hands over Cedara's head and addressed the people. His voice rose and fell in the cadences of the ancient ceremonial tongue that Commander Sisko had heard only two or three times before, drifting out of the station shrine.

Then the vedek spoke so that all could understand. Taking the Kai's letter from his sleeve, he presented it to Cedara, saying, "You are the healer whose coming was foretold through a vision from the Prophets. We entrust the testimony of this vision to your keeping."

Cedara bowed her head over the scroll. Her short hair had been scrupulously washed and dressed so that it curled in a shining cloud about her face. Her earring sparkled with its own galaxy of crystal stars, catching the light of the torches and throwing back a faint, sweetly chiming music.

"If the Prophets grant me the power to heal, I will dedicate that gift of healing to my people," she said.

Vedek Torin turned to the crowd. "As the wisdom of the Prophets welcomes all, the child of prophecy welcomes all. Let any approach who wish to speak with her."

There was a great deal of shuffling and jockeying for place as the secular witnesses formed themselves into a line, but no one pushed or shoved. Vedeks took up positions around the pool, up one stone ramp and down another, in order to guide the line and keep it moving along.

Commander Sisko's admiration for Cedara grew as he watched the ceremony of presentation progress. She had a word and a smile for every soul who came to meet her. She and those who had come to see her spoke too softly for Sisko to hear, but he could see that none left her presence suspicious or dissatisfied.

The *Dessin-ka* delegation was the last to climb the stone ramp. Led by an iron-haired, leonine Bajoran, they presented themselves to Cedara in a body. Sisko saw the leader's brows draw together in a frown as he addressed Cedara. Whatever his words, they caused the attendant vedeks to wince. Vedek Torin stepped forward, hands raised, but a gesture from Cedara made him withdraw again, leaving unsaid whatever admonition or reprimand that had risen to his lips.

With a subtle gesture, Cedara beckoned the *Dessin-ka* leader to incline his head to her. As soon as he was within arm's reach, she seized his ear and pressed her cheek to his. Sisko saw her lips move briefly before she released him. He stared at her, awestruck, then fell to his knees. His followers did likewise. His voice rumbled through the torchlit dark, though he spoke too quietly for Sisko to hear the words.

"Rise." Now Cedara spoke in a clear, ringing voice that carried to the ends of the garden. "I will not be worshiped. I have come to heal, not to stand with my back turned to those who most need healing. Your promise is enough."

Shakily the *Dessin-ka* obeyed, getting to their feet and making a sign of homage. "We will not worship you, if that is your desire," the leader said, and his voice too was finally loud enough to reach Sisko's ears. "But we will live by the words which you have given me this night."

Cedara offered him her warmest smile. "That is all I ask."

As the last of the *Dessin-ka* descended the stone ramp behind Cedara, the vedeks drifted off the platform, back to the shore of the pool. Only Vedek Torin and Cedara were left standing there. Slowly the sectioned causeways lifted to close over their heads as the platform sank beneath the surface of the pool once more. All that could be heard in the garden was the sound of water trickling back into its bed and the muted splash of black and silver fish leaping for the moons of Bajor.

In an intimate anteroom of the Temple, Commander Sisko stood up from his bench just in time to have the wind slammed out of him as Cedara flung herself into his arms. The barefoot child climbed Benjamin's body like a monkey scaling a banana tree and wreathed her arms around his neck.

"They *made* me wear a dress!" she wailed.

"And you looked very lovely in it," Sisko said, trying to keep a straight face.

"Oh, I hope not. Then they'll just make me wear it *again*."

"I have the feeling there's no one on Bajor capable of making you do something you don't like. Certainly not twice."

"Once was difficult enough," said Vedek Torin, coming into the room. "We were fortunate to find a novice who was able to persuade the child to wear the gown for only a few hours."

"I like her," Cedara confided in Sisko's ear. "She's new, but she's nice. When Dejana is all better and we come here to live, I want her to take care of us."

"That should be easy enough to arrange," Benjamin replied. "Incidentally, while I was waiting for you here, I contacted Dr. Bashir. Your sister is recuperating at a fantastic rate and he reports that all traces of the virus have been wiped out of her system."

"Does that mean she can come here right away?"

"Soon enough—*if* she's forgiven you for telling the secret yet."

Cedara sighed. "I'll have to go back and explain to her that we're going to play a different game from now on." She disengaged her arms from Sisko's neck and slid to the floor. Her hair was still elegantly coiffed and her earring twinkled, but she had managed to get her hands on a common worker's tunic and trousers—grubby ones at that. Talis Cedara, child of prophecy, had reverted to being Talis Cedra, child of mischief.

"You know, Cedara, now that you're the *Nekor,* you may have to wear dresses now and then," Sisko teased her.

The girl twisted her mouth. "And I told Dejana that the best part of being the *Nekor* was that no one would ever be able to make her do things she didn't want to."

"Alas," said Vedek Torin. "Even the Kai Opaka was often compelled to assume roles not to her liking." He patted her shoulder gingerly. It was more like touching a holy relic than a simple gesture of comfort.

"Dress or no dress, you behaved very well in the garden," Commander Sisko said. "I understand that it's no easy thing to impress a member of the *Dessin-ka,* even if you are their promised *Nekor.*"

"Was it not a wonder?" Vedek Torin concurred. "She secured the loyalty of the *Dessin-ka* to the provisional government before witnesses. Not even the Kai Opaka was ever able to do that."

"I couldn't hear everything that was said in the center of the garden," Sisko said. "I didn't think the obvious presence of a nonbeliever would be appropriate, so I kept my distance. *Did* she?"

Cedara shrugged. "It was easy. I gave him a present and he gave me the oath of loyalty in exchange."

"What sort of a present?" Sisko asked.

"A few secrets about himself that weren't secrets to me," Cedara replied. "And the name of a man to watch out for. I don't think Kejan Ulli will be able to get by on his word of honor among the *Dessin-ka* much longer."

Commander Sisko threw his head back and laughed. "Good girl!" He offered her his hand. "Are you ready to come back to DS9 now?" Cedara nodded eagerly.

Vedek Torin looked pained. "Is this necessary? I do not

like to have the child removed from the Temple precincts. There is so much to do, so many arrangements to make for her upbringing—"

"And my sister's," Cedara prompted him. "We're *not* to be separated. You can make me wear the stupid dress, but you can't split us up."

"We would not think of it," the vedek promised her. "You have my word. I have already conferred with Commander Sisko: Your sister is to join you here as soon as she is well enough. Do you not trust my oath on this?"

"She's not coming back with me because of Dejana," Sisko soothed Vedek Torin. "It's only to say goodbye to her friends."

Cedara clasped the vedek's hand and looked him in the eye. "I'm not going to run away from my duty anymore. You can trust *my* oath on this."

The farewell party for Talis Cedara at the Replimat was one of long, uneasy silences and sudden, awkward bursts of conversation. Jake sat toying with his ice cream sundae until it was a bowl of brown sludge, and Nog kept giving the Bajoran girl sideways glances that seemed to say, *You're not* really *a female, are you? Yes, you are. No, you're not. How* could *you! As the lone adult overseeing all this, Commander Sisko was honestly thrilled when he recognized Dr. Bashir passing by and energetically hailed him.

"Commander!" Bashir cried, joining the table with alacrity. "I've just had the most marvelous news. I transmitted my findings on the Bajoran camp fever in all its manifestations to Starfleet Medical. My old professor, Selok of Vulcan, did some additional intensive studies on the data. He's just sent back word that the physical configuration of the virus itself is incompatible with non-Bajoran hosts. There's no need to fear an epidemic off the planet." He rested his elbow on the back of his seat and turned to Cedara. "You know, your sister's been showing me how to do that private sign language you two used to fool everyone."

"Sign language?" Jake suddenly forgot the shock of having learned that his former best friend—and roommate—had turned out to be a girl. Nog just snorted.

"We made it up on the road," Cedara explained. "Sometimes, when we had to hide, we had to keep absolutely quiet but we still needed to talk." She giggled. "I told you: People don't use their eyes. When I wanted everyone to think that Dejana was the *Nekor* I just stood behind anyone who questioned her and I used the signs to tell her what to say. That's why she sounded like she knew so much. We even fooled Lieutenant Dax, and she's *old* inside!"

"Your masquerade almost turned a world upside down." Sisko could speak with equanimity now that the crisis had passed. "Couldn't you have found another way to secure Dejana's future?"

"I tried," Cedara said. "At first I thought that if I was extra helpful to Dr. Bashir, maybe he'd take us away when he went back to the station. Maybe he'd even train me to be a healer! On Bajor you have to belong to a healing order if you're going to be respected, but I didn't think I wanted to do that. You have to give up your life to the Temple! Then I heard about the search for the *Nekor* and—well . . ." She giggled again.

"You were very helpful to me, Cedara," Dr. Bashir said. "I think you'd make a fine healer."

"I think—" the girl said slowly. "I think that's what I ought to be. Not the *Nekor,* not just a symbol. Dejana and I are all right now, but what about the others? What about the kids who are still stuck in the camps, with no way out? They need healers—healers like you, Dr. Bashir, who care about their spirits as well as their bodies. I know I'd be more use to Bajor as a doctor than as the *Nekor.*" She sounded downcast.

"'I have come to heal, not to stand with my back turned to those who most need healing.'" Commander Sisko quoted Cedara's own words in the garden. "Why not tell Vedek Torin what you've just told us, Cedara?"

"Do you think he'd listen?" Cedara asked, her eyes full of hope.

"I could come with you and help him see," Dr. Bashir offered. He turned toward Commander Sisko. "That is, with your permission, sir."

"Permission granted. Only this time, try not to take quite so long finding your way back," Sisko joked. Then, sincerely: "We need you here, Doctor."

Julian beamed. "Yes, *sir!*"

"She didn't fool *me!*" Nog exploded without warning. "I knew she was a girl right away!"

"When did you know it, Nog?" Jake asked derisively. "Before or after she knocked you down and sat on you?"

"Why, you—!" The Ferengi jumped on Jake and the two boys began scuffling right in the middle of the Replimat.

"Think you can heal that, Cedara?" Dr. Bashir asked archly.

Cedara watched Commander Sisko wade into the middle of the fray to pull the two combatants apart. *"Men."*

EPILOGUE

DR. BASHIR walked with Vedek Torin in the Temple precincts. He had never seen the wonders of that greatest of Bajoran sanctuaries, impressive even after the Cardassians' attempted destruction. They had been speaking for some time, Vedek Torin contributing little to the conversation beyond the occasional murmur of agreement.

At last the Bajoran said, "You pleaded Talis Cedara's case eloquently, Dr. Bashir. Perhaps you have missed your true calling as a man of law."

"I know what I should be," Julian responded. "It's what I am."

"But you did not know how best to be it," Vedek Torin stated. "Not until you encountered the child."

"Cedara? But she never—"

"I did not say *how* your eyes were opened, or even whether she is the child I meant." The vedek's face was tranquil.

Julian's vision of the cavern came back at the vedek's

267

words. The doctor shook his head. "I can't say I follow you, Vedek Torin. All I know is that somehow I've come to understand that I will always be able to do something for the children of Bajor, even when I can't be right there to see the immediate results."

"It does not matter if we cannot live to taste the fruit; still we must plant the trees," Vedek Torin said.

"By the same token, you should allow Cedara to pursue a career as a healer, even if she chooses never to enter any of the Temple orders. I myself would be willing to take a hand in her education, and when the time comes, to sponsor her studies at Starfleet Medical. She could bring more to your world as a doctor than as—"

"—the *Nekor?* But she is only the *Nekor* to the *Dessin-ka.* Would you have her reject her spiritual calling altogether?"

"Vedek Torin, I escorted Talis Cedara and her sister here at her request." Julian felt hesitant. What he had to tell the vedek was difficult to say. "On the way here, in the runabout, she told me that—that she isn't sure she *has* a spiritual calling. She has gifts, yes, but—"

Vedek Torin's hands emerged from the folds of his robe. He clapped them sharply together and a novice appeared out of the shadows. "Fetch the child Talis Cedara," he said mildly.

A short while later a slightly wary Cedara was brought to join the doctor and the vedek. They stood before a meditation niche where the object of contemplation was a tiny earthenware drinking cup, its spring green glaze exquisite. Beside it stood a small silver cruse in a bronze tripod.

"So, I have been hearing much of your wishes," Vedek Torin said to her. "But not from your lips. Shall I assume that you will need to call upon this man whenever you have something to tell me? That may be awkward."

"I—I was afraid you'd be angry," Cedara replied. "I was afraid that if I told you I wanted to become a healer like Dr. Bashir, you'd say I was betraying the Kai Opaka's vision."

"Do you have the Kai's last letter with you, child?"

Cedara became indignant. "You entrusted it to me. I'd never leave it behind."

"Give it to me."

Still on her guard, Cedara produced the scroll and passed it to the vedek. He unrolled it in the niche and beckoned her nearer. "Tell me what you see here," he said.

"I see I'm going to have to be the *Nekor*," she muttered sullenly, not even bothering to look at the scroll.

Vedek Torin chuckled. "And this is the child who thought that no one used their eyes but she!" he told Dr. Bashir. To Cedara he repeated, "What do you see?" His finger skimmed the surface of the scroll, but it did not touch the lines of black ink. Instead it ran across the thick, ornate border of gold traceries on a background of blue.

Cedara stared at the curling designs; her eyes grew wide. "They're—they're words!" she exclaimed. "Not just designs to make it pretty; they're *words*."

"So I too discovered only recently, while meditating upon the Kai Opaka's last message. The Prophets saw fit to open my eyes and let them truly see what had been before them all this time. If there are words for you here, child, it would not be right to leave them unread," Vedek Torin said gently.

Dr. Bashir peered over Cedara's shoulder. "Words?" he echoed. "In the border design?" His brow wrinkled. "It doesn't look like any form of Bajoran I've ever seen."

"It was written by one who meant her true message for only certain eyes to find," Vedek Torin responded. "It is a form of our language older than the one we use in our ceremonies, hidden from all but a handful of scholars." He smiled at Cedara's expression, intent as she pored

269

over the antiquated script. "Some do not need to be taught what they already know."

"I think—I think I understand this," Cedara said. She began to read aloud: " 'The enemy is gone and we return to our old, contentious ways without a thought to what our madness does to this world, this day, and tomorrow. A healer must be found who can bring together the hundred warring factions of Bajor if we are to survive. The Prophets, in their wisdom, have given me to see that the healer is a child—any child. Where is the monster so heartless that he can look into the eyes of a child who has known war and turn his hand to new battles? The time of the ancient prophecy's fulfillment has not yet come, but the time when our healer must be found is now. The same factions whose quarrels weaken the government and our hopes for unity and peace will vie with one another to see the fulfillment of their own causes in the child of prophecy. They will unite in her name, and in her name healing will be brought to our world, our children, and our souls. May the Prophets in mercy forgive me for what I do in their name, as I invoke prophecy in the name of mercy.' "

Cedara raised her eyes from the scroll. "Then . . . I am not the *Nekor?*" She sounded as if she didn't know whether to be happy or sad.

Dr. Bashir gave her a hug. "What you are hasn't changed. And what you can do stays the same."

"But if the prophecy means nothing, I'm—I'm useless," the girl said in a small voice.

"Child, take this." Vedek Torin handed her the cup from the meditation niche. She cradled it in her palms, uncomprehending, as he filled it with sweet water from the silver cruse. At once the dozens of invisible, unsuspected cracks in the fragile vessel began to leak. Automatically Cedara's fingers moved to cover the cracks so that not a drop of water fell to the ground.

"You see?" The vedek smiled. "To restore a thing of

beauty to wholeness is not useless, whether it is a cup or a world . . . healer." He took the cup from her hands. The cracks were sealed.

Later, Julian walked in the gardens with Cedara clinging to his hand and chattering eagerly about her plans for the future.

"—and I'm going to study with the Temple healers, and I'll write to you and talk to you and visit you whenever I can—I have to; Dejana's got a crush on you and she'll never forgive me if I don't give her *some* excuse to come see you—and it's so lucky because this novice who takes care of us is also studying to be a healer and she's awfully nice and you've got to meet her and— Oh! There she is with Dejana now! Come on!"

She tugged her hand from Dr. Bashir's and ran across the garden to where Dejana sat in the shade of a fruit tree with a lady swathed in the traditional habit of the Temple novices. Julian followed at a more sedate pace. As he approached the little group under the tree, he began, "Talis Cedara says I have to meet you . . ."

The words faded on his lips as the novice lifted her head and he looked into the face of Borilak Jalika.

She rose to her feet with the same breathtaking grace he remembered from the caverns, and her smile cut through him like a knife. As he stared at her, Cedara grabbed Dejana's hand and dragged her little sister away to play hide-and-find among the blossoming shrubs and hedges.

"You do not look happy to see me, Julian," Jalika said, a touch of melancholy in her voice.

"I didn't—I never expected to see you here—to see you like—like—" He gestured helplessly at the all-shrouding robes. With a pang he recalled what she had told him of the life of a novice Temple healer. "There's no room for me in your life here, is there?" he asked hoarsely. "Your whole world's become study, devotion,

271

work— All I can ever hope to be for you now is a—a teacher."

"I could not ask for a better one. If my instructors here permit it—"

"I want more than that, Jalika, and you know it."

"There can be no more than that for us, Julian." Her words trickled away like water over stones. "Not anymore."

He seized her by the shoulders. "How could you do this? How could you make this choice, knowing—?"

"I chose the healer's world freely, Julian," she said, gently shrugging off his touch. "So did you, long ago. Do you remember telling me that it was wrong to keep you in the caverns, to prevent you from going on to help others who might need your skills?"

"I remember." His own words lodged in his chest and burned. "I told you that you knew it was wrong, no matter what we felt for one another." He took a deep breath and let it out slowly. "You will make a fine healer, Jalika. You've chosen well."

"I did not make my choice for or in spite of Father— or anyone else; only for myself. I want you to know that too."

"I would have come back, Jalika," he said. It sounded like a plea for forgiveness. "I promised I'd come back."

"You have come back, beloved." She lowered her eyes. "We have both come back to what we know we must be."

Her pale hand stole into his darker one, tightened for a moment, and was gone. He knew she spoke the truth. Bound by more than any embrace could ever hold, they stood together in the garden. Over their heads, echoing back from the Temple walls, racing through the flowers, came the laughing voices of the children.

About the Author

Esther M. Friesner attended Vassar College and holds a Ph.D. from Yale University. She was severely criticized by her first college English teacher for choosing *Star Trek* as a subject for expository writing. (Hence we learn that Creative Writing does not always mean it, especially when it's listed in a college course catalog.) The author of nineteen published fantasies, her most recent works include *Majyk by Accident, Majyk by Hook or Crook,* and *Majyk by Design.* She is also the editor of the *Alien Pregnant by Elvis!* anthology. Her short stories have appeared in numerous anthologies and such magazines as *Asimov's, Fantasy and Science Fiction,* and *Amazing.* She lives in Connecticut with her husband, two children, two obstreperous cats, and as many hamsters as the market (and the cats) will bear.